The Reunion at
SUGAR SAND INN

SUGAR SAND BEACH
BOOK 4

LEIGH DUNCAN

The Reunion at Sugar Sand Inn
Sugar Sand Beach Series, Book #4

Copyright ©2021 by Leigh D. Duncan

This book is a work of fiction. The characters, events, and places portrayed in this book are products of the author's imagination and are either fictitious or are used fictitiously. Any similarity to real person, living or dead, is purely coincidental and not intended by the author.

Digital ISBN: 978-1-944258-30-6
Print ISBN: 978-1-944258-31-3
Gardenia Street Publishing

Published in the United States of America

Welcome Back to Sugar Sand Beach!

Escape to Sugar Sand Beach with Erin Bradshaw and her best friends for a second chance at all life has to offer.

Forty-five year old Erin has grown restless with her life. Which is odd because she's spent the past twenty years roaming the globe. Between summers in Alaska and winters in the Florida keys, she's climbed the steps of Machu Picchu, hiked long sections of the Great Wall of China, and kayaked down the Amazon. Lately, though, Erin has felt the urge to put down roots, strengthen her neglected relationship with her sister, Reggie, and reconnect with her two best friends, Michelle and Nina.

When Michelle inherits a run-down beach house in sleepy Sugar Sand Beach and invites her friends to help convert it into an inn, Erin jumps at the chance to settle down with the best friends a girl could ever hope to have.

But now that Reggie's garden is flourishing, customers crowd the tables in the Café, and the first of the Inn's guests are due any day, a figure from Erin's past makes a surprising appearance.

When he threatens the bonds of friendship that have deepened over the summer, Erin must choose. Will she return to her nomadic way of life? Or will she put down forever roots in Sugar Sand Beach?

Join Michelle, Reggie, Nina and Erin as they build new lives in Sugar Sand Beach, where fresh opportunities for life, love and happiness are as limitless as the blue Florida skies.

One

Erin

The occasional scrape of a box being unloaded from the back of a pickup truck broke the early morning silence that draped the farmer's market like a heavy blanket. Beyond the pole barn, stars still twinkled in the sky. No birds chirped; not even the earliest had stirred from their nests. Under the metal roof, most of the wooden stalls yawned emptily. Within hours, though, vendors would fill them with produce so freshly picked, it still bore drops of morning dew. Plump, red tomatoes. Yellow and green squashes. Cukes and okra. Beans of every kind.

On a different kind of mission, Erin Bradshaw padded down the center aisle, her footsteps muffled by a thick layer of sawdust.

A faint glow drew her toward a stand in the back corner, where a husband-and-wife team sold organic fruit. Erin's tummy rumbled as she moved close enough to identify a lumpy display as mounds of dust-colored cantaloupe. On the ground, bushel baskets held piles of dark green watermelons with bright yellow patches. Beyond the stall, a shadowy figure unloaded trays of fruit from the back of a truck known best for its fuel efficiency.

"Good morning, Gena." Erin stepped out of the darkness into a circle of light created by a bare bulb that hung on a thin wire from the corrugated tin roof.

"Morning, Erin." Dressed in overalls that were more functional than fashionable, Gena slid a tray of plump, ripe strawberries onto one of the wooden display shelves. "You're out and about early."

"One of those nights, I guess. Couldn't sleep a wink." After Ron left, she hadn't been able to stop thinking about the man she'd once loved or why he'd shown up in her life again. She'd still been wide awake at midnight when soft footfalls on the hardwood floors told her Michelle and Reggie had returned from the movies. By the time Zeke dropped Nina off after the Happy Dolphin closed and the throaty rumble of his

2

truck faded, she'd given up on sleep entirely. "I decided I might as well fix breakfast for everyone this morning."

"Your timing's perfect." Gena straightened the bandanna she wore over the thick braids she'd coiled around her head. "A new shipment of papaya and mangoes arrived last night. Saul said there were even a couple of pineapples." In addition to the berries and peaches Gena and Saul grew, the couple belonged to a co-op of organic farmers that stretched across the Southeast.

"You know me too well," Erin said. On previous visits, she'd mentioned developing a fondness for tropical fruits on her many travels. Her time in the Keys had only reinforced it. She splayed her fingers across her belly. "I'll take some of everything."

When Gena immediately sprang into action, Erin cocked her head. The normally subdued farmer had more than the usual pep in her step this morning. Hoping for good news, she asked, "How is Saul? Still doing well?"

Secrets were hard to keep in Sugar Sand Beach. Everyone in town knew that five years ago, a cancer diagnosis had prompted the young couple to swap their high-stress, big-city lifestyle for a more laid-back approach in the town where they'd grown up. People for miles around had rallied around them, supplying meals and helping out wherever help was needed while Saul underwent a series of treatments. For the past year, his name had shown up on the prayer list at the First Baptist Church every three months like clockwork. That's when the pair made the five-hour drive to the Mayo Clinic in Jacksonville, where Saul underwent a battery of tests.

"Excellent. His doctors gave him a clean bill of health. They don't want to see him for another year." Gena exhaled forcefully. "Words aren't enough to tell you how thankful I am to have that behind us."

"That's wonderful news, Gena. I'm so happy for you." Erin didn't know the couple well, but she hoped their casual friendship might deepen over the years. Assuming she stuck around, that is.

"Clean living, clean food, and good neighbors. That's what did it." Gena shrugged. "Speaking of which, I'll give you some chamomile. Try it next time you can't sleep. What else can I get for you?"

"Any chance you have fresh bread today?" Just thinking about Gena's sourdough made her mouth water.

"I took the honey wheat out of the oven just before we left the house. It's still warm."

"Give me a couple of loaves." Thickly sliced and slathered with butter, the bread would go perfectly with the fruit salad she planned for breakfast.

A rooster crowed in the distance. The inky horizon lightened slightly while Erin added pints of blueberries and blackberries to her order. She reached for a couple of peaches, but Gena shook her head. "This late in the season, they're mealy. Fit only for cobblers and pies."

Erin thanked her for the advice. By the time she paid her bill and, carrying two cloth bags filled with her purchases, headed for the exit, many of the other vendors had arrived and were unloading their wares. A handful of early shoppers browsed the aisles looking for the freshest fruits, the most succulent vegetables for their tables. Erin spotted the owner of Maggie's Diner sorting through a display of tomatoes and stopped briefly to exchange the usual pleasantries with the woman who also served as the mayor of Sugar Sand Beach.

As she moved closer to the exit, the scent of strong coffee mingled with the earthy smell of root vegetables and the grassy-green fragrance that rose from a mountain of early corn. She nodded to the sleepy-eyed teenager who dispensed coffee from a tall urn on a folding table, but she didn't stop. Although a shot of caffeine sounded just like what the doctor ordered, she wasn't quite so desperate that she'd stoop to paying for a cup of the bitter brew. Not when a French press and a supply of hard-to-come-by beans waited for her at the inn.

Taking care not to squash the bread or bruise the tender fruit, she placed her purchases on the floorboard behind the driver's seat, climbed behind the wheel of her Jeep and headed home.

"Home," she murmured as she traveled west on Route 98. Several miles down the road, she'd turn off the four-lane highway onto the graveled drive that led past the "Opening Soon" sign in front of the Sugar Sand Inn. In the last five months, she'd come to think of the two-story Queen Anne-style house as the place she wanted to spend the rest of her life. She and Michelle and Nina and Reggie had spent weeks on end cleaning and painting, repairing and prepping for the grand opening. She'd poured her heart and soul into her role as the inn's activities director—over the last couple of months, she'd learned more about the local waterways and fishing holes than most of the people who'd lived their entire lives in the vicinity. She and Reggie had created bike paths around the lake on the five-acre property, and she'd planned a half-dozen kayaking and canoeing excursions for the inn's guests.

But one look at the man she'd loved and lost, the man she never thought she'd see again, and suddenly, she was rethinking everything. How could she tell the others that Ron's sudden reappearance had shaken her resolve and threatened all their futures?

How could she keep it a secret?

"Well, this is a nice surprise!" Michelle stopped at the threshold to the kitchen and stared at the platters of cut fruit and sliced bread on the granite counter. "Someone got an early start on the day. What brought this on?"

The timer on the stove dinged, signaling the coffee had steeped the appropriate amount of time. Erin gently plunged the grounds to the bottom of the French press while she explained. "With Nina working such long hours at the Happy Dolphin, we've been playing catch-as-catch-can for a couple of weeks now. I thought it might be nice if we could all start the day enjoying a meal together."

"Uh-huh. What else?"

Erin grimaced. Friends since grade school, Michelle knew her well enough to know there was more to her good intentions than just the desire for a friendly get-together. "Okay," she said on a slow sigh as she decanted the perfectly brewed coffee into a carafe. "But I don't want to talk about it until we're all here."

"That's fine with me." Michelle pulled her favorite mug from the cabinet and held it out. "I'm not one to look a gift cup of coffee in the mouth. Especially when you went to all this trouble." She sipped the piping hot beverage. "Oh, this is heavenly," she declared. "Why don't we drink this every day?" Carrying her cup, she crossed the kitchen to the breakfast nook and took her usual corner seat.

"Don't get too used to it. This is the last of the Peaberry beans I brought back with me from Tanzania." She'd hidden the small stash in the bottom of the freezer, waiting for a special occasion. Telling her friends about the visitor who'd stopped by the house last night certainly qualified as one.

"Hmmm. So good." Michelle took another sip and closed her eyes, savoring the taste. "The Keurig makes a good cuppa Joe, but this is beyond great. Has Nina said anything about the coffee she plans to serve in the cafe?"

"I'm still trying to choose between a service or buying in bulk from the box store in Destin." Her face flushed from her usual early-morning workout, Nina stepped into the kitchen wearing yoga pants and a sports bra under a flowing tank top. "But whatever you're brewing over there smells divine. Maybe we should give it a try." The chef nodded to the carafe.

"The cost is a bit dear," Erin pointed out. At upwards of fifteen dollars a pound, the beans were too pricey for every day. Definitely too expensive to serve in what they all hoped would be a bustling restaurant.

"Too bad." Nina poured herself a cup. While Erin slid onto a bench seat beside Michelle, she plucked a blackberry from the fruit on the counter and popped it into her mouth. She chewed thoughtfully. "Wait. These are from Saul and Gena's farm, aren't they?" Her brows drew together. "You've already been to the farmer's market?"

"I went for a run first. Tried to clear my head." It hadn't worked.

"While it was pitch-black outside?" Concern edged Michelle's voice.

"There was plenty of moonlight," Erin said simply. It wasn't the first time she'd indulged in a solitary run before the sun came up. There was

9

something healing about being alone on the beach, the gentle waves lapping the shore, the breeze blowing through the palmetto and sea grass on the dunes, her feet pounding against the wet sand. Usually, everything that troubled her quickly faded away. Not this time. This time, too many memories, too much betrayal had crowded her thoughts.

"I did get some good news at the farmer's market, though."

"Hold that thought." Her sister Reggie made the request as she came through the back door carrying a basket of produce from the garden. "Let me unload this and grab some coffee first." She set the basket on the counter and began transferring cucumbers and peppers, tomatoes and green onions into the big farm sink. Two minutes later and smelling slightly of sun-ripened vegetables and rich earth, she joined the others at the table. She sipped the exotic blend and lowered her cup. "Now, what's the good news?"

"It's about Saul." Erin dabbed her napkin at a few wet spots on the table. "Gena said his latest scans came back clean. He's officially in remission."

"Oh, that's good to hear," Michelle said. She lifted her cup in a toast to the young farmers they all admired.

"I bet Gena's relieved," Reggie said as she clinked her mug against Michelle's.

Erin nodded. "She did look like a weight had been lifted off her shoulders."

"That doesn't explain why you were at the farmer's market before daybreak," Nina pointed out.

"Or why you were running on the beach in the dark," Michelle added.

Erin took a breath so deep her chest shuddered. This was why she'd fixed breakfast, wasn't it? The three women seated before her were the best friends anyone could ever hope to have. She trusted them, relied on them. So much so that she'd gone all in on transforming the house Michelle had inherited into a first-class inn. Which had involved sinking every dime of her savings into the project.

And she hadn't been alone. They'd all pooled their resources, left their old lives behind and joined together in this new venture. Until last night, whenever she'd pictured the future, it had always been the four of them together. A band of sisters, best friends forever. Michelle would serve as the inn's official hostess, greeting their guests and overseeing the day-to-day operations. Nina would finally fulfill her lifelong dream of running her own restaurant, the Sugar Sand

Cafe. Reggie would put her considerable skills as a master gardener to bear on the garden that would supply most of the restaurant's farm-to-table fresh fruits and vegetables. As for herself, she'd spend her days doing what she enjoyed the most in life—sharing her love for the outdoors with others. She'd kayak some of the prettiest waters in the world with the inn's guests. She'd take them camping under the stars. They'd hike through the nearby nature preserve or go for rides along the quiet bike paths.

Then Ron had stepped onto the porch and said the one thing—the only thing—that could tempt her to reshape her future.

She cleared her throat.

"I had an unexpected visitor last night while Nina was at the Happy Dolphin and you were at the movies." She nodded to Michelle and Reggie.

"Who? Orson? Don't tell me that man is stirring up trouble for us again." Michelle's eyes narrowed. A Sugar Sand Beach native, Orson Danner had had big plans for the property Michelle inherited from her birth mother. He hadn't reacted well to the news that she and her friends intended to transform the gracefully aging house into an inn.

"No, not Orson." Erin shook her head. She almost wished the developer had stopped by.

She could easily deal with the likes of him. Her ex-husband, not so much.

"Well, who then?" Reggie asked.

"Yeah, don't keep us in suspense," Nina added. Picking up the carafe, she topped off everyone's coffee.

"Ron." Erin scooted back on the bench while she waited for her friends' reaction. As expected, it came quickly.

Nina immediately lost her grip on the carafe, which fell to the table with a thunk. Michelle's mouth worked wordlessly. Reggie's eyes welled.

"Oh, shoot!" Nina snatched the container from the table and held it up to the light. "It didn't break, thank goodness." Her movements methodical, she set the empty carafe on the table before pinning Erin with a stern look. "Now what's this about Ron?"

"Why on earth would he show up here?" Michelle asked, regaining her powers of speech. "You didn't have any idea he was coming?"

"No." Erin's head swung on a swivel. "The last I heard, his outdoor adventure business in Houston was thriving and he was still living in the house his dad left him." The one that had rung the death knell on their relationship.

"So, what brought him to Sugar Sand Beach? Is he on vacation? How'd he know where to find you? Or did he just stop by on a whim? He's not moving here, is he?" Her lips set in thin lines, Reggie fired off questions in a staccato burst.

Erin eyed her younger sister curiously. Thanks to a ten-year difference in their ages, the two of them hadn't had much in common while they were growing up. They'd never spent lazy summer afternoons talking about boys or comparing notes on kisses. They'd certainly never double-dated. In fact, her baby sister had still been in middle school when she'd married Ron, a union that had fallen apart practically before the ink on their wedding certificate dried. In the years since, Erin had made a point of never bad-mouthing her ex. So why the sudden animosity toward a man Reggie barely knew?

"I'm not sure how he tracked me down, but it wouldn't be difficult. I haven't tried to keep our move here a secret." Erin gestured to the kitchen and the house beyond it. "Quite the opposite. In trying to build interest for the outdoor activities we'll offer here at the inn, I've posted several pictures from my kayaking and fishing trips on social media. It's possible he ran across them."

"Or that he's been keeping tabs on you all these years," Michelle countered.

"I guess." Erin shrugged. Why Ron would do that, she had no idea. After all, he was the one who'd pulled the plug on their relationship. "As far as what brought him here, he had a business proposition he thought I'd be interested in."

"Don't tell me he's selling insurance on the side," Nina said dryly. The dark hair she usually wore in a bun hung loose today. She flipped a long lock over one shoulder.

"Nah." Erin snorted. The idea that Ron, with his sun-bleached hair and sinewy muscles, might trade his oars and paddles in on a suit and a briefcase made her chuckle. "He's working with a couple of investors to expand his business on a global scale. They intend to offer customized tours for well-to-do clients. Kayaking down the Amazon, mountaineering in Nepal, diving off the Great Barrier Reef, African photography safaris. First-class all the way."

"Glamping?" Nina asked. Her eyebrows rose.

"A step or two above that," Erin answered. "Each team will include medical personnel, a chef, transportation specialists, the works. Posh accommodations. Two experienced guides on every trip."

"Where would you fit in?" Not lifting her eyes above the rim of her cup, Reggie polished off the last of her coffee.

"He wants me to sign on as part of his team. He thinks my"—she made air quotes—"extensive travel experience makes me the perfect fit for the job. He and I, along with the rest of the team, would travel the world together."

"That certainly sounds like your dream job," Nina murmured.

"It was. Once." When she and Ron were first married, that was the plan—to spend their lives roaming about the globe, never putting down roots, staying in one place only long enough to earn as much as they needed for their next jaunt. "It's not anymore."

"What'd you tell him?" Reggie demanded. "That you already had your bags packed?"

Erin felt her cheeks warm. It wasn't in her nature to be cruel, and she wasn't particularly proud of how she'd reacted to Ron's new plan. She sighed. "I told him I'd made a commitment here and—unlike him—I honor the promises I've made."

"Ouch. That must have stung," Michelle said.

"If it did, he didn't let it show. He just handed me a brochure and said they were planning to get underway next summer. He seems certain that I'll change my mind before then."

"And will you?" Though Reggie looked cool, calm and collected, a slight waver crept into her voice.

"Travel the world in style? Hobnob with the rich and famous?" She'd spent years touring the world on a shoestring. It'd be nice to travel first-class, but she shook her head. "As tempting as that sounds, I'm not going anywhere." The reassurance seemed to calm Reggie, and it was the truth. At least, she thought it was.

"Hold on a minute now." Michelle held up one hand. "You need to give some serious thought to his proposal before you reject the idea outright."

Erin froze. She'd half-expected that kind of advice from Nina. The cook had carved out her own version of a free-and-easy lifestyle. With only Mr. Pibbs depending on her for kibble and cuddles, Nina had traded jobs and apartments so often, her page in Erin's address book looked like chicken scratches. Reggie's animosity came as a surprise, but Erin had thought her sister might take Ron's side, too. A life on the road with nothing to hold her down would seem appealing to someone who was going through a nasty divorce, right? But Michelle? She hadn't expected Michelle to throw any support Ron's way. Until circumstances beyond her control had turned her life upside down, Michelle had lived in the same house with the same man for more than twenty-five years.

Erin focused on her friend. "Why? Like I said, I've made a commitment."

Michelle met her gaze with an unwavering one of her own. "The man you once loved enough to follow to the ends of the earth waltzes back into your life promising to give you the very thing you've always wanted. And you don't think you should at least stop to consider it? Or have a single doubt about that decision?"

Nina drummed her fingers on the wooden table top. "The fact that you felt you had to bribe us with amazing coffee and organic fruit speaks volumes. Not that I'm complaining, mind you." Her movements as graceful as a dancer's, Nina rose from her seat and crossed to the kitchen island.

While the others followed her example and filled their own plates, Erin asked herself hard questions. Was Michelle right? Should she seriously consider Ron's proposal? Her head told her she'd been there, done that. Ever since her marriage had crashed and burned, she'd lived the life she and Ron had planned on having together. The last couple of years, though, she'd grown weary of not sleeping in the same bed every night, of throwing a dart at a map and then heading off to wherever it landed. She'd started to long for something she hadn't been able to name until she arrived in Sugar Sand Beach. The life she was building here gave her the stability and structure she'd been seeking. If anyone other than Ron had asked her to walk away from it, she wouldn't have given them a second's thought.

But this *was* Ron. The man she'd fallen for head-over-heels while they were in college. The man she'd planned to spend her life with. To grow old beside. A part of her would always love him. Would always want to be with him.

Even if it meant walking away from all she and her friends were building in Sugar Sand Beach? She squeezed her eyes shut, unable to answer the question.

"Who knows what the future will bring for any of us?" Michelle asked from the island as she selected slices of brightly colored cantaloupe. "If there's one thing I've learned this last year and a half, it's that life doesn't come with guarantees."

Erin swallowed. She had to admit it; Michelle was an authority on the subject of how quickly someone could have the rug yanked out from under them. Two years ago, Michelle and Allen had been the envy of their affluent neighborhood in Fairfax, Virginia. Still in love after twenty-five years of marriage, and with their twins off to college, they'd begun to look forward to spending their retirement years in the two-story Colonial they'd bought before their first anniversary.

Those plans had hit a snag when Allen was laid off in a corporate merger and decided to go into business for himself. Confident that his new start-up would succeed, he'd borrowed heavily against the house and emptied his 401K in order to finance his new venture.

On paper, his plan looked good. As a computer programmer, his skills were in great demand. He was healthy. A non-smoker, he ran five miles several times a week and mostly watched his weight. Everyone thought he'd remain fit and active well into his eighties, maybe even into his nineties. Except, before Allen's fledgling company could land its first contract, he'd keeled over from a heart attack.

His death had left Michelle up to her eyeballs in debt. If her birth mother hadn't left her five acres and a house in Florida, she'd probably have ended up selling perfume from behind the counter of one of the high-end department stores where she'd once shopped. Instead of spending her nights in comfort and ease, after work each day, she'd climb the stairs to a cramped, fifth-floor walk-up apartment.

"Truth," Erin nodded. "And I will think about

it. But right now, I don't have any plans to leave. I like it here. For the first time since Ron and I divorced, I'm putting down roots." She smiled slyly as the rest of the group returned to the table. "It's not half as bad as I thought it'd be." Sobering, she added, "But I suppose I should keep my options open. We've poured everything we have into the inn and the cafe. We hope and pray it'll be a success. But, like Michelle said, there are no guarantees."

"And you told Ron all this?" Lingering behind the others, Reggie stabbed a piece of papaya from the platter on the counter.

Erin's face heated. She wasn't dumb enough to spill her guts to a man she hadn't spoken to in a dozen years. She swirled the dregs of her coffee while she swallowed the snarky remark that had sprung to her lips. It wasn't Reggie who'd stirred her ire. That honor belonged to Ron—his visit had left her edgy and restless. The sleepless night hadn't improved her mood. Deliberately, she smoothed her ruffled feathers. "Once I let him know I wasn't interested in joining his team, he just said he'd be around for a while and that we could talk about it more later."

"So you're going to see him again." Nina's voice was heavy with doubt.

Erin shrugged. "If he does stick around, I'm

sure we'll run into one another. He'd be hard to miss in a town the size of Sugar Sand Beach." A part of her wanted to get to know her ex again, while another part warned that having anything to do with the man who'd broken her heart was a big mistake.

"Sounds like you have some things to think over. Don't rush it. Give yourself some time." Michelle took a final bite of bread and pushed her plate away. "No matter what you decide, though, we have a grand opening to plan. I have a huge list of things that I need to tackle before that happens. We all do. So, what's everyone doing today?"

"Now that Charlie's settled in at the Dolphin, I need to focus on getting the cafe ready to open." Three weeks ago, the four of them had teamed up to prove that the head chef and his protégé at the Happy Dolphin were the worst kind of snakes. They'd succeeded in that endeavor. The chef had been fired. His assistant, too. But their sudden departure had left the owner in a bind. Nina had graciously stepped in to run things there while he searched for a permanent replacement. Charlie, an old friend of Nina's, had accepted the job, and she'd been so pleased that she'd worked an extra week at the Dolphin while he moved his family—lock, stock and barrel—from Virginia to Florida. "My first priority is to hire the kitchen staff."

"Are you looking for another sous chef?" Erin asked softly. After what had happened with Nina's last assistant, she figured the cook might be a little gun-shy.

"No. I've put a pin in that idea," Nina said with a half-laugh. "I'm looking for a couple of part-time line cooks. Ideally, I'll find one who can handle the prep work and another to help me with the breakfast and lunch rush. After that, we'll need at least one waitress and a busser. Then I have menus to finalize and supplies to order. A final inspection with the health department." She heaved a sigh. "And a hundred and one other details to take care of."

"I'm moving into the gardener's cottage today," Reggie said firmly.

"Hey." Erin nudged her sister with an elbow. "What about me?" She and her sister had planned to share the small apartment behind the main house.

"Why bother, if you're leaving?" Reggie snapped.

Okay, I guess I deserved that. She had been talking about pulling up stakes and moving on just five minutes ago, but that decision was far from being made.

"I'm not going anywhere. If I do decide to accept Ron's offer—and I'm not saying I will— I'll be right here for another year. At least." Erin tried her best to convince her sister. "For now, though, Michelle needs time to work her magic on our rooms before we open for business."

The two-story house had eight bedrooms— seven upstairs and a large, airy master on the first floor. When they'd arrived, the four women had spread out, each choosing one bedroom and its adjoining sitting room as their own. But that only left four suites for guests. After discussing the matter at length during their usual afternoon get-togethers on the front porch, they'd all agreed to make some changes. As the inn's hostess and their chef-in-residence, both Michelle and Nina needed to live in the main house. They'd opted for adjoining rooms on the second floor, where they'd share a sitting room and bath. Reggie and Erin had offered to share the tiny cottage attached to the gardener's shed. The move would free up two additional suites for paying guests.

Michelle rubbed her hands together. "I can't wait to get started on those rooms. I want to have them finished in time for Aaron and Ashley's visit." The twins were flying down from Virginia in three weeks for a much-anticipated reunion with their mom.

"I'd better get busy. My stuff won't pack itself." Her shoulders rigid, Reggie stood and marched out of the room.

"Sounds like we have our work cut out for us," Erin said as she eyed her sister's hasty departure. She began gathering plates and utensils.

"I'll get those," Nina said. "Now that I won't be working at the Happy Dolphin anymore, it's time this kitchen and I get reacquainted. Besides, I think you have some fence-mending to do. She's pretty upset."

"You noticed that, too, huh?" Erin asked. It wasn't like Reggie to lose her cool over something that hadn't even happened yet and probably never would. Something else must be bothering her. Whatever it was, Erin needed to get to the bottom of it. And fast. Otherwise, sharing a one-bedroom apartment with her sister was going to be mighty uncomfortable.

Two

Reggie

Reggie carried the last box of her clothes across the strip of vibrant, green grass that separated the main house from the gardener's shed. The mid-morning sun glinted off the smaller building's tin roof. Beneath it stood stained and faded walls. In several places, bare concrete blocks peeked through where the paint had peeled off completely.

She gave herself an imaginary pat on the back. When they'd arrived in Sugar Sand Beach, vines had covered the shed from the foundation to the roof line. Broad leaves had grown so thickly over the windows only the faintest trace of light had seeped through the glass. It had taken her a full week of hard work, but she'd ripped down every one of the stubborn plants.

Another long afternoon with a pressure washer had removed the last traces of the vine and left the cottage ready for the painters who'd spend the next two weeks treating the main house and all the outbuildings to a fresh, new look.

Reaching the entrance, she lowered the box she carried to the ground, grasped the handle and tugged the door open. Holding it ajar with one foot, she retrieved the box and elbowed her way into the small apartment. If she'd been in Virginia, she might have propped the door open until she finished moving in. But this was Florida, where all manner of bugs and critters would view an open doorway as an invitation to come on in and set up housekeeping.

Um, thanks, but no thanks.

As the door glided shut on recently oiled hinges, she looked around for a place to put her clothes. Chest-high stacks of tubs and cardboard containers covered every square inch of the tiny kitchen floor. A pile of Erin's camping equipment took up one corner of the living room. Her sister's duffle bag and a backpack filled a swivel chair upholstered in bright yellow. Linens and pillows had been piled on the couch's blue-and-white striped cushions. She sighed and found a temporary home for the box in the breakfast nook. Promising to start unpacking soon, she wandered past the bathroom to the only bedroom.

Once they'd decided to move in here, she and Erin spent two days cleaning the apartment from the ceiling lights to the floorboards. Two coats of cream-colored paint brightened the rooms considerably, and bamboo blinds gave them some privacy while they softened the light that poured through the windows. They'd both taken one look at the queen-size bed and decided it had to go. The twins that replaced it left ample room for a dresser and nightstand.

Reggie pulled the scrunchie from her hair and wondered what it'd be like to share a room with Erin again. The first seven years of her life, she'd drifted off to sleep each night comforted by the sound of her sister's soft breathing. That ended the summer before she started fourth grade, when Erin left for college. Their bedroom felt lonely after that and, on more than one occasion, she'd huddled under her blankets, wishing her big sister was there to scare away the monsters. Life had never been the same after that. On holidays and during the few weeks each summer when Erin and her piles of dirty laundry came home, she and her friends stayed out long after Reggie's bedtime. Once her sister met Ron, even those visits dwindled. They stopped altogether after Erin's marriage failed. Working on the inn had given them the chance to grow close again and now, to share a room again. Only it sounded like Erin wasn't planning to stick around for very long.

The tears Reggie had held at bay all morning surged forward on a relentless tide. She sank onto one of the beds and cupped her head in her hands. Lately, the hits just kept on coming. Could she endure another loss? Another upheaval?

There'd been so many.

This year, after the sixth round of in vitro failed, she'd had to accept that she'd never have a baby of her own. In a double whammy, her husband walked out on their marriage. At loose ends, she gladly threw her lot in with Erin, Michelle and Nina, but the move to Florida meant leaving behind nearly everything that wouldn't fit into a dozen cardboard boxes. Now it sounded like—just when they were getting to know each other better—Erin was making plans to leave. Coming on top of everything else, Reggie didn't know if she could stand it.

"Yoo-hoo! Anybody home?" Erin's voice echoed down the hall seconds before a door snicked shut. "I would have been here sooner, but Michelle needed help moving all the furniture away from the walls in our old rooms.

She wants to get started painting right away."

Reggie hastily mopped her tears with her hands. The last thing she wanted was for Erin to catch her sitting in the bedroom having a pity party. So much for that plan, she told herself, when her sister appeared in the doorway.

"Hey, sis." Erin's voice dropped to a sympathetic whisper. "You doing okay?"

"Does it look like I'm okay?" she answered, unable to curb the harsh note in her tone. Reggie lifted her tear-stained cheeks to her sister.

"Yeah, I kind of got that you were having a hard time at breakfast. Want to talk about it?"

"What's there to talk about? It's another verse of the same old song. You're leaving. Again." There. She'd said it.

"Um, no, I'm not," Erin countered. She sank onto the bed opposite Reggie.

"It sure sounded like Ron made you an offer you can't refuse. Nina called it your dream job," she reminded her sister. "Michelle practically rushed upstairs to pack your bags."

"It's not like that, Reggie. They're just looking out for me. They don't want me to slam the door in Ron's face without considering his offer. But I'm not going anywhere. Not for at least a year. After that? Who knows. There are too many 'if's' for anyone to decide right now."

"Like what?" she asked. Much as she wanted to let Erin's neutral tone soothe her like it had when she was a child, she needed to understand what was going on in her sister's head.

"What if Ron's plans fall apart? Just because he says he's taking his business global, that doesn't mean it'll actually happen." Erin fluffed the pillow atop the bed's pale blue comforter.

Based on what her sister had told them at breakfast, and from the looks of the brochure she'd passed around the table, Reggie thought Ron's plans looked pretty solid. "What else?"

"Well, what if we're wrong and, despite our best efforts, the inn fails?" A tiny divot appeared between Erin's brows. She smoothed the fringe on the pillow. "What if a hurricane makes landfall right on top of us and we lose everything?"

That last bit made her shiver. "I do worry about hurricanes," she admitted. Living in Florida, it'd be foolish not to give some thought to the big storms. Damaging winds could tear the roof off the house. The storm surge could send water rushing over the front steps. Ronnie, one of the co-owners of the hardware store in town, had pushed her to stock up on sandbags, tarps and emergency supplies. She'd picked up a couple of things; maybe she should have bought out the entire store.

"We can't do much about hurricanes except get out of their way, but when I start getting nervous about them, I remind myself to look at the numbers." Erin counted off facts on her fingers. "First, most hurricanes peter out before they do any damage. Second, on average, of the big ones, only one or two make landfall each year." She touched the top of her middle finger. "The odds of a Cat 5 coming ashore right on top of us are like a million to one." Dropping her hands, she finished, "Even if the worst does happen and a storm heads our way, we'll have plenty of time to get to safety before it hits."

"Assuming you're even here," Reggie said stubbornly. "Why can't things just stay the way they are?"

Erin let out a long-suffering sigh. "Leaving Ron out of the equation for the moment, you can't honestly think that nothing's going to change for the rest of our lives. Change is part of life. We move. We grow. We fall in love. Look at Michelle and Dave." She glanced to the right as if she could see through the walls to the main house. "With every passing day, they grow closer. Sooner or later, they're going to want to take that relationship to the next level and see where it leads them."

"You think they'll get married?" No one

could deny the deep fondness that had developed between the handsome attorney and their friend, but until this moment, Reggie hadn't stopped to consider what the future might hold.

"It's way too early to start planning an engagement party," Erin said. "But Michelle isn't the only one who has a new beau. Look at Zeke and Nina." The contractor and the chef had shared a connection while Zeke expanded the dining room. Recently, Nina had been seeing more of him and his two daughters. "And then there's you and Chris..."

"We're just friends. That's all," Reggie protested. She was too smart to let her relationship with a man who'd lost his wife less than a year ago go any deeper than that. Especially not before her own divorce was finalized.

"I'm just saying...we all need to accept that change is inevitable." Erin lifted one shoulder.

Reggie pursed her lips. "But Ron? I don't understand why you'd even consider pairing up with him again. Didn't he let you down the last time? Or did you forget about that?"

"I didn't forget." Erin heaved a breath. "It took a long time after Ron and I went our separate ways before I trusted another man. In some ways, I still don't."

Reggie tucked her bottom lip between her teeth. Erin had the body of a runner—long, lean and athletic. With hazel eyes and the slash of a smile beneath a head of long, blond hair, she could probably snap her fingers and have any man she wanted. Yet, as far as she knew, her sister had never had a serious relationship after her divorce. Why was that? "What happened between the two of you?"

Erin's smile turned melancholy. "You were too young to understand back then. What were you—twelve?"

"More like seventeen," Reggie corrected. She'd even been through her first heartbreak, but her sister and Michelle and Nina had still treated her like she was a kid.

"Long story short, he wasn't the man I thought he was." Erin shrugged. "He knew when we met that I dreamed of traveling the world. He said that's what he wanted, too. Whenever we talked about our future together, he painted a picture of us as a pair of gypsies. We'd live in exotic places, see the seven wonders of the world and make our own list of seven more. I couldn't think of anything better, so when he proposed the day we graduated from college, I said yes."

When Erin stared dreamily into space, Reggie prompted, "But it didn't turn out like that?"

Erin blinked and gave her head a sad shake. "No. Six months later and still on our honeymoon, we were backpacking through Switzerland. I remember that day so clearly. We were in the middle of a field of flowers with water rushing through a rock-lined stream beside us, the Alps in the distance. It was like something out of a travel brochure. That's when Ron got the news that his father had died. We turned around right then and there and headed back to the States."

"That must have been awful," Reggie whispered. Her stomach clenched as she thought about the worst happening while she was so far away. "Mom and Dad told me you'd come back from Europe and were in Houston, but they didn't say anything about Ron's father. I wonder why we didn't go to the funeral."

Erin tipped her head to one side. "Why would you? Mom and Dad barely knew Ron's folks."

That much was true. She remembered meeting Ron's parents on the steps outside the courthouse the day of her sister's wedding. With Michelle and Nina serving as Erin's attendants, they'd gathered in the judge's chambers for a brief ceremony. Afterwards, they'd all gone out to lunch together. As far as she knew, the two families hadn't had anything to do with each other beyond that.

"After the funeral, Ron said we needed to stay in Houston while he handled his dad's estate. I agreed, thinking he meant a month, two at the most. His mom and dad had divorced years earlier, and he didn't have any brothers or sisters, so it should have been pretty straight-forward, right?"

"You'd think so. Was his dad wealthy?" Sam had talked enough about wills and probate in the early days of their marriage that Reggie understood how a hefty bank account or vast holdings complicated things.

"Comfortable, maybe. But he wasn't an oil baron or anything." Erin laughed. "By the time everything was said and done, a year had passed. Ron had inherited his dad's house—we'd been staying there while he sorted everything out. There was some money, too. Enough that we weren't going to starve anytime soon. I told him, this was our chance—we could follow our dream and travel the world. I mean, that was always the plan, wasn't it?"

Reggie's head bobbed. It made sense that her sister and Ron would pick up where they'd left off.

"I started making arrangements. Ron had

always talked about how much he wanted to see the Great Pyramid of Giza, so I was looking into flights to Egypt when, without so much as a by-your-leave, he changed everything. One night, he announced that he'd decided to keep his dad's house, buy a boat and go into the fishing charter business. He went on and on—he'd really thought the whole thing out. When I asked where our dream of traveling the globe fit into this new life he'd mapped out, he said we'd have time for that later—after the kids were grown and on their own."

Reggie held her breath. Like Erin, she'd had the rug pulled out from under her by her husband. It had been the worst night of her life. "What'd you do?"

"I looked at him like he had lost his mind. The whole time we were dating we'd talked about the kind of life we wanted to lead. Living in Houston and running a fishing charter wasn't it. Neither was starting a family. I wasn't even sure I wanted children. That he'd make such a huge decision without discussing it with me, well...We fought."

The memory of the night Sam had called it quits on their marriage came rushing back. Reggie blinked back tears as Erin's breath shuddered.

"We both said things we shouldn't have," Erin continued. "He blamed me for his dad's death. When I pointed out how ridiculous that was, he said if I hadn't been so insistent on gallivanting around Europe, he'd have been there when his dad needed him. After that things got...really ugly. I packed my bags and left. I was so hurt and angry, I just wanted to put as much distance between us as possible. So I did. Six months later, the divorce papers caught up with me in Bangkok. I signed them and kept on going. I never saw him again. Not till last night."

"And he just showed up out of the blue, expecting you to head off to Timbuktu with him? Did he at least apologize for all he put you through?" Reggie tugged on her ponytail.

"He did. I said I was sorry for my part in our breakup, too." Erin waved a hand, dismissive. "It's water under the bridge. We've both moved on, lived the lives we were meant to live."

Despite her words, Erin had dark circles under her eyes. Was her sister as content with how things turned out as she claimed? "I'm surprised you'd forgive him. Much less ever consider working with him."

The same melancholy smile Erin had worn earlier put in a return appearance. "Ten years is a long time to hold a grudge. If you aren't careful, it makes you as bitter as a cup of week-old coffee. I've thought—a lot—about that day when things came off the rails for us. I realize now that Ron felt guilty about not being there for his dad at the end. He blamed me 'cause he couldn't blame himself."

In a way, Sam had done the same thing. When, despite all the rounds of in vitro, they still hadn't gotten pregnant, he'd piled all the blame for their inability to have a child on her. Had he walked out on her, on their marriage, because he was unable to shoulder his share of that burden? Reggie bit her lip. Sam's problems were his own to deal with. For now, it was enough that he'd held up his part of the bargain, signed the divorce papers and divided their assets equally. By Christmas, she'd be free to move on with her life. In the meantime, her sister had given her some good advice. Neither dwelling on the past nor being fearful of the future would help her move forward.

And moving forward was exactly what she wanted to do. She brushed her hands together as if shaking off the dust of old relationships.

"Thanks for telling me what happened between you and Ron. Mom and Dad never talked about it. At least, not when I was around."

She straightened. Erin deserved to know how she really felt. "I hope you decide to stay. It's been nice, getting to know my big sister again."

"Same here," Erin said with a smile. "And like I said, I don't have any plans to go anywhere anytime soon." She looked around the room. "So shall we get started unpacking?"

"Yes. Let's." Whether her sister stuck around for six months or six years, from now on out, Reggie refused to let the specter of things that might never happen ruin the present.

Three

Michelle

"How in the world did Polly hear about our plans for Jack and his friends?" Michelle let out an exasperated sigh.

Sensing she wouldn't want everyone in town to see her frustration, Erin, Nina and Reggie closed ranks around her until they stood in a tight cluster on the lawn in front of the First Baptist Church of Sugar Sand Beach. Flustered, Michelle straightened the shoulder strap of her purse for what had to be the sixth time in the last two minutes. "We weren't planning to start that until after the grand opening."

Several days a week, most of the town's retirees gathered at the Community Center, where they wiled away the hours playing bingo and hoping to win the daily jackpot—a coupon for a free dessert from Maggie's Diner. But on days when the center was closed or for those who didn't enjoy the game, there were few alternatives. Jack's solution had been to stake out a table at his niece's restaurant where, along with his pals, the retired farmer spent his days sipping free coffee and flirting with the waitresses. Thinking one of the inn's roomy parlors filled with comfy couches might offer a better option, Michelle had planned to host Senior Days once or twice a week starting in the fall.

Only spry Polly Denton had jumped the gun. When she read the announcements from the podium nearly an hour ago, Polly had invited all of the town's senior citizens to a weekly coffee klatch at the inn starting *this* Tuesday. Worried about the sudden shift in her timetable, in addition to the million other details that needed to be addressed before the inn's grand opening, Michelle hadn't been able to sit still and enjoy one minute of the morning's sermon.

"The painters are starting work on the exterior tomorrow. There'll be ladders and workmen everywhere," she fretted softly. "What if someone trips and falls over a drop cloth? What if they get hurt? They'll have to eat. What will we feed them?" Her mind raced, and she turned to Nina.

"Can you make cookies for Tuesday? What about crackers? And tea?"

"Relax," Nina soothed. "Now that I'm back at the inn full time, I can whip up whatever we need."

"Well, that's something to be thankful for." Michelle ran down her mental checklist. She'd need to hang fresh towels in the bathrooms, make sure everything was spick-and-span. "The board games and decks of cards I ordered came in last week. I need to put them in the sideboard. And then there's the painters. I'm worried about them."

"We can have them start on the outbuildings first," Reggie suggested. "That's a two-day job. Or, if we explained the situation, they might begin on the back side of the house."

"Why didn't I think of that?" Michelle drew her first easy breath since Polly's announcement had shocked her upright in her pew. "I wish I knew who spilled the beans," she said, hiking her purse strap onto her shoulder again.

As if she expected the culprit to step forward and admit their guilt, she studied the crowd. Five minutes earlier, Reverend Olliver had walked down the center aisle to the exit, where he'd shaken the hands of each and every departing member before they descended the steps to the sidewalk. In no apparent hurry to head home or to the diner for Sunday dinner, people now lingered on the narrow lawn in groups of three or four.

Erin winced like she had a toothache. She smoothed one hand down the pale kimono top she'd worn over blousy slacks. "I think I might know the answer." She aimed her chin toward the spot where Polly and her son Walt stood chatting with Gus, the owner of the only grocery store for miles around.

"How would he…" Michelle put two and two together. "Oh. You told Walt."

"I mentioned it the last time we spoke. When I told him getting ready for the grand opening was taking up all my time right now, he asked what we'd planned for the big day. He's such a whiz at business that it seemed like a good idea to get his input." In addition to the Happy Dolphin, Walt owned at least a part interest in several other restaurants and businesses in nearby Panama City. "I'm so sorry. I never dreamed he'd tell Polly. Or that she'd announce it to the world before we were ready."

"Well, the cat's out of the bag now." Michelle expelled a breath of air. "We're stuck. We'll have to kick off our Senior Days a little sooner than anticipated, that's all." She really shouldn't have gotten so worked up about it. Certainly not when she should have been listening to the sermon. From the little she heard of it, it had been a good one. "We'd better mingle," she whispered to the others. "Meet you at the car in ten minutes?" With temperatures in the mid-eighties and the humidity so high she could practically wring water out of the air, it wouldn't be long before the crowd dissipated.

Reggie grinned. "Great! That gives me enough time to give Hope the toy I bought her." She reached into her purse and pulled out a floppy-eared elephant. "It plays music," she whispered in an awed tone. "She's going to love it." Holding the gift behind her back, she headed toward the spot where her friend Chris spoke with one of the church deacons. Balanced on one of her daddy's lean hips, little Hope pulled on Chris's ear.

"It's good to see her with the baby," Erin said when the smiling six-month-old spotted Reggie and held out her hands. "After all she's been through, I didn't think she'd warm up to little kids. But Hope has my sister wrapped around her little finger."

"Looks like her daddy is a fan, too," Nina observed as the young widower handed his daughter over to Reggie without hesitation.

"Betty Spann promised to bring me her recipe for bread-and-butter pickles today. I'd better go talk to her. We're going to need that recipe. Otherwise, some of the cucumbers from our garden will go to waste." She quickly joined a knot of women from the Ladies' Auxiliary.

Michelle pitched her voice for Erin's ears only. "I'd much rather put some pickles on my sandwich than face another cucumber salad." In the last week alone, they'd had cucumbers in dill sauce one night, cucumber and onion salad the next. She'd drawn the line at cucumber smoothies—enough was enough. "They give me gas." She rubbed her tummy.

Erin grinned. "Can't have that when you're around Dave. Speaking of which, where is our favorite attorney?"

"Yesterday was his daughter's birthday." Sara, an attorney in her own right, clerked for a judge in the state capitol. "He's spending the weekend in Tallahassee with her. We'll probably grab a cup of coffee together later this week."

"So you and Dave, huh?" A speculative gleam brightened Erin's hazel eyes. "Are things getting serious between you two?"

"It's much too soon for that," Michelle protested despite how the mere mention of Dave's name made her pulse race. Not so long ago, she'd been sure her romantic life had ended when her husband of twenty-five years died. But the tall, handsome attorney had rekindled emotions she never thought she'd feel again. At first, she'd been concerned that her interest was one-sided, but he'd recently assured her they shared a mutual attraction. When he'd invited her to attend a play with him—their first official date—she'd felt as giddy as a schoolgirl. She still did.

She fanned her face with one hand while Erin continued to stare at her. Studying the crowded lawn, she felt relief surge through her when she spotted Maggie Henson on approach. She waved to the woman who'd become a good friend in the short time they'd known each other. "I wonder if she was as surprised by Polly's announcement as we were," she mused, hoping to distract Erin.

"We'll talk more about Daaave later," Erin promised in a singsong voice. "But she probably wants to thank you for hosting Senior Days. I'll leave you two to chat. I want to catch Walt before he skedaddles." Erin used her fingers to brush her long blond hair behind her ears.

"You're not going to give him a hard time for spilling the beans to his mother, are you?" Michelle asked. Walt had proven to be a man of principles and integrity during the whole fiasco with Nina's ex. Without his help, things would have turned out much worse for all of them.

"Don't worry. Walt's a good guy. It's not his fault his mother's such a blabbermouth."

Michelle chuckled as Erin hurried off. She turned to greet Maggie. "Why, don't you look nice," she exclaimed. The owner of the diner had swapped the black T-shirt and pants she wore to work each day for a pretty floral sheath dress that brought out the color in her cheeks. "Is that new?"

"This old thing? You like it?" Maggie plucked at the sides of the slim-fitting dress and held them out briefly before letting the material fall back into place. "I love Sundays." She sighed. "It's the one day of the week I get to dress-up." She leaned in close. "Listen, are you sure you're up to hosting Jack and his pals on Tuesday? I know you weren't planning to get started on that quite this soon."

"No, we weren't. But it's okay," Michelle assured her friend. "I was worried because we're having the house painted next week. I spoke with Erin and Nina and Reggie about it, though, and they think we can manage. We'll have to shift a few things around, but everything should be fine."

"Oh, good." Relief flooded Maggie's fine features. "'Cause Jack, he's really looking forward to it. I haven't seen him this excited about anything in years. He left right after church or he'd tell you himself. He was anxious to get home and share the good news with the rest of his friends."

"That's so sweet," Michelle said. That was exactly the reaction she'd hoped for from the aging farmer.

"Although I'd never in a million years say this to Jack, it helps me out, too. Reverend Olliver has asked me time and time again to let them hold their weekly prayer group at the diner. But as long as Jack and his friends took up an entire table, I had to turn him down. Guess where the prayer group is meeting this week?"

"The diner?"

"Bingo!" Maggie grinned. "Reverend Olliver couldn't be happier, and I'm glad for the extra business."

Thank goodness she hadn't jumped to her feet and corrected Polly during today's service, Michelle thought. She almost had, and look at all the people she'd have been letting down. The longer she lived in Sugar Sand Beach, the more she realized this was what small-town life was all about—neighbors reaching out to help

49

neighbors. Her heart softened. "I am glad it worked out. Now don't worry about a thing. Everything will go off just like clockwork."

And it would, too. No matter how many hoops she had to jump through to make it happen.

Tuesday morning, Michelle surveyed the front parlor. A tall dispenser of lightly sweetened lemonade stood at one end of the sideboard. Opposite it, the blue light on the Keurig announced that the coffee maker was raring to go. In between stood stacks of paper cups suitable for either hot or cold beverages, as well a tray filled with an assortment of cookies and crackers.

She'd unpacked the Scrabble game earlier today. The tiles were now facedown on the folding table, strategically placed beneath an overhead light. Four tile racks stood at the ready for contestants. Another table held decks of cards in case Jack and his cronies wanted to play penny-ante poker or Hand-and-Foot. The cupboard doors stood open to reveal a short stack of other popular games. Two fully stocked bathrooms were just down the hall. Comfortable chairs clustered around an occasional table in the far corner, the perfect spot for simply sitting and chatting.

Michelle brushed her hands together and checked her watch. They were ready. She'd no sooner had that thought than a car door slammed. A minute later, footsteps thumped up the wooden steps and onto the front porch.

"They're here!" She called to the others as she moved briskly toward the foyer. A flurry of activity signaled that Nina, Reggie and Erin were converging on the parlor. She swung the front door wide.

Wearing bib overalls and a plaid shirt, Jack marched up the front steps like a king returning to his castle. An entourage of similarly clad elderly men accompanied him. Reaching the threshold, he held out a hand. "Thank you for inviting us to your home, Ms. Robinson," he said.

"Michelle, please," she said with a warm smile as her hand was enveloped in a strong grip. Jack pumped twice. His calloused palms whispered against her skin when he let go.

He gestured toward the small group that had gathered around him. "That there's John, Toby and Eustis. Billy and Frank'll be here in a minute.

Takes them a bit longer 'cause they gotta use the ramp."

As Michelle shook hands with each of their guests, she stole a quick glance out the side window. Two more men had reached the top of the ramp that had been added to the house shortly after the accident that had robbed Nancy Simmons of her ability to walk. Aided by walkers, the pair made their slow way across the porch. She did a quick head count. Six. Two more than the usual cadre of four who met at the diner, but Maggie had warned her that Jack had spread the word to friends who had missed Sunday's announcement.

"Welcome to the Sugar Sand Inn." She smiled brightly at the later arrivals. "Right this way, gentlemen." Her footsteps measured to suit the group's slow pace, she headed down the long hall that ran from the front door all the way to the sun porch at the back of the house. Built in the early 1900s, the house focused on function rather than flow. As a result, entrances to several rooms branched off one wide, main hall.

"I like what you've done to the place," Jack said. He paused at the entrance to the living room, where a fresh coat of white paint brightened the soaring mantel above the fireplace. "Nancy'd like having so many people in the house. Always did like a party, that gal did."

"Uh-huh." Eustis ran a hand through the sparse hair he'd combed over his balding head. "She sure did. Her parents threw a big ol' New Year's Eve party each year. Those were always loads of fun."

Curious, Michelle halted. "You all knew Nancy?" she asked. She hadn't considered it before, but the men had to have been born around the same time as her birth mother.

Jack tugged on his chin. "Well, now, not all of us. Billy, he moved to Sugar Sand Beach two years ago to live with his daughter. And Lou there—his family moved here after Nancy shut herself up in this big ol' house. But me an' Eustis an' Toby was in high school with Nancy. She was a couple o' years younger—in the tenth grade when we was seniors. We didn't run together much back then. Probably would have when we got older, but the accident put an end to all that."

"Tweren't no more parties after that, either," Eustis moaned. "Say, I don't suppose you'll be startin' them up again, will you?" He gave her a hopeful look.

Careful not to promise more than she could deliver, Michelle gave a noncommittal shrug and followed it up with a cheery, "We'll see," before they resumed their trek.

At last, the group arrived at the entrance to the large sitting room that abutted the kitchen. "Once the painters finish with the house, you'll be able to come and go through the sun porch." She pointed toward the rear of the house. A few steps beyond the recently remodeled dining room on the left and the kitchen on the right, light streamed in from the back porch. "It's not quite as much of a hike from there." For Billy and Frank's benefit, she added, "That entrance has a ramp, too."

As she shepherded her small group into the room that would serve as the gathering spot for Senior Days, her friends stepped forward.

"I'm sure you all met Nina, Reggie and Erin at the open house this spring. And you're sure to have seen us all around town. But just in case, Nina is the head chef for the cafe we'll be opening soon."

Nina, wearing a simple chef's jacket over loose cooking trousers, gave a shallow bow.

"Reggie is responsible for all the beautiful plants and shrubs on the property. She's also in charge of our garden. Which, we hope, will soon supply most of the farm-to-table produce for the cafe."

Reggie gave the group a small wave and a big smile.

"Erin is the activities director for the inn. We'll all be around if you need anything, but she'll be your official hostess on Tuesdays."

Wearing a green polo with the name of the inn stitched onto the shirt pocket, Erin stepped forward. "Welcome to the inn! We're all glad you chose to join us today. As you can see"— she gestured toward the tables and chairs scattered about—"we have a few games and activities available for your use. Help yourself to coffee or lemonade on the sideboard. If you need anything else, just let me know. Oh, and the bathrooms are right around the corner." She pointed to a short hallway between the sitting room and the library.

Nina cleared her throat. "Until we have the cafe up and running, we're offering box lunches at five dollars apiece. Today, we have turkey or roast beef sandwiches. I'll be back in a little while to take your orders." Having said her piece, she left for the kitchen, where she'd left an applicant for the prep cook position cooling his heels.

A long couple of seconds passed while Jack and his pals took in their surroundings. Then Jack clapped his hands together. "This here all looks real nice, ladies." He turned to his friends.

"Billy, you grab us that table over yonder while I get us some coffee. That okay with you?"

"Make mine a lemonade," said the man with the walker. He raised the metal frame and moved it a foot closer to the table before shuffling forward. Repeating the process over and over, he crossed the room to the table.

Meanwhile, the others in the group scattered. John made a beeline for the sideboard, where he snagged two cookies, quickly wrapped them in a napkin and stuffed them into one of his overalls' deep side pockets. He grabbed another handful, which he piled onto a plate that he carried to Billy's table. Ignoring the sideboard, Frank propped his walker beside the sofa and sank onto the cushions with a groan. Toby joined Jack, who was giving the Keurig a questioning look.

"You know how to work this thing?" Jack's glance traveled from the K-cup he'd taken from a nearby rack to the brewer.

"Not a clue. Where's the pot?" Toby looked around as if he expected one to materialize out of thin air. When it didn't appear, he beckoned to Michelle. "Is this here a coffee maker?" he asked.

Michelle beamed at them. "Happy to help," she said, stepping between the two men. "It's pretty simple, once you get the hang of it. This brewer makes one cup of coffee at a time, so first, you place an empty cup like so." She positioned a paper cup under the spout. She held out her palm. "Jack, I'll take that K-cup." When he handed it over, she lifted the cover and slid the plastic cup into place and closed the lid. "See that blinking blue button?" she asked. When the two men nodded, she jabbed it with her finger. "Push the button, and in about thirty seconds, voilà, fresh-brewed coffee."

The rich smell of a dark roast filled the air. Less than a minute later, the brewer coughed to signal it had reached the end of the cycle. Eager to try his hand, Toby handed Jack the full cup and centered an empty one like Michelle had shown them. "How come the button's not blinking?" he asked.

"You need to remove the used plastic tub and put in a new one," Michelle told him. Much as she wanted to do it for him, she restrained herself.

"You mean you have to load the thing every time? You can't just reuse the old one?" Toby scratched his head.

"That's the way it works, yes," Michelle assured him.

She watched as, his movements tentative, Toby took another K-cup from the stand. His mouth twisted into a perplexed frown, he wrestled the used portion from the top and inserted a fresh one. He shot Michelle another questioning glance.

"Close the lid," she coached.

He did and expelled a heavy breath when he pressed the flashing blue button. "Seems like an awful lot of work for just one cup of coffee," he muttered.

Meanwhile, Jack picked up the used K-cup and shook it. A few drops of brown liquid splattered on the top of the sideboard. Ignoring them, he examined the holes in the top and bottom of the plastic container. "You recycle these?"

Michelle shook her head. "You can, but it's a lot of bother. You'd have to peel this off." She tapped the thin aluminum cover. "Wash out the grounds. Then the plastic can go in the recycle bin."

"Huh." Jack and Toby exchanged looks of pure dissatisfaction. "You'd think they'd at least make 'em out of cardboard." Carrying their coffees and Billy's lemonade, they headed for the table where the others waited.

Michelle mopped up the few splatters on the countertop and refilled the Keurig's reservoir from a nearby pitcher of water. After removing the used container from the brewer, she examined it closely. She and Allen had limited themselves to two cups of coffee each day, so she hadn't given a whole lot of thought to the number of the tiny tubs she contributed to the local landfill. Now that she was living with Erin, Reggie and Nina, though, they bought their coffee supplies from the big box store in Destin. In *big* boxes. Closing her eyes, she tried to imagine the pile of little plastic cups the four of them had tossed over the last two months. She swallowed hard as she pictured how that pile would grow once the inn had overnight guests. She shook her head hard enough to make her chin-length hair sway. Jack had a point. Tossing the tiny plastic tubs into the landfill where they wouldn't disintegrate for several lifetimes was foolish.

The chatter of several voices coming from the hallway stopped her before she was able to do more than vow to make a change. She spun toward the doorway just as a trio of women she recognized from the Ladies Auxiliary at church spilled into the room. Leading the charge was a neatly coiffed Mrs. Bees, the woman who'd filled in as Hope's emergency babysitter one afternoon last month. Michelle stared at the new arrivals in wonder. Had every resident of Sugar Sand Beach over the age of sixty-five decided to attend Senior Days? Her gaze swept the room. Well, the parlor was large enough to accommodate quite a few more people.

From his table in the corner, Jack let out a loud groan. "What are they doing here?" he groused.

Mrs. Bees shook a finger in his direction. "I'll have you know we have just as much right to be here as you do, Jack Henson. Isn't that so, Michelle?"

Before answering, Michelle shot Erin an amused glance. Mrs. Bees might be so tiny, a stiff wind could knock her down, but the woman had a lot of gumption. She cleared her throat. "It wouldn't be very neighborly of us to leave anyone out, now would it?"

Mrs. Bees's hand landed on her hips. "So there, Jack." She turned to the women who flanked her on either side. "Flo, Hazel, let's sit at that table." She pointed to the one farthest from Jack and his pals. "Hazel, you brought the cards, didn't you?"

Her white hair in tightly permed ringlets, Hazel held up a small cloth bag. "Sure did. But without Dottie, we need a fourth."

Mrs. Bees surveyed the room. "We need one more for Hand-and-Foot. Anyone want to play?"

Michelle hid a smile behind one hand when Mrs. Bees pinned Jack with a hopeful glance. But Jack was having none of it. He shifted his chair away from the women. Muttering loudly, he huffed, "There goes the neighborhood."

When no one else answered Mrs. Bees's request, Erin stepped forward. "I'd love to join you, if you'll have me. Twos and jokers wild?"

"Yep," Mrs. Bees answered. She dismissed Jack with a scowl before turning her attention to Erin. "I didn't think you youngsters knew this game."

"I spent summers teaching kayaking and giving tours in Seward, Alaska," Erin explained. "When it rained—and it rained a lot—we spent the down time playing cards. Rummy. Canasta. Poker. You name it. Hand-and-Foot was my favorite."

"Well, come on then. Let's not waste any time. I'm Ruth, by the way. Ruth Bees."

"Pleased to meet you, Ruth. I'm Erin."

While Erin helped the women get drinks and snacks, Michelle scanned the room. Frank and Eustis sat on the couch, where she doubted very much time would pass before they both dozed off. Jack and the other men chatted amongst themselves. She smiled to herself when she caught Jack sending surreptitious looks in Ruth's direction. Clearly there was more going on between them than either wanted to let on.

She whispered quietly to Erin that she'd be upstairs if she was needed and headed for the stairs to the second floor, satisfied that their first Senior Day was off to a good start.

Four

Nina

"Ethan. Thanks for waiting." With mixed feelings of hope and trepidation swirling in her belly, Nina strode into the kitchen. "Today was our first Senior Day, and I needed to say hello to our guests." When she set up the appointment with the young man who'd agreed to wait in the breakfast nook, she had no idea they'd be playing host to the group this morning.

Ethan relinquished his grip on the glass of water he'd cupped in his hands and jumped to his feet as though he'd been sitting on a bed of prickly cactus. Though she'd only been out of the room fifteen minutes, Nina watched carefully to see if he left a cell phone on the table or slipped one into his pocket. She exhaled slowly when he did neither. Her former assistant had been so tightly glued to her phone that Nina had been certain it'd take pry bars and acetone to separate the two. She wanted the next person she hired to focus more on the job than their social life.

Towering over her own five feet ten inches, Ethan extended a hand that dwarfed her own. "I hope you don't mind. I helped myself to some water while I waited." He indicated a half-empty glass on the table.

She hid a smile for Ethan's sweet, Southern drawl while she glanced at the table. The folded paper towel he'd placed under the glass earned him a couple of points for neatness. She awarded his firm grip and the directness of his brown eyes another two points as she waved him into his seat. After stepping around the table, she took a seat opposite him. She didn't bother reaching for his resume. Maggie Henson had recommended him. That had been enough to get Ethan an interview despite his lack of actual work experience. "Maggie tells me you've lived here all your life?"

"Yes, ma'am. I mean, yes, Chef," Ethan stammered. The sprinkling of freckles across his nose and cheeks darkened as a flush crept up his neck. "My folks run a fish camp on Western Lake. You might'a heard of it? Red's?"

"Can't say I have, but my friend Erin has probably been there. She's an avid kayaker."

Ethan nodded. "There's lots of little lakes around here. Most of 'em are hard to get to. Western Lake's about the easiest."

"Your folks must do a good business, then." Curiosity swirled through her. Why was this young man sitting in her kitchen, applying for an entry-level job, instead of working for his parents? Didn't he want to go into the family business? Did he have some ulterior motive?

The instant the last question crossed her mind, memories of all the problems Krystal had caused flooded back. It took some effort, but she shoved the troubling thoughts aside. The experience with her previous assistant had put her on edge, but Ethan hadn't done anything to raise her suspicions. She needed to give the young man the benefit of the doubt.

"They do all right." Ethan shrugged one shoulder. "Enough to keep food on the table. That's saying something when there's seven mouths to feed."

"So you have brothers and sisters?" she asked, wanting to learn more about him and his reasons for showing up in her kitchen.

"Four brothers. No sisters. The two oldest— Tommy and Curtis—they help Mom and Dad run the camp. The younger ones—Freddy and Mac—they're still in school. But they help out summers and weekends, same as I did when I was their age. Mom and Dad have six cabins and five jon boats and canoes for rent. There's a gas pump and a small store and always work to do."

She pictured wooden cabins tucked among the scrub oak, a long dock stretching into the water, a store that offered just the basics—bread and suntan lotion, a freezer filled with bait and ice cream bars. "You don't want to work for your folks?"

"Nah." Ethan's sandy-colored hair was so closely cropped that it didn't move when he shook his head. "I knew early on I wasn't cut out for a life of haulin' boats in and outta the water, cleaning cabins and waiting on customers. I didn't want to be a fishing guide, either—never saw much point in fishing. For me, the fun part always came at the end of the day when we'd cook our catch. Bring me a mess of bream, and I'll fry you up the best food you ever put in your mouth. Redfish is mighty good eatin' too. There's lots of them in the lake."

"It sounds like you were born to cook." She paused. "Did your mother teach you?"

Ethan snorted. "No, ma'—Chef. Mom thinks dinner comes in a box or a can. It was my uncle who taught me food could be better. He took me to the Back Porch in Destin for my sixth birthday. Have you been there?"

Nina nodded. Popular with tourists and locals alike, the beachside restaurant specialized in fresh seafood. "I like their corn medley."

"It's awesome. I make one a lot like it, but I add a little chopped jalapeno to kick it up a notch."

She pulled the taste of the mix of fresh corn and vegetables from her memory banks, added in a touch of heat and smiled. "Sounds yummy."

The comment stretched Ethan's full lips into a grin. "When my uncle took me to the Back Porch—that was the first time I was ever in a real restaurant. I had no idea what to do when they handed me a menu. I probably would'a got fried shrimp or fish, but my uncle insisted on ordering me a 'grown-up' meal. I didn't know food could look and taste that good! I didn't want that meal to end, and it took me two hours to eat my dinner. After that, I started watching those cooking shows I used to flip past on the TV and, before too long, I was trying out some of the recipes. Had a few flops, but even my flops were better than mac 'n' cheese out of a box."

Nina smiled at the note of pride she heard in the young man's voice. Every chef had an "Ah-ha!" moment when they recognized their life's work. She was glad Ethan's uncle had given him his. "So after high school, you studied food science at Florida State College."

"Yes, Chef. I worked afternoons and summers for my folks all the way through high school. Earned enough to pay for two years of schooling in Jacksonville. I'm the first in my family to go to college, and I graduated at the top of my class. Got my associate's degree in Culinary Management."

Nina caught another hint of pride in Ethan's tone and nodded. He should be proud. Unlike Krystal, whose rich daddy had paid her way through school, he'd set his sights on a goal and worked hard to achieve it. She gave the boy high marks for work ethic and drive. Now, could he follow direction? Was he teachable? Time would tell. She dusted her hands.

"I mentioned that we're hosting Senior Day today. Until the cafe opens, we thought we'd offer box lunches for the attendees. Feel like helping me whip up the sandwiches to go in them?" Putting the simple fare together would give her the chance to see the young man in action, something she probably should have done with Krystal. If she had, she'd never have hired the girl.

"Yes, Chef. I'd like that."

"Okay. Iceberg lettuce and tomatoes are in the crisper." She pointed to the built-in Sub-Zero fridge. "Cutting boards are in the cabinet next to the sink. Why don't you start getting those ready while I find out who wants to order and whether they want turkey or roast beef." She patted the pocket of her chef's pants, where she'd tucked a small notepad and pen.

"Yes, Chef. Is it all right if I borrow one of those?" He aimed his chin toward a wall of pegs where dark green bib aprons hung.

"Help yourself. I'll be in the room next door if you need anything."

Ethan rose. Long, coltish legs took him across the room in four quick strides. He grabbed an apron at random, slipped the neck strap over his head and crisscrossed the ties around his narrow waist before working them into a neat bow in front. Without prompting, he headed for the hand wash station.

Impressed, Nina sent silent thanks to Maggie for recommending the young man. Ethan had shown all the qualities she expected of an eager, young cook. Though she'd hold off on making a final decision until she saw how well he handled himself in the kitchen, so far, she just had one question. Why hadn't Maggie snapped him up for her own restaurant?

Nina sat at the oversize desk in the office she shared with Michelle. Her fingers moved with agonizing slowness across the keyboard as she hunted keys and pecked at them to create an employee record for Ethan. She finished, read the information on the screen and winced. She'd spelled the boy's last name incorrectly. Carefully, she slid the cursor to the wrong letter before she searched the keyboard for the Delete key. She struck it once. When nothing happened, she struck it again. The monitor blinked. The form she'd spent the past fifteen minutes filling out disappeared.

"Ouch!" she whispered.

Give her a cell phone or a tablet, and her thumbs flew across the keys whenever she wanted to send a text. Why did typing on a computer have to be so difficult? Determined to finish the job she'd started, she straightened the paperwork on the desk and began again.

The door to the office swung open. Erin's head appeared in the gap. "You busy?"

"I could use a break." Nina stuck her tongue out at the evil keyboard. She glanced over Erin's shoulder to the kitchen. "How's it going out there? None of our guests have taken up skateboarding in the halls, have they?"

Erin's hearty laughter filled the small office.

"Nope. The ladies wanted to stretch their legs. Reggie's taking them out to the lake in one of the ATVs. The men are either napping or watching a home improvement show on the television." She and Michelle had mounted a flat-screen TV on one of the parlor walls. "While I had a minute, I wanted to find out how things went with your interview this morning. Any luck?"

"As a matter of fact, yes. His name is Ethan Fort, and he accepted my offer for the prep cook position. He'll start work next Monday. He's a sweet kid. I have high hopes. I was just trying to create a new employee record for him, but I hit a wrong key or something 'cause I lost it." She sighed heavily.

"Want some help?"

"I'd wouldn't turn it down if you've got a spare minute."

"Glad to. I don't have anything else to do until Reggie brings Ruth and her crew back." Erin strode across the room.

Nina stood and stepped aside while Erin slid into the spot in front of the computer. "Wow! He won't turn twenty-one till next spring," Erin noted while her fingers flew over the keyboard.

"Remember what it feels like to be that young?" She and Erin and Michelle had been in their junior year at the University of Virginia when they'd reached the legal drinking age. She'd always been on the go back then—racing between classes and labs and a series of part-time jobs in restaurants near the college.

"Yes, and I'm glad that's over." Erin shook her head. "I made some foolish mistakes back then."

"Are you talking about Ron?" Erin didn't talk about her ex much. Not that Nina expected her to. After all, twenty years—give or take one or two—had passed since their divorce.

"Yes and no. It broke my heart when he and I called it quits. I loved him. On some level, I probably always will." Her voice quieted. "I'm still not sure I ever got over him." As if realizing she'd said too much, she straightened. She cleared her throat. "But we would have ended up hating each other if we'd stayed together. I wouldn't have gotten to travel like I did. I've been to so many places, seen so many amazing things. And the people—I met some wonderful people along the way, too." Erin's gaze drifted to the window and beyond.

Huh. That was interesting.

She'd had no idea Erin still harbored feelings for Ron. Was there a chance the two of them would get back together again? Nina combed her fingers through her hair until they reached the tidy bun at the back of her head. "I guess that means you're giving some real thought to going with him?" Much as she hated the thought of Erin leaving, she'd never stand in the way of true love.

"Not seriously." Erin's focus shifted to the screen. Her fingers hit a few more keys. "I mean, I think about it, of course. Who wouldn't want to travel the world on private jets and stay in luxury hotels? But every time I start to go down that path—imagining what it'd be like—I hit a road block. I can't stop thinking I'll uproot my life only to have Ron change his mind. Again."

"You don't trust him." The hope that her friend had rediscovered her soul mate collapsed like a cake taken out of the oven too soon.

"I guess that's what it all boils down to. I loved Ron once upon a time. In many ways, I always will. But do I trust him to make a plan and follow it through?" She pressed one hand to her chest. "My heart says yes." Her fingers rose to her temple. "My head says no. Right now, I'm listening to my head."

"Whatever you decide, you have my support," Nina said slowly. She needed her friend to know she was free to follow her heart.

"Thanks. Now let's get this finished, shall we?" Erin bent over the keyboard. A few seconds later, she hit the return key. "Voilà!" she said with a flourish. "And it's done. One down. How many more to go?"

"Three," Nina admitted. "I still need a waiter or a waitress, someone to bus the tables and a line cook." She wanted more than a line cook, though. She needed a sous chef—someone who could handle the kitchen in her absence. But she'd learned her lesson. After the experience with Krystal, she wouldn't name anyone as her second-in-command until they proved trustworthy.

"I'm not worried about the first two. Those positions will be easy to fill. Once the word gets out, tons of people will want to work here. This is a great place." Erin gestured beyond the office to the sunny kitchen filled with state-of-the-art appliances. A frown tugged at her lips. "That line cook, though. That's a tricky one. Do you have any leads?"

"A couple of people responded to my posts on the job boards. They either didn't have experience or they weren't a good fit." One of them had been Paul, the chef she'd interviewed before she hired Krystal. Preferring to handle everything on her own than deal with the man's abrasive personality, she hadn't bothered to return his call. "There is one other person." She took a breath. "I'm just not sure I can go there."

"Oh?" Erin's hazel eyes filled with questions. Wisps of blond hair framed her face when she leaned forward expectantly.

"Charlie's wife, Viola."

"She applied?" Erin's eyebrows hiked. "How'd that happen?"

"I guess Charlie told her I was looking for help." Nina had spent half her life in various Northern Virginia restaurants, often with Charlie working the grill while she manned a different station. Over the years, their relationship had deepened from the nodding acquaintance she shared with her other co-workers into a real friendship. She thought so highly of Charlie—and his skills—that she'd whispered his name into the owner's ear as a potential candidate for head chef at the Happy Dolphin. Her friend and his family had moved to Florida three weeks ago. "Viola sent me an email this morning. She wants me to consider her for the job."

"What's she like?" Erin asked.

But Nina was already shaking her head. "I've never met her. They had an apartment out in Herndon. The few times she drove into the city, we missed each other."

Erin whistled. "Charlie made that drive every day? That's quite a commute." In Northern Virginia's rush hour traffic, the twenty-five mile

74

drive could take two hours. "I can see why he and Viola would jump at the chance to move here." Rush hour in Sugar Sand Beach consisted of two cars at the town's lone stop sign. She eyed the computer. "Does she have any experience?"

"Not professional experience. She made cakes and pastries out of her kitchen in Virginia. Did pretty well at it, from what I hear. Charlie says she had quite a lengthy client list, including a few restaurants. He showed me pictures. Some of her designs were works of art."

Erin licked her lips. "Think you could ask her to bring us a chocolate cake as, you know, part of her application? I could use a slab of chocolate right now."

Laughing, Nina jostled Erin's elbow.

Erin sobered. "In all seriousness, she must understand deadlines and how to get things done on time. That's part of the battle, isn't it?"

"True." Nina scraped her teeth over her bottom lip. "The thing I'm worried about is how this'll affect my relationship with Charlie. If I hire Viola, if I even interview her, and things don't work out, I'm afraid it could damage our friendship."

"That's a tough one, but I don't think you have any choice—you have to ask her to come in. If you don't, that'll damage the relationship, too." Erin traced a circle on the desktop with her finger.

"Damned if I do. Damned if I don't." Nina sighed.

"Yeah, so err on the side of doing," Erin advised.

"You're right. I'll call her as soon as I finish up here. Hopefully, she'll be able stop by tomorrow sometime." Nina crossed her fingers. She hoped to fill all the staffing positions before Friday, when she and Zeke were driving into Destin to pick up his girls for the weekend. The thought made her smile. Saturday was Zeke's forty-eighth birthday. He was going to grill steaks while she and Megan and Lily made twice-baked potatoes, green beans amandine and Caesar salads. Afterward, since Zeke wasn't particularly fond of cake, they'd make Baked Alaska together, something the girls were very excited about.

The printer whirred. Seconds later it spit out two copies of Ethan's employment records. Nina removed them from the printer and stuck the paperwork in a file folder she'd labeled earlier.

"Erin!" Jack's voice bellowed through the house.

"Oops. That's my cue. Gotta run." The blonde moved quickly toward the door. "Good luck."

Her fingers waggling, she disappeared around the corner.

"Thanks," Nina whispered. She tugged on one ear. She'd take all the luck she could get.

Nina lowered the wooden tray onto the rattan and glass coffee table on the front porch. Loaded with extra goodies, the tray weighed more than usual, and her back sent up a warning flare. She straightened and rubbed her thumbs firmly over the pressure points just below her waist. The pain eased immediately, and she returned to the task at hand—doling out glasses of sweet tea to three of the best friends a girl could have.

"Hey, what's this?" Reggie snagged the tin box from the tray.

"Viola's job application," Nina answered with a grin as Reggie thumbed the latch. The lid sprang open. Nestled in white paper, neat rows of ginger snaps, pecan sandies and thick, rich brownies filled the inside. She caught a whiff of the heady scent of sugar, chocolate and spice even though Reggie sat several feet away.

"What do you mean, her job application?"

Michelle leaned forward to take a glass of iced tea from Nina's outstretched hand.

"Viola, Charlie's wife, was an admin assistant, but she hasn't worked outside the home since Malcolm and Dimella were born." The youngsters would both be in middle school next year and, according to Viola, were looking forward to making new friends when school started in the fall. "No formal training, but she's taken tons of cooking classes. So, in lieu of references, she brought brownies and cookies."

"Oh, man!" Reggie said around a mouthful of chocolate. "These might be the best brownies I've ever tasted."

"Don't hog them all to yourself." Erin reached for the box. "Hand 'em over, sis." A playful tug-of-war ensued until, with a groan, Erin wrested the tin box from her sister's hands. After eyeing the selection carefully, she chose a brownie and one of each of the cookies, which she settled on a napkin she took from the tray. "I could get used to eating dessert before dinner," she said, handing the box to Michelle.

"Mmmm, those do smell good." Michelle cast a look of pure longing at the sweets. "But I think I'd better not for now. Maybe after supper. Do you want one?" Still studying the treats, she cast the question in Nina's direction.

"No, thanks." She patted her stomach. "I had more than enough while Viola and I were chatting." Recalling the texture of brownies that were soft without being gooey, she licked her lips.

Michelle closed the lid and returned the box to the tray. "What did you decide about Viola?"

"I offered her the job." Nina sank onto one of the cushioned chairs and sipped her tea. She hadn't known what to expect of Charlie's wife, but Viola had exceeded her fondest hopes. Smart and personable with a generous smile and intelligent brown eyes, the younger woman had displayed more knowledge about working in a commercial kitchen than she'd expected. That she wouldn't have to teach Viola the basics of food safety had weighed heavily in the woman's favor. And Reggie was right: Those brownies were some of the best she'd tasted. "If she accepts, I think she'll make a good addition."

"She didn't say yes right away?" Erin frowned.

"She wanted to talk it over with Charlie." When Erin's frown didn't waver, Nina hurried to add, "Which I understand perfectly. They only moved here a couple of weeks ago and, with two school-age kids, taking on a full-time job right now might be a bit too much."

"Would it be full-time, though?" Michelle prodded. "At first?"

"No, and I explained that." The cafe wouldn't open at all for another month or so, and then only for breakfast and lunch. By then, Malcolm and Dimella would be in school. As for a dinner service, Nina wouldn't even consider adding that until after the first of the year. "At the same time, I told her we'd need a firm commitment from whoever takes the job." The fiasco with Krystal made her wary of hiring someone whose dedication was subpar.

"When's she supposed to get back to you?"

Nina had given Viola until tomorrow at five to make a decision. After that, she'd have to move on to the next candidate on an all-too-short list. She'd opened her mouth to give Erin all the details when her phone buzzed. She held up a finger. "One minute," she said as she retrieved the device from her pants pocket. She pressed her cell to her ear. "Nina Gray here."

"Chef Nina, this is Viola. Viola Wilson." The woman's voice trailed up at the end like she was asking a question.

Nina pointed to her phone. "It's her," she mouthed. She tamped down a sudden rush of nerves while she spoke into the receiver. "Hey, Viola. I'm sitting here with my friends Michelle,

Erin and Reggie. We were just talking about how much we hope you'll join the team at the Sugar Sand Cafe."

"Oh, good! I spoke with Charlie this afternoon. He feels the same way I do—this opportunity is too good to pass up. If the offer still stands, I'd like to accept it."

A rush of warm relief swept through Nina. Making a thumbs-up sign with her fist, she signaled the rest of her friends. "That's awesome," she said, meaning it more than she'd expected. "When can you start?" Much as she'd like to get Viola situated before Ethan started work on Monday, she didn't hold out much hope of that happening.

"Would tomorrow be too soon?" Viola asked hesitantly. "I know you're taking a long weekend, but I'd love to plunge right in."

"Tomorrow would be perfect," she assured the woman who'd just become her favorite new employee. "We'll take care of your paperwork, and then you can start getting familiar with the kitchen before Ethan reports on Monday." The cafe's waitress and busboy wouldn't report to work until the week before the soft opening.

"Thank you, Chef Nina. I know you're taking a chance by hiring someone like me. I want you to know, I won't let you down."

"I'm sure you won't," Nina responded and hoped she was right. "I'm looking forward to working with you. See you tomorrow."

"See you tomorrow, Chef."

The line went dead as Viola ended the call. Nina turned to her friends. "Well, that went better than I'd expected." Earlier today, she'd hired Gwen Wambles, a waitress who lived in Miramar Beach but had been commuting back and forth to wait tables at Boshamps in Destin. A phone call to the local high school had hooked her up with Dax Falk, a student who'd earn credit in the Culinary Arts Program by bussing tables at the cafe. She clapped her hands together.

"This calls for a toast." Reggie lifted her glass of iced tea.

"Here, here," said Erin and Michelle in unison. Glasses clinked. A thrill of expectation shot through her. With Viola, the cafe was fully staffed, which brought Nina's dream of operating her own restaurant another step closer to fulfillment.

Five

Erin

"That's the last of the tools." Her arms full, Erin stepped out of the bright sun into the cool shade of the garage. After dumping an armload of pruning shears into a five-gallon bucket, she began handing the trimmers to Reggie, one by one. Her normally carefree sister had a plan for exactly where each implement should go. As Reggie put each item in its place, Erin eyed what, not so long ago, had been a bare wall. Hand trowels and all manner of garden tools hung in neat rows from the pegboard Reggie and Chris had installed. Along the back, more racks held hoes, spades and rakes. The scent of fresh-cut lumber rose from a newly constructed workbench. On its broad top stood baskets of garden gloves, seed packets and a flat of tiny, heirloom tomato plants Reggie was showering with extra TLC.

"Do you want Chris and me to take down the pegboard in the gardener's shed?" Reggie added the last pair of shears to the wall and leaned back to admire her handiwork. She smiled her satisfaction at the tools she'd arranged in order from smallest to largest.

"Nope. You've done more than enough," Erin assured her sister. When she'd pointed out her need for a dedicated space to organize the inn's activities and store her boats and equipment, Reggie had volunteered to move the tools and gardening paraphernalia from the shed to the garage. Erin had protested, but her sister had pointed out that the four bays—which had once been crowded with vehicles Michelle inherited from her birth mother along with the rest of her estate—now sat largely vacant. One of the big used car retailers in Pensacola had given them top dollar for Nancy's sedan, money they'd added to the inn's general fund. The wheelchair-accessible van, loaded with donated goods for Sugar Sand Beach's hometown hero, now sat at Jimbo Dutton's garage, where local businesses and concerned citizens regularly added more contributions. Reggie kept the tractor inside the pole barn she and Chris had erected near the garden. With the ATVs parked by the back door, where they were handy whenever anyone wanted to go for a ride, the roomy garage offered plenty of space. Erin had still argued that moving all the gardening equipment seemed like a lot of work, but Reggie had insisted, and Michelle and Nina had taken her side. Chris, who'd been finding more and more excuses to work with Reggie lately, had started prepping the area the very next day.

A week later, she and her sister had worked from sunup to midafternoon hauling tools and equipment across the yard from the shed to the garage. The task was nearly complete, and Erin admitted the equipment did look nice displayed on the walls of the garage.

Eager to get to work transforming the now-empty shed into the Activity Center, she stretched and worked out a few kinks in muscles that were more used to pulling on paddles than toting boxes and tools. "Anything else I can do?" she asked Reggie.

"No, I think that's about got it." Her strawberry-blond hair stuffed inside a baseball cap, Reggie grabbed a refillable water bottle from the corner of the work bench and drank. "I'm going to spend the afternoon in the garden. I spotted a few weeds in among the green beans.

Can't let them get a toehold or they'll take over the place."

Erin smiled. Her sister had dreamed of having a garden of her own from the time their grandmother had shown them how to plant butterbeans on her hardscrabble farm in West Virginia. "You do that," she said. "I'm going to grab a broom and a mop and get started on the shed."

She paused. Calling it a shed was really a bit misleading. Constructed of concrete block topped by a gravel-and-tar roof, the solid building was far from the wooden lean-to its name implied. "Thanks again for letting me turn that area into the Activity Center. I really appreciate it."

"Don't be silly. I definitely didn't need that much space for tools and such. Besides, it'll make your morning commute that much shorter."

Erin laughed as she headed out the door. Reggie was right about one thing—she wouldn't have far to walk to get to work each morning. The apartment she and Reggie shared was right next door. Which would be perfect for those mornings when she needed to be on the water by sunup.

At first, she'd been concerned the shed wouldn't hold all the kayaks, the canoe and the bicycles. Those fears had quickly vanished. Now that they'd emptied out the room, she saw the area was larger than she'd realized. The building had more than enough floor space for her boats, plus the few pieces of office equipment she'd need. And the wide barn door at one end would make getting the kayaks in and out a breeze.

She quickly reviewed her plans. After scrubbing every inch of place from floor to ceiling, she'd paint the walls a soft blue that reminded her of the sky on a sunny day. The pegboard that once held gardening tools would work great for storing paddles and life preservers. First, though, she'd treat the wood to several coats of paint the color of whitecaps on a windy day. Next, she'd haul a spare desk and side table from the house. The furniture would form an inviting office area where she'd display schedules and signup sheets for the inn's activities. And with her laptop plugged into the cottage's Wi-Fi, she'd have weather reports at her fingertips, crucial information to have when taking guests out on the water. She rubbed her hands together. It was time to get to work.

Hours passed while Erin swept and scrubbed and mopped. By the time she finished scouring every inch of the room, she'd emptied so many buckets of dirty water outside that it stood in puddles beyond the shed. She was finally rinsing out her mop bucket after making dozens of trips to refill it when she caught sight of a vehicle pulling onto the graveled parking area beyond the garage. Her heart skipped a beat as the well-aged Land Rover slowed to a stop. Seconds later, a rusty door hinge complained loud enough for her to hear it from where she stood. Suddenly self-conscious, she tugged at the hem of her shorts as the man she least expected—or wanted—to see today stepped out of the boxy SUV.

"Ron." His name came out as whisper because her mouth had suddenly gone dry. She glanced down at the clothes she'd worn for a busy day of moving and cleaning. Dirt streaked the T-shirt that was better suited for the rag bag than her closet. A dark smear of grease stained her shorts. Her left pinky toe poked out of a hole in her shoe. She wasn't in much better shape than her clothes, either. Most of her hair had escaped its ponytail and hung in damp, limp strands around her face. She hadn't worn a speck of makeup, not that there'd be any left if she had. Beneath the brim of her baseball hat, sweat bathed her cheeks and neck.

The urge to duck out of sight behind the shed rushed through her a second too late. By then Ron had spotted her. To make matters worse, he stood beside his car looking like someone who'd just stepped off the pages of a magazine. The lightweight fishing shirt he wore tucked and belted into a pair of walking shorts did nothing to hide the wide set of his shoulders, his narrow waist or his muscular legs.

She lifted her hand in a weak wave. In the time it took his long strides to eat up the ground between them, she raced to do a little damage control. Rubbing her hands under the tap, she washed the worst of the grime from her arms and face. She whipped her hat from her head next. Tucking it under one arm, she captured her loose hair into a haphazard pony tail. She ran out of time before she could do anything more. Figuring it would have to do, she jammed the cap back in place.

"Ron," she said when he'd gotten close enough to eliminate the need to shout. She gave herself a mental fist bump for keeping her tone even despite her heart's uneven rhythm. "What are you doing here?"

"I wanted to check in with you. See if you'd given any thought to my proposal."

Ron was taller than her, so tall she had to tip her head back to see his face from under the bill of her ball cap. "I told you no the first time you asked. What makes you think I'd change my mind?"

Disbelief flickered in Ron's baby blues. "I thought you'd jump at the chance to leave all this behind." He sent a pointed glance to the bucket at her feet.

One of Erin's hands landed on her hip. The other kept a firm grip on the handle of the mop. "There's nothing wrong with putting in an honest day's work."

"I'm not saying there is." Ron gave his head a slight shake. "But don't you deserve better?"

Erin tsked. She couldn't blame Ron for having doubts. He hadn't been with them when they first arrived in Sugar Sand Beach. He hadn't seen the shuttered windows, the spiderwebs draping every surface, the broken railing hanging off the porch like a drunken ladder. He only saw the house as it was now, with its neatly trimmed hedges and gleaming glass panes, with painters and scaffolding and graveled walkways. He had no idea how much of their hearts, their souls, and, yes, their savings they'd poured into the Sugar Sand Inn. More specifically, he had no idea of her own plans for the place.

Leaning the mop handle against the outside wall, she beckoned him to follow her inside. "I know it doesn't look like much right now," she said as soon as they'd stepped beyond the barn doors, "but you're looking at the future home of the Sugar Sand Inn Activities Center." The hours she'd spent on the space had paid off. Light bounced off the white walls. Not a single scuff mark marred the bare concrete floor, where scattered spots were still drying. Even the metal pegs sticking out of the unfinished pegboard walls shone. She let her chest fill. "A little paint and furniture, and this place is going to be fantastic."

"So, what? You're going to spend your days playing ping-pong and badminton?" Ron looked skeptical.

"No, silly." She started to give his upper arm a light tap like she used to do once upon a time but thought better of it and stuck her hand in the pocket of her shorts. Until he'd put in a surprise appearance recently, she and Ron hadn't exchanged more than a dozen words in the twenty years they'd been apart. Picking up where they'd left off was a bad idea. A very bad idea. She straightened.

"The last couple of months I've spent countless hours getting to know the lay of the land around here. Or, more to the point, the water. I've logged over a hundred hours in the Gulf, and I'm pretty sure I've kayaked every stream or lake between Panama City and Destin." Idly, she rubbed a red welt on her forearm. She'd had to hack her way through dense brush to get to some of those lakes and still had the mosquito bites to prove it. "I'm doing everything I can so that, when the inn opens a couple of months from now, I'll be ready to take our guests kayaking or canoeing wherever they'd like to go. We'll offer fishing trips and biking excursions, too. They can hike across our five acres or follow one of the many trails through the Topsail Hill Preserve."

"So, no ping-pong?" Ron said, only slightly more impressed by the activities she'd planned.

"Don't mock me, Ron." She waved a hand, a warning that she was serious. "This is going to be great. There's plenty of room to store the kayaks and the canoe, plus I can use the pegboard for life vests and helmets and such. There'll be a counter here"—she indicated the spot—"and a desk in that corner. Eventually, we'll offer activities to non-guests, but that'll be down the road a bit."

Some of the doubt eased from Ron's features as his gaze flitted about the room. "Not exactly what I thought you meant when you said you'd signed on as the Activities Director for a bed-and-breakfast."

"An inn," she corrected. "The Sugar Sand *Inn*. Unlike a B&B, where people stay a night or two, our guests will stay with us for a week. Some even longer. We have to offer them more than board games in the front parlor." Although there'd be those, too, if they wanted them.

"This is nice and all, but seriously, it's a little off the beaten path, don't you think?" Ron's brows rose with the question. "I mean, Sugar Sand Beach isn't exactly a thriving metropolis. Or a hot tourist spot like Panama City."

"True, and we love that about this place. It's part of the charm. Believe me, you haven't lived until you've lived in a small town. People here have opened their arms to us, welcomed us into their homes and helped us get started. We're trying to return their hospitality by donating to local causes and supporting local businesses."

"You mean there's a downtown? Seriously?" Ron stuck his hands in his pockets. He shook his head. "I couldn't find one on the map."

"Yes, there's a downtown," she said, defensive of her new home. "It's just a few blocks from here. We even have all the usual stuff—a grocery and a hardware store, souvenir shops and a florist. Until we open the Cafe, there's only one restaurant, but Maggie's Diner has the best key lime pie north of Key West. You ought to try it sometime."

"No time like the present," Ron said

smoothly. "But only if you'll lead me to it," he challenged.

Well, she'd walked into that one, hadn't she? But how was she supposed to know Ron had never lost his taste for the luscious pie that had once been his favorite?

She checked the waterproof watch strapped to her wrist. Normally, she and Michelle, Reggie and Nina would gather on the front porch within the hour to catch up on the day and discuss plans for the weeks ahead. While the painters were working on the exterior, though, they'd stored the porch furniture and postponed their meetings until after dinner. That gave her two hours, more than enough time to show Ron the town of Sugar Sand Beach and grab a slice of pie at Maggie's.

"Tell you what," she said, accepting his dare, "let me take a quick shower, and you're on."

In the third booth from the back at Maggie's Diner, Erin broke a bite-size piece of graham cracker crust off her slice of key lime pie. She scooped the morsel onto her fork tines, debated whether or not she wanted to eat it, then set it aside. The pie looked and smelled every bit as delicious as she'd assured Ron it was, but she'd lost her appetite.

Though she blamed the few bites of a sausage dog she'd eaten earlier, she knew she was only fooling herself. The real reason her tummy felt as leaden as the ocean on a windless day sat across from her, blissfully forking down pie as if they'd spent the last twenty years together instead of apart. As if he hadn't torn her life to shreds when he'd called it quits on their marriage. As if he fully expected to snap his fingers and have her jump at the chance to run off into the sunset with him.

No, sir. Thank you very much, sir.

She wasn't going to run away with Ron but, purely in the interest of being neighborly, she had spent nearly two hours showing him everything of interest in Sugar Sand Beach. They'd started at the hardware store, where he'd studied a display of camping equipment while she ordered the paint she needed for the Activity Center. With no one around to issue tickets for jaywalking, they'd crisscrossed the single main street several times. At the surf shop, Ron had admired the owner's custom-made boards, and the two men had spent fifteen minutes discussing the merits of the new foam core boards over the traditional polyurethane models. Later, Ron had purchased a tiny figurine fashioned out of sea shells and glue from the souvenir shop. Together, they'd studied the display in the window of Polly's Posies, which, much to Erin's relief, had closed for the day. Her life was complicated enough without having to explain Ron's presence to Polly, or worse, have her blab the news of Ron's visit to Walt. Not that she and Walt were anything more than friends or ever would be. But still.

For their final stop, she'd led Ron to the grocery store, where they'd traded the usual greetings with the owner Gus. The portly older man had insisted her guest try the store's specially smoked sausage so, a few minutes later, they'd each ordered one "with all the fixin's" from Gus's grandson. Taking their purchases to the picnic tables outside, they'd unwrapped the tinfoil around their dogs and bitten into what Erin considered the best sausage in the South.

Today, it might as well have been sawdust.

Though she'd kept up a cheerful patter— careful not to get too personal, careful to avoid any talk of their past together—the questions that bubbled inside her had soured her stomach. She longed to ask Ron why he hadn't been honest with her when they first met. Why he'd pretended to share her goals for the future. And just as important, what he really wanted now. As a result, she'd only managed a bite or two of her sausage dog while Ron had wolfed his down.

"What do you think of Sugar Sand Beach?" she asked now as she pushed crumbs from her untouched slice of pie around her plate.

"It has its charm," Ron admitted. He licked a tiny bit of filling from his bottom lip. "You were right about the pie. It's perfect." He blotted his lips with his napkin. "As for the town, I honestly didn't think places like this existed anymore. I can see why you like it here. But to stay here for the rest of your life?" He scooped up a last bite. "You'll be bored and ready to move on in a matter of months."

"I don't think so." She'd never say "never," but that was one thing she was certain of. "I spent half my life living out of a duffle bag. The last few years, though, being on the go lost its magic. I started dreading the end of the summer when I had to leave Seward, or the end of the winter when it was time to pack up the cottage in Key West and head out to parts unknown."

"You always did have the travel bug. Give it a little while." Ron pushed his plate aside. "You'll get it back."

His confidence in the prediction irked her. "I

thought you had it, too. You sure pretended you wanted a life on the road. Apparently, you lied."

Ron held up his hands like stop signs. "Don't get me wrong. I loved being with you, seeing the world through your eyes. But our honeymoon was the first time I'd ever been out of the US. After six months, I'd had my fill of hostels and never knowing what I'd end up with when I ordered something in a restaurant. My dad's death helped me see that life was too short to spend it doing something I didn't love."

"Or spending it *with* someone you didn't love." That was the crux of the matter. He hadn't loved her enough.

"But I did love you, Erin. Look." Ron spread his hands flat on the tabletop. "We both had hopes and dreams. They were just...different. I won't apologize for the choices I made. I've lived a good life, built a good business in Houston. I enjoyed being outdoors, meeting people. I spent most of my time on the water—either fishing or parasailing. It was what I was supposed to do. But make no mistake, I loved you. Losing you was—is, it is the biggest regret of my life. If you'd stayed, we could have had a good life together."

She shook her head. "The life *you* wanted. Doing what *you* wanted to do. That wasn't my dream. You knew from the very beginning I wanted to travel the world. I thought we'd do that together."

"And I thought you'd stay."

She shrugged. They'd loved each other, but neither of them had been willing to sacrifice the lives they were meant to live for someone else's dreams of the future. Rehashing the decisions they'd made twenty years ago was not going to resolve things between them. It was all water under the bridge, and like that water, they'd both moved on. It was high time she quit blaming him—or herself—for the choices they'd made. "So did you ever get married?"

"No. You?"

Wordlessly, she shook her head. She could tell him he'd broken her heart, that it had taken years for her to trust another man again. While that was true, it was also true that she'd never found anyone who made her feel the same way she felt when she was around him.

She was curious about one thing, though, and sensing it might be her only chance to find out, she asked, "After all these years, why the change? Why do you suddenly want to hit the road again?"

Ron's features smoothed. "To be honest, I saw it as the opportunity of a lifetime. A chance to make amends to the one person I regret letting down the most. You and me together again, traveling the globe. It'll be like old times, only better. Imagine, no hostels and no backpacks. Only first-class accommodations and porters to carry our bags for us." He cast a searching glance at her.

Did she dare believe that he was trying to earn her forgiveness? Give them a second chance? If so, he was going about it the wrong way. Slowly, she shook her head. She'd let her hair air-dry after her shower, and the strands swung loosely around her shoulders. "No. I told you. My years of waking up in an unfamiliar bed in an unfamiliar city on an different continent are over. I'm putting down roots here in Sugar Sand Beach, and I'm surprised by how much I like it.

"Here? To help run an inn?" Ron hiked an eyebrow. "I give it two, three months, tops. Then you'll be ready to move on. I'll be waiting when you are."

"You'll be waiting a long, long time."

"This I gotta see."

There was something else in play here, something she didn't quite understand. Ron could have his pick of traveling partners. She personally knew of a half dozen people who could ferret out the best cafe in Istanbul as well as they could spot an orangutan hanging from a limb in the Sumatran rain forest. Yet he'd chosen her, and when she'd turned him down, he hadn't moved on to his next candidate. Why was that? And how far was he willing to go?

She tilted her head. "It's a free country. You're welcome to stay if that's what you want," she dared him.

"Careful what you wish for. You might just get it." Something in his voice said he'd planned on sticking around all along.

This should be interesting, Erin thought. The longer Ron stayed in Sugar Sand Beach, the better her chances of finding out what really brought him here. In the meantime, she'd use the time to sort out her own feelings for the man she'd once loved.

Six

Nina

"What smells so good?" Michelle stood in the doorway to the kitchen.

"Bouillabaisse," Nina answered without glancing up. The hearty sauce was Aaron and Ashley's favorite. She'd started this batch before either Viola or Ethan had arrived this morning. After it simmered most of the day, she'd store it in the back of the fridge for the twins' visit.

"I can hardly believe they'll be here this weekend. Speaking of which, I'm headed to Destin to pick up a few last minute things. Can I get anything for you while I'm there?"

In the middle of critiquing Ethan's work, Nina held up a finger. "One second." She scanned the plastic tray of tomatoes the young cook had peeled and sliced. "Those look great," she told him. "Cover them with absorbent paper. Then add another layer on top." The paper would soak up the excess tomato juice that otherwise turned sandwiches and salads sloppy.

"Yes, Chef," the young man replied. She took another second to take a deep breath. Mixed with the good smells coming from the pot of sauce on the stove, the aroma of baking bread floated in the air. According to the scent, it wasn't quite time for the loaves to come out of the oven. Still addressing Ethan, Nina told him to store the sliced tomatoes in the fridge when he finished. "Which shelf?" she asked, testing him.

"On a lower shelf, but above the meat, Chef."

After nodding her approval, she gave Michelle her attention. The brunette had dressed with care in cream-colored pants and a teal-blue blouse. A wide gold belt tied the two together. Gold sandals and jewelry polished off the outfit. "You're looking awfully sharp for a shopping trip. Lunch with Dave?" she guessed.

"An appointment with a new hairdresser," Michelle corrected. "Fingers crossed, right?"

No wonder her friend looked like she was ready for a photo shoot. Nothing sent shivers down a woman's spine faster than walking into a salon she'd never visited before. Would the stylists wear an air of snooty condemnation along with fashion-forward wardrobes? Would they listen when she said she only wanted a light trim? Or would she end up spending the next six months dealing with a style she couldn't manage?

Nina gave Michelle a second once-over. "Are you nervous?" she asked, already certain of the answer.

"A little. This place comes highly recommended. but you never know... I just wish I could fly my hairdresser down from Maryland. Shirley always did such a great job with my hair." Michelle fidgeted with the strap of her purse.

"You can do this," Nina assured her friend. "Remember, you have the power of the tip in your hand, and you're not afraid to use it."

"She's right, Michelle," added Viola from her spot behind the Aga range, where round shapes bubbled in hot oil. "You got this."

Nina smiled. From the day Viola had reported to work two weeks ago, she'd been on a first-name basis with Michelle, Erin and Reggie. With everyone, in fact, except her. To Nina, Viola gave a respectful "Yes, Chef" and "No, Chef" despite the warm camaraderie that had developed between them.

"There's just one thing." Michelle tugged on a strand of the shiny black hair that no longer ended at her cheek line but swung halfway to her shoulders. "I found a few gray hairs. I'm afraid the new stylist will want to do something drastic to cover them up. But I'm too young to go gray."

"Oh, shoot. Those are your battle stripes. Wear 'em with pride. I do." Viola patted the colorful scarf she wore over her own short baby curls.

"My battle stripes?" Michelle repeated slowly. "I've certainly earned a few of those these last couple of years, haven't I?"

Nina felt Michelle's doubtful gaze. "You have been through a lot, but you've come out on top. Some women would have let the challenges you've faced define them. They would have spent the rest of their lives moaning about the past and never moving forward. Not you. You used it as a springboard to start a new life for yourself." She glanced around the busy kitchen. At the counter, Ethan continued slicing tomatoes for the chicken pesto sandwich she planned to put on the cafe's menu. Viola lifted perfectly browned donuts from the fryer with a slotted spoon. "Not just for yourself but for those around you. I'd never be opening the cafe, Ethan would be looking for work, and Viola and Charlie might still be in Virginia. Who knows what would have become of Reggie, or if Erin would still be lost and wandering the world? All of that changed because of you. So what if you have a few gray hairs? You earned them. Wear 'em with pride."

"That was quite the speech," Michelle said, her hand dropping from her purse strap. Her shoulders straightened. "But I get the message. I won't let this new hairdresser bully me into something I don't want."

"That's my girl," Nina said while, at the stove, Viola nodded her agreement. As for Ethan, if the youngster paid any attention to the conversation, he wisely kept his thoughts to himself.

"So there's nothing you need from Destin?" Michelle asked, circling back to her original question.

"No. We're good here," Nina assured her. She'd checked off every item on her grocery list during a trip to the big box store in the city earlier this week. The pantry and the fridge were full of all of Aaron and Ashley's favorites.

"Okay, then. I'm off." Michelle headed for the back porch. She reached the screen door just in time to hold it open for Reggie.

Nina felt her eyes widen at the sight of the overflowing bushel basket the redhead carried. "Tell me those aren't all red peppers," she begged. Once the cafe opened, they'd go through mountains of fruit and vegetables each day. But until it did, they were already hard-pressed to use up all the tomatoes and cucumbers Reggie picked every day. The red peppers presented a challenge Nina wasn't sure she was up to.

"Yep." Reggie proudly sat the basket on a low table by the sink. "Some of the prettiest red peppers I've ever seen. The plants are just loaded with them." One by one, she transferred the vegetables from the basket to the counter nearest the sink. "I figure three, maybe four days before the next batch ripens."

Nina pressed a hand to her heart. Reggie was right, the peppers were lovely, but what on earth was she going to do with so many? There was a limit to how many stuffed peppers her friends would eat.

Finished frying the donuts, Viola began dunking each one in a cinnamon sugar mix. "That there'd make a nice batch of pepper relish," she commented as she flipped the first donut over and coated the back side. She placed the finished treat on a cooling rack.

"What else does the recipe call for?" Nina asked. When she worked at Chez Jacques in Arlington, she'd created a red pepper sauce from blackened bell peppers, roasted almonds and crushed hazelnuts, but she'd never tried a relish.

"For each dozen red peppers, you'll need seven Vidalia onions, three cups of cider vinegar, two cups of sugar, mustard seeds and salt, two dozen banana peppers and three or four jalapeños," Viola recited from memory.

"You must make this often to have the recipe down pat like that," Nina commented as she mentally combined the ingredients Viola had listed. The result was an interesting blend of sweet and hot. It was also oddly familiar, and she wondered where she'd had it before.

"I make it every year." Viola pretended to ignore it when Reggie snagged a donut from the cooling rack, but she smacked the younger woman's hand when she reached for a second one. "It's Charlie's favorite. He'll slather it on bread and eat it straight. Me, I like it on turkey sandwiches."

"I remember it now. If it's the same relish I'm thinking of, Charlie gave me a little bit at lunch one day. It was delicious. When I asked him for the recipe, he said it was a family secret." Disappointment curved Nina's shoulders. Much as she'd like to whip up a batch of the relish, she wouldn't copy someone else's recipes.

"He told you that, huh? That's just like a man." The loose ends of her scarf flapped when Viola shook her head. "Everyone in our family makes pepper relish. Brothers, sisters, cousins, second cousins, third cousins once removed. It's definitely not a secret. Besides, y'all are like family. Family looks out for one another, and that's what you did when you recommended my Charlie as head chef at the Happy Dolphin."

"You wouldn't mind sharing it with me, then?" Nina asked.

"Not as long as you don't mind sharing some of the finished product with me."

"Fifty-fifty?" At Viola's nod, Nina quickly reviewed the schedule. With Michelle's twins flying in on Friday, she'd been working all week preparing their favorite foods for the weekend. Thanks to Ethan and Viola, she was a day ahead of schedule. They could make the relish on Thursday and have all day Friday for the final push before Ashley and Aaron's arrival. The thought of topping her burger at Saturday's cookout with the tangy relish helped her make the final decision. "We'll make it tomorrow then."

"It takes a dozen red peppers per batch." Viola spared a quick glance at the sink full of peppers. "Looks like you have enough there to make two batches, with some left over. Better plan on spending the biggest part of the day working on it. It's a mite on the labor-intensive side." Viola finished dusting the last of the donuts. "Do you have canning supplies?"

"We do." Nina nodded. She'd found the immense pot outfitted with wire racks on the top shelf of the kitchen pantry. Boxes of quart and pint jars, as well as lids, sat nearby. She paused. She had one more favor to ask Viola and knew it was a big one. "Do you mind if Megan and Lily join us?"

Zeke's ex-wife had had to fly out of town on an unexpected business trip. The contractor had picked up the girls from their home in Fort Walton yesterday. After talking it over with Michelle, Reggie and Erin last night, Nina had offered to let the girls hang out at the house during the day while Zeke was working.

"I'd be shocked if you didn't. Those young ladies are never underfoot and always welcome." Her generous hips swaying, Viola carried what was left of the sugar mixture to the trash can and dumped it.

"You can bring Dimella and Malcolm, too, if you'd like." Fair was fair, after all. If Nina was babysitting, it was only right to let Viola bring her kids to work, too.

But Viola shook her head no. "They both have basketball camp all week, but they'll be here for the cookout on Saturday."

Nina's heart warmed. Charlie had filled their

lunch breaks with stories about Dimella and Malcolm. "I can't wait to meet them. I've heard so much about them, it's almost like I know them already."

Seeing that Ethan had finished with the tomatoes and had begun cleaning his station in preparation for the next task, Nina headed for the pantry, where she retrieved a gallon jar of bright green olives. She plunked it down on the counter near her young apprentice. "Cut in half for the sandwiches," she told the prep cook.

"Yes, Chef," Ethan replied. He gave the counter another swipe of disinfectant and went right to work.

The aroma of fresh baked bread in the kitchen intensified. Nina crossed to the oven, where she removed four loaves of ciabatta seconds before the timer dinged. Once the loaves cooled, she'd top the bread with house-made pesto, grilled chicken, onion, kale and a tomato slice. Sprinkled with olives, the hearty sandwiches would be tonight's supper. Of course, there'd be extras— lots of them. She'd send most of the leftovers home with Ethan and Viola. The rest, she'd drop off at the church along with the donuts. The Ladies Auxiliary had been more than happy to incorporate the dishes she was testing for the cafe into their meals-on-wheels program.

She looked around the kitchen. Everything was proceeding smoothly. "Then it's set," she announced. "Tomorrow, we make relish."

Thursday morning dawned hot and humid, typical for August, according to longtime residents of Sugar Sand Beach. One look at the thermometer mounted outside her window told Nina the temperatures had already climbed into the eighties by the time she completed her daily yoga routine. As she rolled her yoga mat, she thanked her lucky stars that Nancy Simmons had installed central air throughout the house before she died. Without it, she'd be as crotchety as Mr. Pibbs when he didn't get his supper on time.

"You like the air-conditioning, too, don't you, Mr. Pibbs?"

The big tabby yawned and stretched. She'd been concerned about how he'd adjust to their new quarters at the end of the hall. Their room was smaller than the one she'd stayed in when they first arrived in Sugar Sand Beach, and they shared a sitting room with Michelle. As far as the big tabby was concerned, however, that just meant there was another pair of hands to pet him.

"Are you finished in the bathroom?" she asked, though she knew she was wasting her breath. Mr. Pibbs had no sense of personal space. No matter how long he lingered in the litter box each morning, nine times out of ten he'd be crying at the bathroom door, begging to join her before she'd showered and dressed for the day. Most of the time, she let him. She shook her head. Yes, she spoiled him rotten, but she wouldn't have it any other way.

Twenty minutes later, showered and dressed in a snug white jacket over her favorite pair of chef's pants because, well, because she'd see Zeke this morning, she headed downstairs with Mr. Pibbs at her heels. As she'd done most days since they'd finished the remodel, she brewed coffee, set out mugs and retrieved the bowl of fruit Ethan had cut up the day before. Next, she put the finishing touches on the breakfast casserole. Today's was one of two dozen she planned to offer guests of the cafe on a rotating basis. This one featured a base of thickly sliced bread. Over that, she'd layered chopped smoky sausage links, grilled onions and cheese. She quickly cracked eggs into a bowl, whisked them until they were frothy and added milk. Once she'd poured the mixture over the rest of the ingredients, she slid the casserole into the big Aga oven and set the timer.

While she waited for the casserole to bake and the rest of the household to stir, Nina sat in the breakfast nook. As she sipped coffee, her gaze roamed the kitchen. There were so many pitfalls to avoid in opening a restaurant, not the least of which was fitting in with the competition. Lucky for her, there was only one other eatery within twenty miles of the inn. Maggie's Diner opened at six. Nina had no intention of honing in on the other owner's early morning business. She'd decided early on that her cafe would open at a much more reasonable 8 a.m., although she planned to offer coffee service for guests and staff starting at six each day. She'd discussed the hours with Viola and Ethan, who'd both agreed to clock in by seven.

She sipped more coffee as she pictured the three of them hustling about the kitchen. Viola was a whizz at the stove; she'd be in charge of turning out the cafe's perfectly fried eggs, thick-sliced bacon and pancakes with soft centers and crispy edges. The wait staff would handle beverages from the handy coffee station Zeke had added during the remodel. Throughout the morning rush, Ethan would make toast, butter biscuits and watch over the waffle maker. Nina, meanwhile, would serve up the day's casserole selections and oversee the plating of each dish that left the kitchen. In the lull between breakfast and lunch, they'd prep the fillings for sandwiches, chop the lettuce for salads and take care of a hundred other tasks that went into running a successful restaurant.

It should work. She whispered a short prayer, not that everything would go smoothly—she wasn't naive enough to believe they'd open without a single hiccup—but that they'd leap over whatever hurdles they encountered.

She finished her coffee just as the aroma of baked eggs and sausage wafted through the kitchen. The timer dinged a few seconds later. By then, she'd already moved the casserole dish to an electric food warmer that was guaranteed to maintain it at the proper serving temperature.

A metallic click broke the quiet. A familiar swish told Nina the door to the sun porch had swung open on well-oiled hinges. The sound of boots striking the floor echoed through the kitchen. A moment later, Reggie appeared in the doorway. The redhead blinked sleep from her eyes. "Coffee ready?" she asked.

"It is. So's the casserole, if you're hungry."

"Not now, thanks." Reggie grabbed a to-go

cup, which she filled from the carafe. "I want to get the last of the tomatoes in the ground before it gets too hot this morning. They say it'll be in the nineties by early afternoon."

"It's a little late to plant tomatoes, isn't it?" Her own thumb was admittedly black, or at least a toasty shade of brown, but Reggie had raised the subject of a winter garden at one of their nightly get-togethers. The woman who stood before her in thick, white socks, khaki shorts and a peach-colored T-shirt had stressed the importance of transplanting the seedlings by mid-July.

"I planted two rows last month. These are extras. I started them a little later just to see how they'd do. We'll lose them if we get an early frost, but I thought it'd be worth the risk." Reggie rubbed her chin. "If these produce, despite the late date, we might want to put up a greenhouse next year. Not a very big one. Maybe just large enough for herbs and tomatoes, cucumbers and some melons. That way we can have fresh veggies throughout the winter."

Nina nodded slowly. Although the farmer's market operated year-round, most of the winter fruits and vegetables would be shipped in from warmer climates, and prices would rise accordingly. "Not a bad idea. Let's talk about it with Michelle and Erin tonight."

"Hmmm. I'm not quite ready to go that far. Let's see how these tomatoes do first." Reggie screwed the lid onto her to-go cup. "Right now, though, I'd better get moving. Save me some of that casserole," she called as she retraced her steps to the porch. "I'll be back in about an hour."

"Will do," Nina agreed. She crossed to the window, where she watched her friend climb into a battered pickup truck, coffee in hand. While she was still standing there, Nina spotted a pair of headlights cutting through the early morning fog as a vehicle turned off the main road. A warm feeling spread from the center of her chest outward. Zeke and his girls were right on time.

Eager to see the girls and, especially, their dad, she hurried through the house to the front door. By the time she made it onto the porch, Lily had already spilled from the contractor's truck and was racing up the steps. Nina had just enough time to aim a warm smile at Zeke before the ten-year-old's little body slammed into her. Thin arms wrapped around Nina's waist.

"I'm all ready!" the chipper little girl exclaimed. She was already wearing the dark green kid-size apron Nina had given her, the one with the Sugar Sand Cafe emblem on the bib. "What are we making today?"

Nina returned Lily's embrace with an affectionate squeeze. Over the last few months, she'd come to think of the youngster as the child she'd never had. And though she knew the girl's hobbies might change over the years, for now, she was doing her best to encourage Lily's interest in cooking. "Today we're making a special pepper relish," she said in a hushed voice, as if she were sharing a secret. "It's a very special family recipe Miss Viola has offered to show us."

"Really? What kind of peppers? Will we get to wear goggles and gloves like the kids on *Young Chefs* when they worked with habaneros?" On Lily's current favorite television show, pre-teen chefs competed against one another for prizes and scholarships.

"Maybe gloves," Nina answered with a reassuring smile for Zeke. "We'll be using mild banana peppers and jalapeños. Nothing nearly as hot as habaneros." The spicier pepper scored as much as 300,000 heat units on the Scoville scale and required special handling. Definitely not something she wanted near Lily. By comparison, the tamer jalapeños they'd be working with today topped the scale at a mere 8,000 units.

"Oh, man!" Lily pouted. "I've wanted to see a habanero for my whole life!"

"Your whole life, huh?" She chucked Lily

under the chin. "So dramatic! But I'm afraid you won't find one of those in my kitchen." She liked spice as much as the next person, but a little bit went a long way. Only one or two of her recipes called for that much heat, and she had no intention of fixing them when Lily was anywhere around. "But we'll have fun. You'll see."

"I'm glad to be here, Chef Nina," Lily said. "Mommy had to go out of town, and it'd be boring if we had to sit at Daddy's all day."

"Now, now." Zeke's deep rumble sounded from midway up the porch steps. "I thought you and Megan couldn't wait to play that new video game I got for you." He gave Nina a sheepish smile. "They've only been begging for it for months."

"Kids," Nina said with an understanding shrug as, in the distance, a door closed. Leaning into the quick peck Zeke brushed across her cheek, she tamped down the urge to step into his arms for another of the deep kisses that, by mutual agreement, they indulged in only when they were far away from his daughters' inquisitive eyes. Like the nights he'd picked her up after the Happy Dolphin served its last patron of the evening and closed the doors. She'd been touched by Zeke's insistence on making the ninety-minute drive into Panama City each night so she wouldn't face the long, solitary trip home at the completion of her twelve-hour shift. Though she should have been dog-tired by midnight, just seeing Zeke's truck in the parking lot had buoyed her spirits. The miles had sped by as they swapped stories, covering topics from their childhoods to the latest escapades of the diners in the restaurant or the challenges of his latest contracting job. Once they'd pulled in front of the inn and he'd parked the truck, though? She stifled a sigh at the memory of how she'd melted in Zeke's arms, the warmth of his embrace. Even thinking of how those deep kisses got her motor running tempted her to step close enough for another one.

Except she couldn't. Not with Lily standing not two feet away. Or Megan...

Nina snapped out of her reverie. So far, Lily's older sister hadn't put in an appearance.

"Where's Meg?" she asked, using the nickname Megan had recently insisted on.

"She ran straight over to Erin's. I wanted her to wait so I could walk her there, but she wouldn't hear of it. I guess they're going fishing this morning."

Nina nodded. Although Megan had recently turned out a perfect flatbread pizza, cooking wasn't the twelve-year-old's first love. When

Erin had offered to take the girl fishing for, in her words, "something you can serve that pepper relish on," Megan had no doubt jumped at the chance.

"You're welcome to join us for dinner tonight," she said to Zeke. "It sounds like we're having fish and pepper relish. I'm sure Lily and I can find something else to put on the table."

"Thanks, much as I'd like that, Mega—Meg insists she has nothing to wear to the picnic this weekend." Zeke let out a long-suffering sigh. "I promised to take the girls shopping for new outfits."

"We're going to eat at the food court in the mall," Lily piped. Her little face scrunched. "Meg always wants yucky old salad when we go out to eat. But I want chicken nuggets. Daddy says we can all get what we want at the mall and no fighting."

"I guess that's sisters for you." Nina nodded with a grin. She didn't have one of her own, but she'd watched enough of Erin and Reggie's good-natured sparring over the years that Lily's observation sounded familiar.

"Maybe I should go check on her," Zeke said without moving. His intense gaze bore into the house as if he wished he could see through it to the gardener's shed where Erin and Reggie lived.

"Don't worry, Dad." Nina patted the muscles of Zeke's forearm. "I heard the back door slam a moment ago. She and Erin are probably in the kitchen right now, helping themselves to breakfast before they take the kayaks out." She glanced at Lily. "Looks like you'll have to be my sous chef for the day. For your first task, how about running inside and checking on your sister so your dad won't worry?"

Not that Zeke was worried in the least. They'd both heard the soft murmur of voices and the occasional faint scrape of a fork against a plate that told them Erin and Megan were right where they were supposed to be. No, if she was reading it right, the teasing glint in Zeke's brown eyes said he wanted to kiss her, and with Lily out of sight for the moment, Nina moved close enough to give the man exactly what they both wanted.

Seven

Michelle

On the last Friday in August, Michelle sat in the well-appointed waiting room of Dave's law offices. Aware that she was in full view of the firm's receptionist, she resisted the urge to tap her foot on the polished, hardwood floor or drum her freshly manicured nails against the tabletop. Instead, she scrolled through her Facebook feed as though each item contained fascinating news. In reality, she had little interest in the dozen or so posts touting Ten Fresh Ways To Fix Chicken or Six Never-Fail Chocolate Chip Cookie Recipes. She had even less use for the countless ads for cheap shoes and clothes she'd never wear. Or the finger-pointing politicians, no matter which side of the aisle they represented.

No, only two things occupied her thoughts:

Aaron and Ashley. When she picked them up at the airport this afternoon, would her children still be miffed that she'd sold their old house in Fairfax? Would the twins understand the choices she'd made in the wake of their father's death? Or throw their support behind her new life in Sugar Sand Beach?

About the time the twins were boarding their flight from Charlottesville to Atlanta, where they'd change planes for the final leg into the Destin-Fort Walton Beach Airport, Michelle absently tugged on her hair. She was momentarily surprised when her fingers slipped from the ends sooner than expected. The motion tempted a smile from her pursed lips. Her new hairstylist, Debra, had been all right. Cheerful, bright, and not too chatty. Most importantly, she'd listened—really listened—when Michelle described what she wanted. Debra had given her exactly what she'd asked for, a precise, chin-length cut that flattered her face.

"Ms. Robinson? Mr. Rollins will see you now."

Michelle looked up from a Facebook post she hadn't read to see Josh at the entrance to the waiting area. Standing, she smiled politely at the young receptionist despite the slight nausea she felt whenever she thought of seeing her children again. "Thanks, Josh. How have you been?" she asked as she followed the slender clerk down the hall to the firm's large corner office.

"Couldn't be better, ma'am. How about yourself?"

She cast about for a safe topic and landed on the weather. Florida's could be fickle. Lately, the soaring temperatures and near-100 percent humidity had been on everyone's lips. "I'll be glad when we get a break in this heat."

"Looks like we might have a little cooldown for the weekend." Josh's footsteps slowed outside Dave's office, where the door stood ajar.

"That'll be nice, as long as we don't get one of those big thunderstorms." *Oh great, something else to worry about.* The last thing she needed was bad weather the entire time Aaron and Ashley were in town. Distracted by the thought, she walked into Dave's office when Josh stepped aside for her.

"Michelle, good to see you." Dave's deep baritone soothed her jangled nerves as he took her hand in a reassuring grip. "Have a seat while I talk to Josh for a sec, will you?"

She nodded, blinking away a sudden prick of tears while Dave turned to his receptionist. He handed the young man a sheet of paper he took from his desk.

"This is that recommendation you wanted. It's been a while since I wrote one of these, so look it over. If I haven't sung your praises highly enough, let me know, and I'll change it."

"Thank you, sir. I'm sure it'll be perfect," Josh answered. Without giving the paper even a cursory glance, he began his usual retreat from the senior partner's office.

"Josh, I'm serious," Dave said, stopping Josh in his tracks. "This is your career we're talking about. Let me know if you see any area I need to beef up a bit."

"Yes, sir." A rosy flush crept up the young man's neck. "I'll read it carefully while you're meeting with Ms. Robinson."

As Josh pulled the door closed on his way out, Michelle turned to Dave. "He's leaving?"

"No. Well, not right away, at least. He still has to complete his final year of law school. But he'll apply to take the bar during this third year, and for that he needs character references." Instead of taking a seat in his padded leather office chair, Dave perched on one corner of the big desk, where he was closer to Michelle.

"He's working here and going to school at the same time? At Florida State?" Michelle blinked as she considered the logistics. FSU was a good two-hour drive from Destin.

"He's a very driven young man. Did I ever tell you about him?"

Michelle thought back. She and Dave had had lunch together practically once a week ever since she'd arrived in Sugar Sand Beach. Over sandwiches and salads, they'd talked about the inn, each other's childhoods, their children. She couldn't recall any discussion of Josh, though, and shook her head.

"His mom works for our cleaning service. One night, when we were both working late and Josh was still in high school, she asked me to give him a job. She's a sweet lady, a single mom, and she was concerned about some of the friends he'd made recently. She wanted to make sure her only son stayed on the right path."

Michelle crossed her ankles. As a preteen, her headstrong daughter had given her and her father plenty of reasons to worry. Their heart-to-heart talks with Ashley had as much effect as beating their heads against a brick wall. But they'd been lucky. Though Ashley could be stubborn, she was also smart enough to look down the road and see where her friends' bad behavior would lead. She'd taken it upon herself to make changes, and by the time she hit high school—much to Michelle and Allen's relief—Ashley's circle of friends consisted of students who were voted most likely to succeed or win a Pulitzer, rather than those who were destined to end up on *America's Most Wanted*.

"I can certainly understand that," Michelle said.

"We don't usually hire kids that young, but I made an exception and agreed to meet him. I'll always be glad I did. Even then, I could see Josh was the kind who could go places. We started him in the mail room. It didn't take long, though, before he was helping the paralegals and junior law clerks with their duties." Beneath his starched white shirt, Dave's chest swelled ever so slightly. "When he decided to go to college and then to law school, the firm covered his tuition and books. Now he works for us during the summers, and on school breaks and holidays."

Michelle's hair gently swayed as she shook her head. "Your good heart never ceases to amaze me." As the senior partner in the firm, Dave paid the money for Josh's college expenses straight out of his own pocket. "And Josh—it takes a lot of dedication to juggle school and work like he's doing. I'm impressed!"

Not one to toot his own horn, Dave said, "Josh is an impressive young man. Smart. Driven. Hungry. He'll make a fine attorney." His smile faltered a bit. "Probably not here, though."

"Oh?" She thought that'd be a given after all Dave had done for the boy.

"I'll offer him a position with Rollins & Rollins, but I'm afraid he's too good to stay on with us following graduation. Some big firm in Atlanta or Miami will snap him up. He'd be foolish to turn down an opportunity like that, and I'd be wrong to stand in his way."

Dave stopped. The skin around his mouth softened. "But enough about Josh. Let me take a look at you."

Michelle stilled while her friend's gaze flicked over her.

"I like the hair. You had it cut, didn't you? And is that a new outfit? The color of that blouse looks good on you." He nodded his approval.

Straightening slightly, Michelle ran a smoothing hand over the cream-colored linen pants she'd paired with a peach blouse. One thing about Dave, she could always count on him to notice the little things. "I was worried about the hair, but Debra did a good job, didn't she?" Knowing the ends would fall in a sleek line around her face, she tossed her head.

"Great," Dave said with a smile. "You're picking up Aaron and Ashley at the airport later?"

Michelle checked her watch. "In two hours, if their flight is on time."

"I'd ask if you were all set for their visit, but I know you are. You've been looking forward to this for weeks."

"Everything is ready. Or as ready as it can be. I put fresh flowers in their rooms this morning." As they geared up to open the inn, she and her friends had decided to hire two women from Sugar Sand Beach to help with the cleaning. Thanks to their hard work, every room was spotless, not a speck of dust to be found. Still, Michelle's hand fluttered about her heart. "There's no reason for me to be so nervous, but I'm wound up as tight as a drum."

She wasn't the least bit surprised when Dave leaned down to capture her nervous fingers in his warm hands. His deep blue eyes searched for hers and held them in an unwavering gaze that filled her with a quiet steadiness.

"It'll be all right. They're your children. You've showered them with love and given them the best you had for their entire lives. They'll accept and support the decisions you've made, no matter what."

Dave's certainty spread throughout her like warm butter on toast, calming her pulse and soothing her nerves. Her heart melted for this man who always knew just the right words to put her soul at ease. "Erin and Nina and Reggie tried to tell me the same thing last night over dinner. They weren't nearly as successful at it as you are."

More than anything she wanted to press her lips to his in a proper thanks, but as quickly as the thought occurred to her, she shoved it aside. She and Dave were still exploring the very edges of their relationship. It was much too early to predict how far they'd travel. But whether their journey lasted a lifetime or ended next week, she looked forward to taking it with him.

She leaned back in her seat, her sense of well-being intact for the first time in weeks. "You are coming to the cookout tomorrow, aren't you?"

"Wouldn't miss it. Sara's driving over from Tallahassee this afternoon. We'll be at your place by two."

"Perfect. I can't wait to meet her. You've spoken about her so often, I feel like I already know her. Ashley and Aaron are looking forward to spending some time with her tomorrow night, too." Sara had inherited her father's generous heart and had volunteered to take the twins to a few of the local hot spots.

Dave gave her hands a final squeeze before he straightened. "I'm looking forward to finally meeting your children. From the stories you've told me about the twins, it's clear the three of you share a deep bond. That's why I'm confident everything will go smoothly this weekend."

"Well." She laughed. "From your lips…" She didn't bother to finish the saying. Checking her watch, she uncrossed and recrossed her ankles. Dave had asked her to stop by so they could review the final changes she'd requested in the partnership agreement. "I hate to rush, but I'm going to have to leave for the airport soon."

"Let's get to it, then." Reaching across his desk, the tall attorney took one of two blue binders from the blotter and handed it to her. Rising, he circled around to his chair. Springs squeaked as he took his seat.

Michelle thumbed through the paperwork that would equally divide ownership of the estate she'd inherited from her birth mother between Erin, Reggie, Nina and herself. Little yellow flags at the edges of a half-dozen pages marked the corrections. Paper whispered as she flipped to the first stickie.

"On Page 4, we've changed Erin's birthdate to reflect her actual birth year," Dave intoned in his most lawyerly voice. He clicked the end of his pen. "Do you agree that's the correct date?"

Having been through the review process with several earlier iterations of the contract, Michelle answered, "Yes." Dave scribbled his initials in the margin, and they moved on to the next flag. Over the next half hour they slowly and methodically worked their way through the rest of the document before Dave made a final notation and closed his binder.

"That does it," he announced. "Except..." His voice trailed off.

"Except what?" It had taken several months to iron out the wrinkles in the partnership agreement. Michelle was eager to get it signed and be done with it.

Dave met her questioning gaze with his steady one. "I have a fiduciary responsibility to point out the value of the property and make sure you understand that, by transferring three-fourths of the ownership to your friends, you're reducing your own assets by that much."

"I understand. And I appreciate that." She let out a long, slow breath. She'd done her research and had a rough idea of what five acres of beachfront went for these days. She'd be set for life if she sold the land outright. But that's not what she wanted to do, not what any of them wanted to do.

"If you still want to form the partnership, then, I'll bring the paperwork out to the house on September 17th as planned."

The hesitancy in Dave's voice puzzled Michelle.

Why wouldn't she go through with it? She'd been land-rich and cash-poor after inheriting the house and property from Nancy Simmons. Without the money Erin, Reggie and Nina had invested, in all likelihood, she would have lost the land to the tax collector in a year or two. With their help, though, they'd shared a goal of turning the rundown house into a first-class inn. They'd all worked side by side for nearly six months and now, finally, they were close to achieving their dream. It was something she could never have accomplished on her own.

Peering up at Dave, she asked, "Is there some reason why you don't think this is a good idea?" From the very beginning, he'd supported her plan to give her friends equal say in the inn's future. She held her breath, not sure how she'd react if he'd changed his mind at this late date.

Dave aligned his pen with the edges of the blue binder. "As your lawyer, I'm required to carry out your wishes and remain impartial."

Michelle frowned. That didn't sound like what she wanted to hear. "But…" she prompted.

"But as your friend, I can honestly tell you I have no qualms about going forward with the partnership agreement. None at all." He smiled broadly.

"Whew!" Air seeped from between Michelle's clenched teeth. "You worried me there for a minute," she scolded gently.

"We're talking about a serious amount of money. I had to make sure you didn't have any doubts. Otherwise, how would I earn my fee?"

"Oh, and what would that be?" Michelle teased. Dave had refused to charge her for any of the legal services he provided. He insisted it all fell under his duties as executor of Nancy Simmons's estate.

"Well, you are going to see *Harvey* with me, aren't you?"

Mirth and something that made Michelle's pulse race danced in his blue eyes. Dave had invited her to attend the play's opening night at The Destin Community Theater next month. A familiar tension tightened her midsection, and she laughed lightly. He wasn't the only one looking forward to their first official date.

"The nineteenth, wasn't it? Or was it the twentieth?" she asked, pretending to forget the date that was circled in red on her calendar.

"The eighteenth," Dave corrected.

"Oh, I knew there was something special about the eighteenth." She sighed dramatically. "That's the day I have to give you up as my legal representation."

Dave was nothing if not aboveboard. To avoid even the slightest whiff of impropriety, he'd insisted on handing her legal affairs off to another member of his firm before their relationship went one step beyond weekly lunches at Maggie's Diner or meeting for the occasional cup of coffee.

"Don't worry. You'll be in good hands with Mark."

She had no doubts that the man Dave had chosen to represent her would do an admirable job. Which didn't keep her from feeling sad at the prospect of working with the other attorney.

"I'll miss meeting with you like this," she admitted. She enjoyed the easy give and take she and Dave had developed. But what really hurt was knowing she'd no longer have an excuse to drop by and see him whenever she was in Destin.

A sly smile tugged at one corner of Dave's mouth. "Don't worry. If you ever have questions—about anything—you can always drop in for a chat."

Michelle stared into his eyes. She had no doubt at all that she'd do exactly that. She sat back in her chair as warmth flooded through her with the realization that Dave shared the same reluctance to give up their time together.

Michelle held her breath as the big, white Escalade crested the small hill that blocked the view of the house. Aaron and Ashley had showered her with love and peppered her with questions about Sugar Sand Beach from the moment she'd picked them up at the airport. But as soon as she'd turned off the main road onto the long, graveled drive that would take them the last hundred yards, a quiet tension had filled the car. The moment of truth had arrived. How would the twins react when they saw the house she and her friends had invested so much of themselves in? Would they approve?

Michelle sent up a silent prayer while she concentrated on seeing the inn they'd soon open through her children's eyes. Slowly, the Queen Anne-style house came into view. The afternoon sun glinted off the metal roof. Beneath it, pale green trim provided contrast against the fresh white paint that reflected the light. A wide wrap-around porch invited family and friends to linger in the cool shade. Everywhere she looked, glass sparkled. A splash of color came from the stained-glass window over the balcony.

The view was so different from her own first glimpse of the place that Michelle's breath caught in her throat. Only a few months ago, heavy metal shutters had covered the windows of the house, which had been sitting vacant for five years. The railing around the warped and rotted porch had listed to one side like a drunken sailor. So many weeds and vines had grown up among the trees and plants, only Reggie had known better than to take a backhoe to the entire lot.

"Oh, Mummy. It's prettier than I ever imagined," Ashley gasped at last.

"Sick!" Aaron said, offering his highest compliment. He loosed his seatbelt and slid forward to peer between the two front seats. "Look!" He pointed. "Someone hung a welcome sign."

Michelle blinked. How had she missed that? She gave the house a second glance. Sure enough, a white banner stretched across the balcony welcoming Ashley and Aaron to the Sugar Sand Inn. Recognizing Erin's handiwork, Michelle made a mental note to thank her friend.

They'd barely reached the parking area before Reggie, Nina and Erin rushed out of the house. Her friends—bless them—took their cues from Michelle and greeted the twins with warm hugs and honest affection. A festive mood descended as they helped Aaron and Ashley with their bags and got them settled in two of the larger suites at the top of the stairs.

The celebration continued all through dinner while they feasted on Nina's Pasta Bolognese, salads made with produce fresh from Reggie's garden and a simple chocolate cake with ice cream that had been her children's favorite when they were younger. It was good to hear the twins laugh again, Michelle thought while they caught one another up on all that had happened in the months since the anniversary of their father's death. Later, as she said her nightly prayers, Michelle whispered a special thanks to the Lord above for restoring her relationship with her children.

The occasional ca-chink of metal against metal came from the pit where Megan and Malcolm had teamed up against Dimella and Lily for a surprisingly competitive game of horseshoes under Erin's supervision. Clouds of smoke rose from the grill Chris had set up beneath a canopy near the garage. The scent of charcoal and sizzling hamburgers drifted across the yard. Vases of fresh flowers from the garden anchored the red-and-white checkered tablecloths on a line of picnic tables. Seated in an assortment of lawn chairs, most of the adults talked and laughed and, as far as Michelle could tell, genuinely enjoyed themselves in the shade of the large oak trees.

A peaceful sigh seeped from between her lips as the last of the nervous tension that had been her constant companion of late finally faded. She inclined her head toward the spot where Sara, Aaron and Ashley sat sipping tall glasses of the inn's signature punch.

"The three of them seem to have hit it off," she commented. "I'm so glad Sara was able to make it. She's every bit as wonderful as you said she was."

Dave nodded, his eyes filled with tenderness as he studied the pretty blonde who sat on the edge of a lawn chair. She waved her hands animatedly, a move that elicited laughter from both Aaron and Ashley.

"The apple of my eye, that one." His gaze shifted toward Michelle. "Is this reunion going as smoothly as it looks?"

"It's been wonderful," she replied, unable to keep herself from gushing a little. "I gave them the grand tour when they got in yesterday. They each love their rooms, and they've had nothing but good things to say about our plans for the inn and cafe. Aaron ran around all morning taking pictures for the website. Ashley looked at the turret with me earlier and gave me some decorating hints that were perfect for the honeymoon suite I want to turn that into." This morning, Ashley had also joined her for a long walk on the beach, though they hadn't talked much. Her daughter had set a killer pace that left Michelle huffing and puffing, but she'd still been happy that they were together.

"Sounds like everything is going well, then." Dave leaned over and gave her hand a quick squeeze. "Good. I know how worried you were about this visit."

"I am relieved." Michelle took a big breath and let it out slowly. It was nice that she and Dave had the kind of relationship where they didn't have to hide their feelings. "I know we still have some things to work out. We've set aside most of tomorrow for mom-and-me time, and some of our conversations will be... difficult." Among other things, she needed to explain the precarious financial situation she'd found herself in after Allen's untimely death. She'd put that discussion off for over a year, telling herself the time just wasn't right, when in reality, she hadn't wanted to tarnish the image her children had of their father. "But after today, I'm sure we'll get through it."

"Aaron and Ashley are great young adults. You should be proud of the job you and Allen did in raising them."

Michelle smothered a laugh. Dave hadn't seen the twins' temperamental side. With any luck, he never would. She cast another glance toward the spot where they sat with Dave's daughter. As she did, she caught Ashley's eye and smiled. Her children were on their best behavior, and one of the reasons sat right in front of them. "It really helps to have Sara here," she told Dave.

His voice quieted. "I don't mind telling you she was a little nervous about today. She was afraid she'd be letting you down if Aaron and Ashley didn't like her."

"Me?" Michelle started in surprise. "Why would she worry about me?" She fanned herself with one hand. Had Dave been in the sun too long, or was there another reason for the faint pink that stained his cheeks?

He cleared his throat. "Your name may have come up in our conversations. Enough for her to figure out I care for you. She wanted to make a good impression."

"And she did. But I'd expect nothing less. After all, she's your daughter, isn't she? From what I can see, that apple you were talking about didn't fall far from the tree." Along with his height and clear blue eyes, Sara had inherited her father's innate grace. Plus, she exuded a Southern charm that won a soft spot in Michelle's heart the instant they met. "But honestly, the shoe is on the other foot here. I was a little afraid she'd hate me on sight."

"Nonsense. She's smart enough to know a woman has to be pretty special to catch my interest."

The deep tenderness in Dave's eyes sent Michelle's pulse rate climbing. More and more, she wanted to explore the feelings he stirred in her. But that would have to wait until she was no longer his client and they were someplace other than within twenty feet of their three children, no matter how old they were. Trying to make light of the situation, she pressed the back of her hand to her head in her best imitation of a Southern belle. "Why, sir," she declared. "I believe you're flirting with me."

Dave played along, pretending to twirl the ends of a nonexistent mustache. "Maybe just a little, my dear." As aware of their surroundings as she was, he sobered quickly. "But I meant every word," he added, half under his breath.

Shouts from the horseshoe pit signaled the end of the game and spared Michelle the necessity of answering. She swung a look in that direction in time to see Dimella and Lily doing a little victory dance. She pointed at Viola, who sat nearby. "Did you bring in a ringer?"

Viola laughed. "Dimella has played before."

"She won the championship three years running at Camp Willamuck," Charlie was quick to add. The Black man beamed with pride.

As he should, Michelle thought. Located in the Shenandoah Valley, the sleepover camp consistently won awards for its summer programs. Aaron and Ashley enjoyed their own summers there enough that they signed on as camp counselors each year until they graduated from high school.

"It was so sweet of Dimella and Megan to include Malcolm and Lily," Michelle observed. The younger children could barely lift the horseshoes. When it proved impossible for them to toss the heavy weights the entire forty feet, Erin had moved each of the little ones closer to the stake, where she'd "helped" them take their throws. Even with the added help, Michelle doubted whether either of the youngsters had scored more than a few points.

Reggie, who'd been hanging out near the grill

with Chris and keeping little Hope entertained, meandered across the lawn with the baby on her hip. At Michelle's chair, Reggie leaned down to whisper in her ear. "Do you know where Nina is? She wanted me to let her know when we were ready to serve the food. Chris says the burgers and hot dogs are done."

Just then, Michelle caught movement out of the corner of her eye. Tracking the motion, she turned slightly toward the dirt road that led to the garden and the lake beyond it. She spotted Nina as she came around a bend in the path. Her friend wasn't alone, and Michelle wasn't a bit surprised to see her drop Zeke's hand when they came in sight of the rest of the group.

"Right on time, as usual," she said, pointing to the chef, who had an uncanny ability for knowing when food was cooked to perfection.

"Come on, Hope." Reggie hiked the little girl a little higher on her hip. "Let's go tell Aunt Nina it's time to set the table."

Michelle waited until the pair were out of earshot before, her voice low, she mused, "I wonder what those two were up to out by the lake." Judging from Nina's mussed hair, she had a pretty good idea the normally put-together chef hadn't merely been showing Zeke how well their garden grew. A fresh worry shot through her. "I hope she's not setting herself up for a heartbreak."

Dave's low voice banished her concern. "You don't have to worry about Zeke. He's as solid as they come. The man doesn't mess around."

Relief shot through Michelle. Nina had been badly burned in the past. She deserved the kind of man who was steady and dependable. "That's good to know." She stood and smoothed her loose T-shirt. "Don't bother to get up," she told Dave. "Stay here and enjoy yourself while I help Nina and Viola bring the dishes out from the kitchen." The shelves of the refrigerator groaned with all of Aaron and Ashley's favorites.

The rest of the afternoon went off without a hitch, so it surprised Michelle—shocked her, actually—when, after everyone else headed home, Ashley pleaded a headache and suddenly backed out of the plans for a night on the town with Sara. His sister's illness put Aaron in a quandary. Michelle could tell her son had looked forward to spending more time with the bright, engaging young attorney, but she also knew how fiercely loyal the twins were to one another. In a move that only left her more confused, Ashley uncharacteristically insisted her brother keep the date before she retreated to her room.

Michelle lingered downstairs until Aaron left

for the evening. An hour later, she and Erin chatted as she bustled about the kitchen fixing hot tea and dry toast—an old family recipe for whatever ailed her children. After loading the simple items onto a tray, she climbed the stairs to Ashley's room.

"Ash?" Her voice soft, she tapped on the door. "I've brought you some tea."

"Go away. Leave me alone."

At the brusque tone, the one that had grown so familiar over the last six months, Michelle stiffened. Clearly, something more than a headache bothered her daughter. Her motherly antenna fairly vibrated with the sense that Ashley had placed the blame for whatever it was squarely on her shoulders. Since moving to Florida, she'd had no choice but to wait for her daughter's temper to cool. This time, however, a thousand miles didn't separate them. This time, only a door stood between her and learning what had upset her child. Determined not to let things fester into an even bigger problem, she reached for the knob.

"Ash, I'm coming in," she announced.

"Go a—" Ashley's sharp retort died as the door swung wide.

Expecting to find the room darkened and her daughter huddled under the blankets, Michelle blinked in the light that spilled from every lamp in the suite. Still wearing the pretty sundress she'd worn to the picnic, Ashley paced across the room, her back to her mother. Michelle's heart clenched when her redheaded child spun around and she got her first real look at her daughter's tear-streaked face.

"Ashley, darling. What's wrong?" she whispered.

"You know very well what's wrong." Accusation freighted every word of Ashley's voice.

Slowly, evenly, Michelle responded, "I'm afraid I don't," while she eyed a nearby occasional table. She wanted nothing more than to lower the tray onto its surface, to sweep her daughter into her arms and offer reassurances that, whatever was wrong, they'd resolve it together.

But one glimpse of the anger in Ashley's eyes convinced Michelle that would be the worst thing she could do. By the time the twins had celebrated their second birthdays, her daughter's temper tantrums had become the stuff of family legends. Michelle had tried every trick in the parenting books to deal with them. Ignoring them hadn't helped. Hugs hadn't worked any better than trying to reason with a screaming two-year-old. In desperation, she'd even tried one so-called expert's recommendation to shock the little girl out of her snit by spritzing her with water from a spray bottle. Which had given Michelle a much better understanding of the term "madder than a wet hen."

She'd eventually learned that her daughter calmed down fastest if she gave her some space and let her vent. So she stood, frozen, while she thumbed through her memories of the day like they were pages in a flipbook. Despite her best efforts, she couldn't spot a single interaction that should cause this much angst.

"It's that man. Sara's father," Ashley said at last.

"Dave?" Michelle's confusion deepened. Dave had been his usual charming self all day. Surely, he hadn't done anything to offend either of her children.

"Yes, Dave," Ashley spat. "I saw how he looked at you. He squeezed your hand when he thought no one was watching. But I saw him. I also noticed that you didn't tell him to get lost."

"Dave is my attorney," Michelle protested. "I told you about him. He was the executor of my birth mother's estate. Without him, I wouldn't have ever found out she left me this house." She paused. In the interest of full disclosure she added, "He's also a friend. A good friend."

"There's more to it than that, though, isn't there?" Insinuation turned Ashley's voice a darker shade of ugly.

Air whooshed from Michelle's lungs. She liked Dave, and he liked her, but there was nothing more than mutual attraction between them. Maybe their relationship could develop into something else. She wouldn't deny that possibility. If and when it did, though, that day was so far in the future, it certainly shouldn't concern Ashley.

"Is he the reason you sold our home? The reason you moved here?" Red splotches mottling her face, Ashley gestured wildly. "Did you spend all Daddy's money—our inheritance—on this house so you could be close to your lover? Geez, Mom. Dad's barely been gone a year, and you've already found someone to take his place!" Her red hair flying, Ashley swept an arrangement of dried flowers from the dresser. The basket smashed to the floor, the petals scattering across the hardwood.

Pain lanced Michelle's heart as she stared at what was left of the arrangement she'd carefully selected from Polly's Posies. It was as broken as her relationship with her daughter. Could either ever be repaired?

Her mouth opened and shut like a fish gasping for air. She turned, unable to summon the words to counter her daughter's temper tantrum or the hurtful words that had spewed from Ashley's lips. The tray still in her hands, she walked out of the suite, down the stairs and into the kitchen, where Erin sat nursing a glass of wine.

The moment Michelle spotted her friend, the floodgates opened. The frustration and heartbreak she'd felt over the strained relationship with her daughter came pouring out. Tears rolled down her cheeks.

"I'm so disappointed," she said, when her sobs finally slowed to a trickle. "I thought this weekend was a turning point, that we'd finally healed the breach between us. If anything, things are worse than ever. I've lost her," she whispered, finally giving voice to her deepest fear. "I've lost my baby girl, and there isn't a thing I can do about it."

Erin handed her a wad of napkins she'd plucked from the holder on the table. While her friend gave her a tight squeeze, Michelle blotted her eyes and wiped her nose. When she'd finished, the blonde placed both of her hands on Michelle's shoulders and held her at arm's length. She stared at the grim determination that tightened Erin's features.

"You and Allen made me the twins' godmother. Do you still trust me with that job?"

"Y-yes." Michelle hiccupped. She dabbed at her eyes again.

"Okay, then. Trust me to take care of this," Erin said.

"What are you going to do?" Michelle asked, her voice sounding small and far too vulnerable.

"I think it's high time my goddaughter and I have a little heart-to-heart. Not tonight. From what you've told me, she's too upset to listen to anyone right now. But tomorrow, first thing, we'll take the kayaks out. You know how much she loves being on the water. She won't be able to stay mad while she's paddling. When I'm sure she's good and ready to listen, I'll make it abundantly clear that's she's wrong about Dave...and a whole lot more."

"Well." Michelle let her breath out in a long sigh. "The way things stand between us right now, you can't make the situation any worse."

Eight

Erin

"Out of bed, lazybones." Though it took every ounce of strength she had, Erin resisted the urge to rip the covers off Ashley's bed. She settled for giving them a firm tug. "You and me have a date with a couple of kayaks."

"Go 'way—wait." Ashley sat up, her long red hair falling in soft curls about her shoulders. She rubbed sleep from her eyes. "What'd you say? What time is it?"

"Early." Sunrise was at least an hour away. Erin forced herself to keep her tone light and breezy. "I'm in the mood for a long paddle this morning, and I need a partner. Are you coming?" Knowing her goddaughter loved a good challenge, she dared, "Or has college life made you too soft?"

153

"Ha! Not on your life." Ashley's feet hit the floor. "Give me five minutes to get ready." Grabbing a holder from the bedside table, she captured her hair in a messy bun.

"Make it three. Don't forget your sunblock." As mean as Ashley could be, she didn't deserve to get burned. Knowing a rogue wave or two was all it would take to wash away even the protection, Erin tossed one of her swim shirts onto the bed. "Wear that. Can't have Miss Precious turning red as a tomato. I stowed a pair of water shoes in a go bag on the boat for you." After an emotionally drained Michelle had turned in last night, Erin had checked today's weather forecast before loading all the necessary gear into her two best seafaring kayaks.

"Is Aaron coming, too?" Ashley asked while she rummaged through her suitcase for a pair of shorts.

"Nope. Just you and me, Toots. He and your mom are going to work on the inn's website this morning." Erin pretended not to notice the way her goddaughter's lips tightened or how Ashley's brows slammed together. Turning on one heel, she ducked out the door. "There's a travel mug by the coffee pot. Meet me in the Activity Center as soon as you're ready."

Ashley snatched the swim shirt off the bed and, carrying her shorts, headed for the bathroom. "I'll be right there."

On her way down the stairs, Erin whistled tunelessly. Nobody behaved toward her friends the way Ashley had treated Michelle. It was time her goddaughter learned that important lesson... and she was just the right person to teach it.

"We have to carry the kayaks all the way to the water?" The corners of Ashley's mouth turned down in what Erin was afraid might become a perpetual frown. Which would be an awful shame for such a pretty young woman. "Why?" the redhead continued. "Can't we use the cart the rest of the way?"

Using it, they'd rolled the watercraft from the Activity Center, past the house, and as far as the dune line.

"It'll be impossible to push through the sand. The wheels will bog down. Carrying them is easier." Erin shrugged. "Don't worry. We'll take them one at a time." She could easily shoulder a fifty-pound kayak through the tall grass and over the sandy path by herself. But today was all about teaching her goddaughter the give and take of teamwork. And family. And to respect her mother.

"Grab the toggles on your end." Erin stood with her back to the first craft and reached behind her for the bow lines. "Okay, lift," she instructed. She waited a beat for Ashley to get used to the weight before she trudged the fifty or so yards to the beach. Leaving the boat near the water's edge, they repeated the process with the second kayak.

When they finished, Erin opened one of the forward hatches and pulled out a waterproof bag, which she handed to Ashley. "Stow your cell phone. Put on a life jacket. You can change into water shoes and leave your flip-flops here." She kicked off her own sandals and retrieved a pair of rubber-soled shoes that were impervious to saltwater.

She'd perched on the edge of her kayak to brush the sand from her feet when a disturbance in the water caught her attention. She pointed to a spot about twenty yards out where the surface boiled. "Look. A mullet school." While they searched for food, the fish regularly swam along the shoreline in large groups.

Ashley had no sooner looked that way when dozens of the gray fish began leaping out of the water. "Why are they jumping up and down like that?"

"Something's hunting them. Watch. We might find out what it is."

Not thirty seconds later, a much larger fish leaped high into the air.

"Silver king," Erin whispered. Four feet long if it was an inch, the tarpon jumped so high, its tail brushed the surface. The hunter grabbed one of the mullet on its way back down, hit the water with a loud smack and disappeared.

"Wow!" Ashley's mouth hung open. "That was a big fish."

"Not as big as that one." Erin pointed again, this time aiming at a pair of dorsal fins another ten yards out. Nearly identical in size, the two fins sliced through the deeper water. "Hello, shark."

"Uh? Maybe we shouldn't go out after all," Ashley suggested.

Erin heard the nervous edge in her goddaughter's voice and sought to reassure her. "That one's a lemon shark. They're more afraid of humans than we are of them."

"I doubt that," Ashley countered.

It was true though. Unprovoked attacks were extremely rare, especially when it came to lemon sharks. Mullet and tarpon, on the other hand, were prey, and the ones they'd been watching had sensed the predator's presence. Erin wasn't a bit surprised when the school of nervous baitfish picked up speed as it moved east and farther down the beach. "Just to be on the safe side," she announced, "we'll head in the opposite direction."

Ashley shielded her eyes while she scanned the water for more dorsal fins. "I didn't expect it to be so flat. What happened to the waves?" Now that the fish had moved on, the surface lay unbroken for as far as they could see.

Erin followed her goddaughter's gaze. The eastern horizon had turned rosy in the half hour it had taken them to get the boats to the water. For now, not a breath of wind stirred the surface, and only tiny ripples eddied against the wet sand. Once the sun came up, though, an onshore breeze would drive waves in towards the shore.

"This is the best time to get on the water. We'll have a fast paddle while it's calm like this. I want to get past Topsail Hill before it gets choppy." The sixteen-hundred-acre preserve spread out behind the next three miles of pristine beachfront. If they moved at a good clip, they'd reach the other side in an hour or so.

Erin floated her kayak and easily climbed aboard while she kept one eye on Ashley.

Though the young woman's motions weren't quite as graceful as she'd have liked, the girl managed to seat herself in the cockpit with her feet tucked into the hull, all without capsizing. Erin nodded. Michelle's daughter could be difficult, but at least she'd remembered the basics from the lessons Erin had given the twins through the years.

"You all set?" she called. When Ashley replied that she was, Erin positioned her paddle so the wide twin blades hung evenly over either side of the boat. Without hesitation, she dug in. First one side, then the other, her blades cut through the water in a circular motion as familiar to her as brushing her teeth. The kayak shot forward. For the next hour, they sped along the shoreline at a challenging pace.

Challenging for Ashley, that was. Erin had barely broken a sweat by the time they scooted past the point where the shoreline's natural beauty gave way to houses with green, manicured lawns. Her paddling partner, however, lagged a good thirty yards behind. One look was all it took for Erin to identify the problem—the more Ashley relied on arm strength to propel her kayak, the less she let her stronger, core muscles handle the effort. That made paddling a tiring business. She tossed an anchor overboard and waited for the younger woman to catch up.

"Ready for a little break?" she asked. She grabbed Ashley's deck line as the other kayak came alongside. While she waited for the girl to catch her breath, Erin tied their boats together.

"You weren't...kidding when you said...we'd get a...workout," Ashley puffed.

"We'll take it a little slower on the way back," Erin promised. They wouldn't have much choice. As the weather reports had predicted, a brisk breeze had stirred the waves once the sun cleared the horizon. Making headway against the light chop would slow their pace considerably. "When we get going again, sit a little straighter and push on the pegs with your feet. It'll help you remember to use your stomach and leg muscles." She removed two bottles from her hatch and handed one to Ashley.

"Did you bring anything to eat?" the redhead asked. She twisted the cap on her water bottle and took a long drink.

"Yep." Erin dug in her bag. Ashley's request had given her just the opening she needed to start a long overdue conversation, the real reason she'd wanted them to spend time together this morning. After giving her godchild a granola bar, she patted her stomach. "Me, I'm still full from the picnic yesterday. I don't know what I liked the most, the hamburgers or that pepper relish. Did you try it?"

Ashley's face, which had been animated only a few seconds earlier, shuttered as if someone had closed the drapes. Her voice clipped, she said, "It was all right."

Erin stretched. "It looked like you and Aaron got along well with Sara. It was too bad you didn't feel well later."

"I lied. I didn't have a headache." Frowning, Ashley gave the cap of her water bottle a vicious twist. "If you must know, I was upset with Mom. I could have done without her mooning all over Sara's dad like some kind of cheap floo—"

Erin's hand shot up. "Stop it right there, Ash. Your mother is my best friend. I will not listen to you badmouth her."

"Not even if she deserves it?" Ashley ripped the granola bar's foil packaging. "You saw the way they were looking at each other. Like a pair of lovesick teenagers. It was disgusting. I'm just thankful Daddy wasn't here to see it."

"He wasn't, though. He's gone. He's been gone a year and a half now." Despite the pain she knew she was causing her godchild, Erin delivered the words in a matter-of-fact tone. She sighed. "That's the sad, bitter truth of it. As for your mom—she's trying hard to rebuild her life. She hasn't had an easy time of it. Even before your dad passed, things were rough. But she put on a brave face so you and Aaron wouldn't worry."

"Are you trying to tell me my parents' marriage was in trouble?" Ashley gave her head a vehement shake. "You're wrong about that. Mummy and Daddy couldn't have been happier."

"Listen to me carefully, Ashley. Your mom loved your dad with her whole heart. She still does. But even when two people love each other, that doesn't mean everything is sunshine and smooth sailing." Her own marriage had taught her that particular lesson. "A marriage takes work. Hard work. After everything she's gone through, and then losing your dad the way she did, you need to give your mom a break, don't you think?"

Ashley's lips thinned. "What I think is this Dave person is after my mom's money."

Interesting. Erin's head tipped to one side. "What money?"

"You know," Ashley said, sounding exasperated. "Daddy's retirement. His pension and his 401K. His life insurance policy. The house, our house. The one where Aaron and I grew up. A two-story Colonial in that neighborhood? It was worth a small fortune."

You poor delusional child, you.

Ashley's naïve reasoning made Erin laugh. *How much of the truth had Michelle hidden from her children?* All of it, apparently. It was time to straighten that out right now.

As gently as possible, she said, "Oh, honey. Your father was a brilliant engineer, but he was a lousy businessman. He invested every dime your parents owned—and more—in that little company of his. His retirement fund, his IRAs and savings—he emptied all of those accounts in order to pay the start-up costs. Your mom had no choice—she had to sell the house when she did. She couldn't afford the mortgage payments, and the bank was threatening to foreclose."

"Oh, now I know you're wrong." Ashley's head jerked as if she'd been slapped. "Daddy and Mummy paid off that mortgage the year Aaron and I graduated from high school. I remember 'cause they opened a bottle of champagne and let us each have a sip even though we weren't twenty-one yet." She folded her arms across her chest as if she'd stated an undeniable fact.

"Do you have any idea how much it costs to form a company and develop a new software product?" Erin waited until Ashley slowly shook her head before she said another word. "Well, it costs a whole lot more than your folks had saved. The only way they could swing it was to take out a new loan on the house. That barely covered the operating costs. When your dad died, there was nothing left."

"But Mom—Mummy would have told me if she had money problems."

Erin's heart lurched when Ashley's eyes begged her to take back everything she'd just said. "I'm sorry, Ash. But it's the truth. Your mom was flat broke before we moved here."

"Why didn't she tell us?" Ashley's face had gone so pale, the freckles on her cheeks stood out. "Why didn't she tell me?"

"She tried to. But both you and Aaron practically worshipped your father." Erin hurried to add, "As you should have. As you still should. He was a good man, your dad. Your mom didn't want to do or say anything that would tarnish his image."

As far as she was concerned, that was part of the problem. Michelle should have at least told her children about the precariousness of her financial situation. Erin took a breath. That, too, was water under the bridge.

"It took her a year, but your mom was going to come clean about everything. Remember the anniversary of your dad's death? How she'd wanted you to come home that weekend?"

"How could I forget it?" Ashley's voice dropped. In a monotone, she said, "We told her we weren't coming. Aaron and I planned to surprise her. Only nothing worked out the way we thought it would."

Knowing Michelle shouldn't be alone that weekend, Erin—along with Reggie and Nina—had taken her friend out to dinner. It had been nearly midnight by the time they'd come home to find Aaron sleeping and Ashley impatiently waiting for them. Things had gone from bad to worse when Michelle let it slip that she was putting the house on the market. Ashley had reacted by throwing a hissy fit. Things between Michelle and her children had been strained ever since.

"Losing your dad was tough enough for your mom," Erin said, laying her final cards on the proverbial table. "She doesn't need the added grief you've given her."

Ashley's lower lip trembled. "So where does this guy Dave fit in?"

"Your mom didn't lie to you. He's her attorney. They've become friends. One day, maybe, they'll be more than that, but for now, that's all they are—friends."

Erin hesitated. Had Ashley heard enough, or did she dare push the girl even further?

In for a penny...

She took a deep breath and plunged ahead. "Your dad is gone, Ash. That's the sad, sad truth. There's nothing you or I can do to change that. But your mom, she's still alive. And, God willing, she'll be around for another thirty or forty years. Do you think she should spend all that time alone? That she doesn't deserve to have someone special in her life?"

Tears trickled from beneath Ashley's sunglasses. They glistened on her cheeks. She picked up her paddle. "You've given me a lot to think about, Aunt Erin. If you don't mind, I'd like to head back now."

Erin stretched out one hand and grabbed hold of the lines that bound the two boats together. "On one condition," she said.

Ashley stilled. "What?" she asked in a small voice.

"That you promise to treat your mom with the love and respect she deserves from here on out." She'd hate to dump her godchild in the Gulf, but she'd do it in a heartbeat if that's what it took to knock some sense into Ashley.

"Don't worry, Aunt Erin. I know how badly I've messed up. I'm going to talk to Aaron. We're going make things right between us and

Mummy." She dipped her paddle into the water. "Trust me."

Erin let the breath she'd been holding seep through her lips. Ashley could be bullheaded, and her temper got her into trouble more than it should. But she could also admit it when she was wrong. And when she put her mind to it, she could put that stubborn streak of hers to work for good.

Erin slipped the knot that set the boats free from one another. Her kayak drifted back as she let Ashley take the lead. Despite the choppy water, the girl set a killer pace all the way home.

Erin played the hose over the kayaks, which she'd propped upside down on a pair of sawhorses outside the Activity Center. A stray piece of seaweed dripped from one of the grab handles. She plucked it from the nylon ribbing and continued spraying until the last bit of suds sluiced to the ground. When the fiberglass glinted in the sunshine, she left both boats to air dry. Picking up the armload of gear she and Ashley had used earlier, she headed inside to put it all away.

Had she done the right thing by letting her godchild dash off in search of her mother instead of helping with the equipment?

She hoped so, but she'd have to wait and see how things turned out before she knew the answer. She did know she'd broken one of her cardinal rules by hauling everything back to the house on her own. But she'd probably do it again if it helped heal the breach between Michelle and Ashley. Whatever it took, she hoped they'd resolve things soon. It hurt to see two of the people she cared the most for at odds with one another.

Inside the Center, she returned the sunblock and the go bag to their rightful places, hung the life jackets from hooks on the pegboard wall and left her water shoes on the mat by the door. She smiled approvingly at the room. The space had come together nicely. She'd been right about the colors. The white pegboard looked great against the blue walls. The desk she and Reggie had lugged down from the turret lent the room a polished, professional air while another find—a tall entryway table—made the perfect place to advertise all the outings and classes the inn would soon offer its guests. One or two more finishing touches and the Center would be ready for business.

On her way back out, she grabbed a bottle of protectant from a shelf and plucked a clean rag from a nearby basket. The spray worked like sunblock on the kayaks. And like sunblock, she wouldn't go out on the water without it. Her fingers tightened their grip on the plastic bottle, though, when she spied a man lingering near the boats.

A thief? Nah!

She scolded herself for the momentary flare of concern. Wild hogs roamed the five-acre property. Snakes and the occasional alligator hid in the tall grass. But she didn't have to worry about thieves in Sugar Sand Beach. Deliberately, she relaxed her shoulders while she gave the unexpected visitor a second look.

An altogether different kind of worry surged through her when she recognized the tall, broad-shouldered man. She shook her head. Ron certainly had a knack for catching her off-guard. Here she was, fresh off the water, without so much as a lick of makeup on her face, her hair a windblown mess. And there he was, looking like he'd stepped out of a photo shoot. Again.

Things could be worse, she reminded herself. At least he hadn't caught her washing the kayaks in a skimpy bikini. She tugged on the hem of the swim shirt she wore over the top of her bathing suit and shorts. On second thought, a bikini might not be such a bad idea. Not that she had any intention of actually stripping down to hers. But she wouldn't have minded letting her ex get a glimpse of what he'd missed out on when he divorced her. She might be in her mid-forties, but she watched what she ate, got plenty of exercise and was actually in better shape now than she'd been when she was in her twenties. Unable to do anything about her hair or makeup, she threw back her shoulders and covered the distance between them in long strides.

"Ron," she said when she got within hailing distance. She would have said more, would have asked him what he was doing here or why he hadn't hightailed it back to Houston once she turned down his job offer. That's what she intended, anyway. The trouble was—much to her consternation—her mouth went bone-dry the instant he turned to face her. She'd say one thing about her ex-husband—he certainly wore the rugged outdoorsman look well.

"Erin. You were out on the water this morning?" He gestured toward the kayaks. "I would have come with you."

Like I'd let that happen.

"Uh, no," she managed, pulling her wits about her like a shawl. "Michelle's kids came down for a visit this weekend. I took Ashley out for a little one-on-one time." *And a nice long talk.*

Ron scuffed one foot through the grass. "Ashley and"—he paused—"and Aaron, right? Gosh, they must be in their twenties by now." He ducked his head as if in apology. "It's been a while."

"More than twenty years," she reminded him. The twins had been toddlers when her marriage to Ron had fallen apart.

"Are they doing okay? You know, after losing their dad?"

His concern surprised her for all of two seconds. That's as long as it took her to remember how upset he'd been when his own father passed. How it had changed him. Ron Senior's death had been the beginning of the end for their marriage.

"They've had their ups and downs, as you can imagine," she replied softly. She wasn't about to share more than that. Their friendships had been among the assets she and Ron had divided when they divorced. She'd kept Michelle's, Nina's and Reggie's. He'd retained others. Her eyes narrowed. "How'd you hear about Allen?"

"Small-town life. Word gets around when four single women move to town. Everybody's talking about you."

Hmph. He'd stayed in Sugar Sand Beach after all. The man was full of surprises. After they'd stopped at Maggie's Diner for pie, she'd thought for sure he'd strike her name from his list of possible employees and move on to the next candidate. Apparently, she'd been wrong about that.

"We've made a lot of friends around here," she said, her way of warning him to tread carefully.

An easygoing smile spread across Ron's face. "I'm not surprised. In the—what's it been—six months, give or take? You've done a lot for people around here. That van you're donating? Your business alone has given the hardware store a much-needed shot in the arm. At the grocery store, Gus can't say enough good things about you. Or should I say, y'all?"

"Whatever floats your boat," she answered with a shrug she hoped would let him know his actions were none of her concern. She had to admit, though, his attempt at the accent sounded odd. Despite spending his childhood in Houston, Ron had never developed a proper Southern drawl. "It's been a two-way street. People around here have done a lot for us."

Her weight shifted from one foot to the other. For someone who was just here to offer her a job,

Ron had sure been talking to a lot of folks. Why the sudden interest? She watched him carefully, waiting for him to explain.

He stuck his hands in the pockets of his fishing shorts. "Have you given any more thought to accepting my proposal?"

"I've thought about it." Though she'd never say it out loud, his offer kept jumping to the forefront of her mind whenever she had a spare moment, much like the mullet had leaped out of the water that morning. To be honest, the prospect of traveling the globe held absolutely zero interest for her. Even first-class travel had lost its appeal. But Ron? The way his smile lit up a room? The lock of hair that fell onto his forehead and added to his boyish charm? His strength?

Oh, yeah.

His reappearance in her life had stirred memories of the love they'd once shared. She'd brushed them aside, thinking he'd headed back to Houston. But here he was, a week later and still hanging around. They said timing was everything in a relationship. If so, theirs couldn't be worse. The last time they'd been together, she'd wanted to travel and he hadn't. Now the shoe was on the other foot.

She gave him the only response she had to

give. "The answer is still no. I have no intention of coming to work for you."

Ron jingled the keys in his pocket. "You can't blame me if I think you'll change your mind. The offer stands. In fact, I'll give you three months to decide. I'm betting sometime between now and November, you'll wake up one morning and start packing your bags."

"That's a pretty specific timeframe," she pointed out.

"I'm willing to wait that long. But after that, I'll have to move on."

Something on the ground near his feet seemed to catch his attention. He nudged a clump of grass before his gaze met hers again. "In the meantime, I need to ask you for a favor."

Finally. It was about time he got around to the real reason he'd shown up at the inn. She canted her head. "Yeah? What's that?"

"The other day when we were talking, you said you'd explored the area pretty well. Does that include Campbell Lake?"

"It does." Erin felt her brows draw together. Sand dunes and little else separated the fresh-water lake from the salty Gulf. Only a handful of such bodies of water existed in the world, so naturally, she'd spent as much time as possible exploring this one.

"I was wondering if you could give me a tour. You know, show me the best parts."

She shook her head. She couldn't if she wanted to, and she didn't think she wanted to. But he deserved more than a simple no.

"I can't take my kayaks there," she explained. "Campbell Lake is part of the Topsail Hill Preserve, and they don't allow outside boats." That rule prevented something as small as the bit of seaweed she'd pulled off her grab handle from contaminating the pristine coastal dune lake. Until recently, a concession stand had rented a handful of canoes and kayaks solely for use in the Preserve. Unfortunately for Ron, though, the little shop had closed last month and wouldn't reopen until late fall. She finished by saying, "I'm sure you'll be long gone by then."

"Well..." The crow's-feet around Ron's eyes wrinkled as his smile deepened.

Why did he remind her of Mr. Pibbs that time the cat caught a mouse? Unease rolled through her midsection. She wasn't going to like the answer.

"Did I forget to mention that I've taken over the Park's concessions? Just for three months... until the new owners come in. That'll give us time to get to know each other again. In case, you know, you get a bad case of wanderlust. In the meantime, I can't rent somebody a kayak to take out on Campbell Lake if I've never been there myself. I need someone to show me the lay of the water, so to speak."

She eyed him. *Who did he think he was fooling?* The idea that he needed a guide to show him the ins and outs of Campbell Lake was ridiculous. Ron was every bit as adept at paddling as she was. He had to be. He owned an outdoor sports company, for crying out loud.

Ron was also the man who'd broken her heart into a million pieces. Who, once upon a time, hadn't lived up to his side of the bargain they'd made. Who'd changed the rules in midstream without so much as a conversation. She shouldn't, couldn't give him a second chance to break her heart, could she?

Still, she couldn't deny that the opportunity to spend a few hours with him appealed to her on several levels. From a purely business standpoint, agreeing to show him the area was the smart move. The inn would, no doubt, have at least one guest who wanted to tour Topsail Hill in the coming months. A little quid pro quo could work in her favor later. Then, there was the man himself. The two occasions she'd seen Ron over the last couple of weeks had stirred up feelings she thought she'd put to rest long ago. Spending a little more time with him would give her a chance to work him out of her system. In all likelihood, she'd be over him once and for all well before he left town. Throwing caution to the wind, she extended a hand.

"I guess you've got yourself a guide," she said.

But as Ron's warm grip enveloped hers, a still, small voice warned that agreeing to see more of her ex might just be the biggest mistake she'd ever made.

Nine

Michelle

"Ahhhhh." Michelle collapsed onto the cushion of her favorite rattan chair. "As beautiful as the house looks with fresh paint, I am so glad we can meet out here again." Weeks had passed since the last time the four of them had gathered on the porch to review the day's activities and make plans for the future. Nina had prepared a pitcher of the inn's signature punch in honor of the occasion. Michelle raised her tumbler and held it out to the others.

Glasses clinked. Chairs creaked as she, Erin and Reggie got comfortable while Nina doled out stuffed cherry tomatoes on tiny plates. "These are a bit of an experiment," she explained. "The original recipe called for bacon, and I made one batch with that. Ethan suggested giving the appetizer a true taste of Florida and provided a secret ingredient to use in the second batch. Let me know what you think."

Ever hungry, Reggie popped one of the tomatoes in her mouth and chewed thoughtfully. "Ummmmm?" Barely able to raise her napkin fast enough, she spit. "Whatever that is, I give it a big ol' thumbs-down." She grabbed her glass and gulped.

"Nice! Tell me how you really feel," Nina said with a frown.

"They can't be that bad," Michelle protested. Nina's failures were so far and few between, she couldn't remember the last time the chef had served something they hadn't loved. Nina even made asparagus—the one vegetable Michelle loathed—taste good. She studied the two little tomatoes on her plate. Small chunks of meat dotted the cream cheese filling. Assuming the brown flecks were bacon, she chose the other one and took a cautious bite. The mystery meat had an unpleasant, rubbery texture.

"Chewy," she said, glad she'd only taken a little taste. She returned the rest of the tomato to her plate.

"The bacon ones are good." Erin pushed one with the mystery filling aside. "So, what was the secret ingredient?"

Nina sighed. "Ethan swears people around here consider alligator a delicacy."

"I'm sorry. Did you say alligator?" Reggie wadded up her napkin and placed it on her plate. "Aren't they a protected species?"

"You have to get a special permit, and you can only hunt them from August to November with a licensed trapper. Ethan's dad is one. He takes a share of the meat as part of his fee for helping hunters"—Nina made air quotes—"bag a gator. They serve it at their fish camp. Fried."

Michelle shook her head. "Can't recommend putting it on the cafe's menu."

"Yeahhhh," Nina drew out the word. "I don't think I'll be taking Ethan's advice again anytime soon, either. I can bring more with the bacon filling from the kitchen. Anyone want some?"

"None for me, thanks." Michelle returned her plate to the serving tray. The gamey taste and the odd texture had turned her appetite all the way to "off."

Erin stacked her plate on top of Michelle's. Stretching out, she propped her heels on the edge of the glass-topped table. "Did the twins' flight take off on time? How was the drive back from Fort Walton Beach?" She sipped her punch.

"A ten-minute delay, which was practically nothing. They'll text when they get in." Michelle glanced at the phone she'd left, faceup, on the table. With any luck, the twins had made their connecting flight in Atlanta and would land in Charlottesville within the hour. "I was a bit teary-eyed on the way home. We had such a good visit, I hated to see them leave." Her gaze captured Erin's and held it. "I don't know what you said to Ash, and I don't want to know, but whatever it was, it did the trick."

"Underneath that stubborn streak of hers, your daughter has a good heart." Erin resettled her sunglasses on the top of her head. "I just told her what she needed to hear and let her figure out what to do with the information."

"Well, thanks. I mean it. I'd about given up hope of ever resolving things between us." She and Aaron had been uploading pictures to the website he'd built for the inn when a weeping Ashley found them in the library. Between sobs, her daughter had begged for forgiveness and had sworn she'd never think ill of her mother again for as long as she lived. Michelle had cautioned her eldest-by-fifteen-minutes child against making promises she couldn't keep— Ashley was, after all, Ashley—but she couldn't deny how wonderful it had been to have both her children wrap their arms around her. They'd talked for hours afterwards, and she'd never felt closer to the twins. She owed Erin a huge debt for making that possible.

"You can repay me by letting me run something by you." Erin nodded to Nina and Reggie. "By all of you."

"Let's hear it." Michelle straightened. Erin didn't often seek advice.

"Ron stopped by earlier today." Trouble muddied Erin's hazel eyes.

"Your ex, Ron?" Nina squinted.

Reggie's lips immediately arrowed down at the corners. "What's he still hanging around for? I thought you sent him packing."

"Apparently, he doesn't take *no* very well." Erin hesitated. "He's, um, he's taken a temporary job at Topsail Hill."

Nina's mouth dropped open. She knew— they all knew—how badly the divorce had hurt their friend. "Why on earth would he do such a thing?"

"That's what I'd like to know," Erin said slowly. "I can't figure out what he's up to. I'll admit I'm somewhat of a world traveler—"

"I'd say that was an understatement," Reggie broke in.

Erin stuck out her tongue at her sister. Turning to the rest of them, she continued. "But I can name a dozen people more qualified to shepherd a bunch of well-heeled sightseers around the globe. I've turned him down twice. No, three times. So why hasn't he moved on already?"

"Maybe he thinks you need rescuing from all of this." Nina waved a hand at the inn, which would soon open to its first guests.

"You think he sees himself as the right man for the job?" Erin shook her head. "I don't buy it." Damp spots on the shoulders of her T-shirt widened as the still-wet ends of her hair brushed her shoulders.

"Okay, then. Let's approach it from the opposite direction." Nina backtracked with the ease of someone who was simply trying out ideas to see if one fit. "You said he hasn't traveled outside the U.S. much. Maybe he thinks he's in over his head with this new venture and wants someone more experienced to team with him. He chose you because, well, because you have history."

"I suppose that could be it." Though Erin nodded, doubt heavily laced her tone. "I just can't help thinking there's something he's not telling me." She took a drink.

"Oh, I know!" Reggie waved one hand. Her voice dropped to a conspiratorial whisper. "Maybe he has a secret baby he's kept hidden from you all these years. He wants the two of you to get reacquainted before he says, "Surprise! Meet your son. Or daughter!"

Caught off-guard by Reggie's off-the-wall suggestion, Michelle laughed out loud. She laughed even harder when Erin's snorts sent punch dribbling from her mouth.

"Ahhhh!" The blonde blotted her shirt with a napkin. Peach-colored stains dotted the front. "Now see? I've ruined my shirt." She threw Reggie a look full of accusation. "I think I'd be the first to know if Ron and I had gotten pregnant."

When Reggie feigned innocence, Erin turned to Michelle. "What do you think? Got any ideas?" She tossed a scathing look over her shoulder at her sister. "Real ones?"

Michelle shifted in her chair. She could think of one possibility, but she didn't think Erin was ready to hear it. To buy herself a few extra seconds before she answered, she drained the last drops of punch from her glass.

The truth was, she'd always liked Ron. There wasn't a doubt in her mind that he'd worshipped the ground beneath Erin's feet while they were dating and those first few months of their marriage. She knew the perfect couple didn't exist—she and Allen had proven that—but Erin and Ron had come pretty close. So she'd been shocked to her core when a very upset Erin called her from Houston one night to confess that she and Ron had split up. Michelle's first instinct had been to catch the next flight to Texas to console her friend. Or help her find some way of salvaging her marriage. But the twins had just learned how to walk and were literally into *everything* and Allen was away on travel and, between the cost of baby formula and diapers, she hadn't had two spare nickels to rub together. She'd begged Erin to come see her. Instead, the willowy blonde had taken off for parts unknown. To this day, she still carried a fair load of guilt for not being a better friend when Erin had needed her. Now that Ron had popped back into Erin's life, she didn't want to miss the boat this time.

Aware that Erin was waiting, watching her like she had all the answers, Michelle cupped her chin in her hand.

The reason Ron had shown up in Sugar Sand Beach seemed awfully obvious. So obvious, she was surprised Erin hadn't considered it herself. Why was that? Was she not ready to admit that her ex-husband still had feelings for her? Did she return those feelings?

Michelle shook the ice in her glass, listening

to the chink-chink of the cubes. "You said he's going to be around for a while?" she asked.

"Three months," Erin nodded.

"Well. We'll have plenty of time to figure out the real reason he came to Sugar Sand Beach, then." Having said all she was going to say, she sat back. Surely by November, Erin would reach her own conclusions. "We'll just have to, you know, wait and see."

Erin's lips twisted into a lopsided grimace. "That's the best you've got?"

"For now," Michelle nodded. She was all for helping her friend solve a problem, but this was one situation where Erin needed to figure things out on her own. Wrapping her napkin around the bottom like a makeshift coaster, she set her glass on the table. The sun had nearly dropped below the horizon. It was time to move on to the business portion of their evening.

"Aaron has nearly finished our website. Do you want to see it?" A nervous thrill shot through her as she retrieved the laptop she'd wedged between her cushion and the chair's rattan frame. Would her friends appreciate all of Aaron's hard work?

"Let me take this stuff to the kitchen." Nina quickly loaded the plates of uneaten appetizers onto the tray. "I won't be a minute. We're having leftovers for supper, so there's nothing I have to do to get dinner ready." Plastic containers full of salad, baked beans and coleslaw from the picnic crowded the shelves of the fridge. There were plenty of grilled burgers and hot dogs, too.

"Sounds good." Reggie slid from her chair onto the porch's wide wooden planks. There, she assumed a cross-legged pose.

Erin evenly divided the rest of the punch between their four glasses while Michelle booted up the computer. She clicked a few keys. Using the shortcut Aaron had shown her, she navigated to the rough draft of their website.

"Welcome to the Sugar Sand Inn and Cafe" read a banner above a stunning photograph of the house.

"Here," she said, flipping the laptop around so the others could see the home page. "What do you think?"

"Oh, my goodness," Reggie gasped. "That's amazing. Aaron did that?"

"I have to admit, when you said he'd offered to design our website, my expectations weren't that high." Smiling, Erin peered closer.

Michelle grinned. She couldn't wait to pass along Erin and Reggie's compliments to her son. "There's a lot more. I'll show it to you as soon as Nina comes back."

Seconds later, the front door swung open.

"Guess who decided to join us," Nina said as she strode onto the porch with Mr. Pibbs in her arms. Her footsteps slowed as she glanced down at the laptop. "Wow!" she exclaimed. "That's nice." She bent low enough to hold the big tabby's face up to the computer screen. "See? That's you, right there on the front steps."

Clearly not as impressed as his owner, Mr. Pibbs only yawned.

"Where'd you get the picture?" Nina sank onto her usual chair.

"Aaron took all the photos," Michelle said proudly. The fancy digital camera had been his birthday present two years ago. "There are some candid shots of the picnic, too."

She clicked through the various headings. The first page provided a warm welcome and a brief history of the house. An entire section devoted to lodging offered drop-down menus that showed each of the inn's six, beautifully appointed suites. Once it went live, Michelle explained, the site would update an app on her phone whenever someone made a reservation. A gallery held photographs of the gardens, land-scaping and parlors. She pressed a tab marked "Activity Center," and Erin chuckled at a shot of her and Ashley launching their kayaks at the beach.

"Aaron must have been hiding in the bushes. If I'd known, I'd have worn lipstick," she teased.

Nina raved about the pages Aaron had created for the cafe. She pointed to the dark wainscoting and light-colored walls. "Zeke and his crew did such excellent work. Everyone's going to want to eat here."

"I just need a couple of things before we can make the website live and start taking reservations," Michelle pointed out once they'd flipped through all the pages again.

"The sooner, the better," Erin said. "How can we help?"

"Aaron reserved a spot for the cafe's menu. I'll need that as soon as you can get it to me." Michelle's pointed glance landed on Nina. The chef still hadn't given her a final list of what they'd be serving.

Nina held Mr. Pibbs aloft and walked his hind legs across her lap. "Good boy," she cooed. The tabby batted the air with his front paws. "It's on my desk," she said, peering around the cat. "I want to go over it with Viola first thing in the morning. I'll have it to you by noon."

"Perfect," Michelle declared. "That just leaves the opening dates for the inn and the cafe."

Reggie leaned against the chair behind her. "You're not asking for much, are you?"

"I know." Michelle gave them all a sympathetic look. They'd already had numerous discussions about the topic. So far, they hadn't reached a consensus. "It's hard to pin down a date. We all have more improvements we want to make to the place. I'd love to finish off the turret before we open. But Zeke can't get to it before December, and I don't think we want to wait that long. We'll miss the tourist season if we do."

"The beach bikes are on back order. I probably won't get those for another month or so," Erin pointed out. The special-order bicycles were outfitted with extra wide tires for riding on sand. "And I want to hold a dry run for the campouts I've planned." Unless she was willing to let the heat and mosquitoes turn the experience into a form of medieval torture, she needed to do that on a weekend of low temperatures and even lower humidity. Which probably wasn't going to happen in August in Florida. "Otherwise, I shouldn't need more than a week to get the Activity Center ready."

"Whatever date we pick works for me." Her arms bent at the elbows, Reggie twisted from side to side. "I just need to know ahead of time so I can make sure the flower beds and hedges look their best. I'll want to mow, too, of course."

"We should hold a soft opening of the cafe a week or so before our first overnight guests arrive. Once we finalize the menu, by noon tomorrow"—Nina shot Michelle a grin as if to say, "See? I got it!"—"we're all set. Viola and Ethan know their way around the kitchen as well as I do. Gwen and Dax are just waiting for me to say the word so they can come for training. Two days, tops. That's all they'll need."

"Oookay," Michelle said slowly. She brought up the calendar function on the laptop. August was already winding down. She scanned the appointments and deliveries scheduled for September. "Dave wants us to sign the partnership agreements on the seventeenth. We can't open before then. What about October 4th? That's a Monday. We probably wouldn't have many guests until the weekend, which would give us a chance to work out any kinks. Does that sound good?" She searched for confirmation in the faces of her friends.

Reggie was the first to speak up. "Works for me," she said, rolling one shoulder.

"Me, too," Erin chimed in.

"I'm good." Nina leaned down to Mr. Pibbs. "Are you okay with that?" The cat blinked slowly. "He's good," she said, running her hand over his silky fur. "We'll invite a few special people to have breakfast at the cafe the last week of September."

"Then it's decided," Michelle said with a relieved sigh. "The official opening date for the Sugar Sand Inn and Cafe is October 4th." She gave an exaggerated shiver as she closed the laptop. "I'll tell Aaron tomorrow. He'll make the final changes to the website, and we can go live with it right away. It's getting real, y'all."

"I, for one, can't wait." Nina hugged Mr. Pibbs to her chest. She stood.

"It's nice to have that all nailed down. I always did like deadlines." Erin began gathering the now empty glasses.

Michelle was about to head indoors when Reggie cleared her throat.

"Um, wait a minute," the younger woman called out.

Noting how Reggie's thick auburn eyebrows had knitted together, Michelle stilled. "What?" she asked.

"That's it? We're just going to set a date and open the inn?"

"You were expecting a parade?" Erin joked.

"Not a parade exactly, but..." Reggie scanned the group, her large eyes narrowing.

"I'm not sure what you..." Michelle stared expectantly at Reggie.

"Well." Reggie pressed her palms flat against the floorboards, her elbows locked. "Everyone for miles around has supported our dream of converting this house into an inn," she pointed out. "When we first got here, people could have sided with Orson and supported his plans for developing the property. They didn't, though. They chose us. When Tobias implied—"

"He did a lot more than imply." Nina lowered Mr. Pibbs to the floor. The big tabby scooted through the open front door and disappeared into the house before she sank onto her chair.

"Fine." Reggie's lips firmed. "When Tobias *accused* you of stealing his recipes—falsely, I might add—Walt didn't have to give you the time of day. But because we were friends with his mom, he…"

"He gave us a chance when he didn't have to," Nina finished. The owner of the Happy Dolphin had recognized the truth when he heard it.

Reggie nodded. "We've all felt the enthusiasm and excitement everyone in town has for our inn. I can't walk into the hardware store without Ronnie or Frank asking how things are going out here."

"When Gus learned I was driving to Destin for ghee, he started stocking it at the grocery store." Nina shook her head. "He has to be losing money on it. I'm the only one who buys clarified butter." In the distance, a night bird sang.

"Polly gave us a really good deal," Michelle mused. She'd placed a standing order for fresh flowers on her first visit to the florist shop in Sugar Sand Beach.

"With that kind of support, it doesn't feel right that we'd open the inn without some fanfare." Reggie nodded at her sister. "A party. A picnic. Something to show our appreciation to the town. I'm just spitballing here, but what if we held another open house?"

"The last one was terrific, but maybe we could make this one a more family-friendly event?" Nina suggested. "I'm thinking of Lily and Megan, Malcolm and Dimella."

"And Hope." A tender smile played across Reggie's lips as she said the baby's name.

"It makes sense to plan some activities for children," Michelle said, testing out the idea. "I expect we'll have mostly couples staying at the Sugar Sand Inn, but we'll probably get the occasional family. We could hold an open house and make it fall-themed."

"Chris and I could build a hay maze near the garden," Reggie suggested. "We can hook the trailer to the tractor and offer hayrides."

"I'll have Viola and Ethan make sugar cookies in fall shapes, like leaves and pumpkins. We can let the kids decorate them during the open house." Nina flexed her fingers. "Maybe even offer a little decorating class."

"What about a parent-and-child fishing tournament?" Erin asked. "We'd supply the fishing rods and the bait. We can give prizes for the biggest fish, the longest one, the oddest one." She glanced at Nina. "What if we gave out coupons for dessert at the cafe as prizes?"

"I like that idea," Nina nodded.

Her friends were so happy about the prospect of an open house that Michelle hated to dampen their excitement like a wet blanket. But, as the one who oversaw the inn's finances, she had to stop this before it went too far. Wishing she hadn't agreed to the idea in the first place, she cleared her throat.

"While this sounds like the right thing to do," she said when she had everyone's attention, "and I'm sure the whole town would turn out for it, we have a problem. A big one."

Understanding dawned first in Nina's dark eyes. "Food," she said simply.

"Right." Michelle's hair swayed as she nodded. Nina had nailed the problem precisely. "We can't afford to feed the entire population of

Sugar Sand Beach. Plus..." She drew in a breath and divided her focus between Reggie and Erin. "With the cafe's soft opening in just a few weeks, Nina and her staff have enough on their plates without having to think about feeding more than a hundred people."

For a long second, an air of resignation descended on the group. Michelle felt sure they were seconds away from canceling the event when Reggie bolted upright.

"I've got it!" The younger woman smacked the heel of her palm to her forehead. "We'll throw a potluck. Like the church picnic last month."

Considering the idea, Michelle tucked her hair behind her ears. To celebrate the 100th anniversary of the Sugar Sand Beach Baptist Church, members of the Men's Ministry had erected long folding tables under the trees behind the sanctuary. The Lady's Auxiliary had filled five-gallon coolers with sweetened iced tea and provided the paper products. Each family had brought not just enough food for themselves but enough to share. By the time the minister said the blessing, the tables fairly groaned beneath hundreds of dishes.

"Everybody does love a good covered-dish supper." Erin rubbed her stomach. "Do you think

Ms. Polly would bring some of those greens she makes? They're awfully good."

Even a potluck presented challenges. Michelle looked to Nina for guidance. "What do you think?"

"They are kind of a tradition around here," Nina pointed out. Over the last six months, they'd all attended one or two. "Erin and Reggie are right—everyone loves them."

A small seed of anticipation took root in Michelle's midsection. Now that she had Nina's blessing, she let it grow. Smiling, she moved on to the next question. "Okay. So when would we do this?"

"How about on the Sunday afternoon before the official opening?" An eager Reggie leaned forward.

Michelle swept the group. Three other heads bobbed along with her own. The matter settled, she sighed happily. "Okay, then. I'll make some flyers and we can start spreading the word." She paused for a second. "Oh, and Reggie?"

The redhead peered up at her.

"Thanks for coming up with this idea, but you'd better watch out. You keep doing this and we'll have to make you the official event planner for the inn."

Reggie's brows drew together. "Huh?"

"Well, it was your idea to hold the first open house," Michelle recalled.

"And you suggested we get a booth at the craft fair," Erin pointed out.

"Now this. You're batting a hundred. Don't think we haven't noticed." Michelle gathered up her things while she enjoyed the look of happiness that glowed on Reggie's cheeks.

Good.

The youngest of their group had spent far too long under the harsh thumb of her soon-to-be ex-husband. Praise for her accomplishments and appreciation for her contributions would go a long way in helping Reggie heal. She wouldn't be ready to move forward with her life until that happened, something Michelle, along with Nina and Erin, was eager to see take place.

Ten

Reggie

"How's your mom's ankle?" Reggie slid the forty-pound bale across the floor of the flatbed. She'd been so concerned about Erin and Ron this morning that she hadn't remembered to ask. Placing one hand on the end of the trailer, she hopped to the ground. Her boots landed in a soft mix of grass and loose hay. She tugged the heavy bale onto one shoulder.

"Her doctor removed the walking cast last week. She hobbled around for a couple of days, but she's walking normally now. To see her, you wouldn't think she'd fallen and sprained her ankle." The bale Chris had hauled across the field landed on the grass with a thunk. He shoved one end to align it with the chalk marks. "She insisted on watching Hope today, and I'm seriously glad she did. I love my daughter, but now that she's crawling, it plumb wore me out to chase after her twenty-four seven."

"Oh, you poor thing," Reggie teased. Not that she thought he'd had it easy the last few weeks while his mom was laid up and couldn't care for the nine-month-old. She knew firsthand how tiring it was to keep the active baby fed, dry and entertained. She'd watched Hope on several occasions so Chris could drive his mom to the grocery store or the hair salon. Those nights, she'd barely made it into her bed before she fell asleep. But seeing the little cherub's blue eyes light up in delight, hearing the surprisingly deep sound of her laughter, or playing peep-eye—or her new favorite, pat-a-cake—with the baby was worth every exhausting minute.

"When I'm at work, I get a lunch break." Chris pointed to the back of Reggie's pickup truck, where he'd left his empty lunch pail. "I can stop for a drink of water when I need it."

"Slacker." Reggie jostled Chris's elbow as they passed each other heading in opposite directions.

"You jest," he said, taking a swig from the water bottle he'd left on an upended bale. "But wait till you're on your own with her for twenty-four hours. You'll see."

Which probably wasn't going to happen any time soon, Reggie thought. Although her friendship with Chris deepened every day, neither of them was in any hurry to take the next step in their relationship. He still mourned the woman who'd died giving birth to Hope. As for herself, little more than six months ago she'd clung to the belief that a sixth round of IVF would be the charm. That the stars would align and give her the baby she longed to have. Not only had that not happened, but her husband had called it quits on their marriage the same day she got the news that the latest fertility treatment had failed.

So, no. Neither of them were in any shape to make a long-term commitment. Certainly not one that would end up with her helping Chris raise his daughter. Although, one day...

Glad the load on her shoulder kept him from seeing the bright sheen of tears in her eyes, Reggie strode across the unfinished maze. Her back to Chris, she positioned the new addition just so.

"Are you slowing down on the job?" he asked. Faster than she'd expected, he stepped to her side and dropped the next bale into place.

Reggie removed her baseball cap and pretended to wipe sweat from her brow. "Just, uh…" She scanned the sky. The towering cumulus clouds she'd spotted on the horizon earlier had boiled closer. "Geez," she said, pointing. "The weatherman lied. He said we weren't going to get any rain today." She quickened her steps to the truck.

"This is Florida. It always rains." Chris fell in beside her. "Are you worried about the hay getting wet?"

"No. If we were using it for cattle, that'd be a problem." Ranchers were careful to store the feed in a dry barn where it wouldn't turn moldy and possibly sicken the cows that ate it. "I'll use some for mulch and just spread the rest out. No, I'm concerned about that."

She angled her chin down toward the chalked outline of the maze. It had taken a full day to stake out the design, marking the turns with brightly colored flags. She'd borrowed a line chalker from the equipment shed at the Little League field and spent another half day carefully drawing thick white lines between the flags. A hard rain would undo all the work she'd done. "If the chalk gets washed away, it'll all have to be done over again."

Chris's strides lengthened. "We better move faster then. At the rate that storm is building, I'd say we have two hours, tops, to get the job done."

For the next hour and a half, they lifted and toted in unison. At times, they moved so quickly Reggie wasn't sure whether she was coming or going. Still, there was only so much they could do, and by the time the clouds rolled in front of the sun and cast the field into shadow, they'd only completed three-quarters of the maze.

The first drops of rain struck as Reggie marked a turn by setting a bale at right angles to the one before it. "I guess that's as much as we can do," she said with a dissatisfied sigh.

"It's only rain. We can get a few more." Chris headed to the trailer for another load.

Reggie's gaze shifted between the remaining bales of hay and the gray clouds overhead. In minutes, they'd be soaked. She shrugged. Well, she wasn't a witch; she wouldn't melt. She followed at Chris's heels.

They finished two more rows before Chris waved Reggie to a stop. "Lightning," he said simply as thunder rolled across the sky.

"Six more trips, that's all we need." The rain fell steadily now. It had already washed away most of the chalk, but there was still enough left to complete the interior of the maze. They could probably handle the rest without the outline.

Chris plucked at her wet sleeve. His voice rose over a rising wind. "We are the only things standing upright in a large, flat field in the state that records more lightning deaths per year than any other. I don't want either of us to become a statistic. We need to get in the truck. Now."

Well, if he was going to get all technical on her...

A clap of thunder sent her scurrying. She clambered onto the tall seat and hauled the door shut behind her while Chris did the same thing on the passenger side. Rain had plastered her clothes to her skin. Now water ran off her in rivulets, soaking into the cloth seats and puddling on the floor mats. Despite jeans that felt like lead weights, she twisted around so she could reach into the storage compartment. She kept several rag bag rejects in her duffle for occasions just like this. Pulling out a couple of towels, she handed one to Chris.

"They're frayed but clean," she told him.

Removing her hat, she shook out her curls. She towel-dried her hair first, then patted the rest of herself as dry as she could manage. There didn't seem to be much point in wringing the water out of her jeans so she ignored them for the moment.

When she finished, she glanced at Chris. The rain had turned his blond hair into a mass of dark ringlets. His wet T-shirt had molded to his chest. Despite water all around them, her mouth went dry. She tore her gaze upward from sculpted muscles and thick biceps.

"Think this is going to last long?" she asked, peering through rapidly fogging windows at the downpour beyond the glass. Thunder sounded on the heels of a bright flash. She shrank against her seat.

"You know what they say—don't like the weather in Florida? Wait five minutes."

"Unless it's in the middle of summer, when you can count on 'hot and sticky' in the daily forecast."

"True." Chris inclined his head toward the nearly completed maze. "Sorry about that. I know you were hoping to finish it today."

Reggie shook her head. Trusting the forecast, she hadn't thrown any tarps in the back of the truck. Not that they'd had the time to cover the hay, not with lightning striking all around them. Now the bales, like their clothes, were soaked and heavy. Too heavy for her to lift. Or Chris, either. They'd need to let everything dry out before they could handle it again. "Who was it that said something about the best-laid plans? Michener?"

"Steinbeck. 'The best laid plans of mice and men often go awry,'" Chris quoted. "He lifted it from a Robert Burns poem."

"Well, whoever said it, they sure nailed it right on the head." Now that she wasn't trying to beat the storm, her mind circled around to the one person who was never far from her thoughts these days. She hadn't realized how much she'd missed having her sister in her life until Erin had shown up in April. Since then, they'd helped each other in countless ways. She hated to think about how much she'd miss the closeness between them if her sister disappeared again. But that's exactly what would happen if Erin and Ron got back together. She sighed heavily.

"What's up?" Chris shifted in his seat until he angled toward her. "You've been—not moody, exactly, but definitely not yourself all day. Something on your mind?"

"No," she said far too abruptly.

Way to prove his point, Reg.

"Yes," she corrected. "Maybe?" She ran a hand through her hair. "I don't know."

She did know she shouldn't blame Chris for being concerned. He was right, after all. She had been 'in a mood.' And forgetful. Today was the first time they'd been able to work together since his mom's fall. She should have greeted him with fanfare and welcome smiles. She hadn't. Just like she hadn't remembered her lunch and had had to make do with a granola bar she'd scrounged from the truck's glove box. She'd been entirely too worried about Erin and Ron. She took a deep breath and let it out slowly.

"Looks like we're not going anywhere for a while." Chris motioned toward the fogged-up windows. Although the worst of the lightning and thunder had passed, rain drummed on the roof and bounced off the hood of the truck. "Want to talk about it?"

Propping one knee on the bench seat, she shifted toward him. She needed to talk to someone. Who better than Chris? "It's Erin," she said, feeling her way. "Her ex-husband, Ron, is in Sugar Sand Beach."

Chris's T-shirt pulled tighter across his chest. His eyes narrowed as the man immediately went on alert. "This Ron, is he a good guy? Has he threatened her in any way?"

Reggie smiled. Chris was normally so laid-back and easygoing, she'd been surprised by the fiercely protective side he'd shown when her own ex came to town. Sam, though, had thoroughly deserved to get tossed off the inn's property.

Ron? Not so much.

"Easy, cowboy," she soothed. "Ron and Erin were married for less than a year. They went their separate ways decades ago. He's stayed in

Texas all this time. That's where he's from, Houston."

"So, what brings him around now? He didn't just show up out of the blue. Not here in Sugar Sand Beach. What's he want?" Chris frowned.

"That's the question, isn't it?" She'd been pondering that ever since Erin told them he'd stopped by. "He says he wants to hire her as a guide for his new business venture," she said, not bothering to hide her doubts. "Some kind of global travel service for the über-rich."

"Sounds like it'd be right up Erin's alley."

"Yeah, but..." Leaning forward, she brushed away enough moisture to create a peephole on the glass. Outside, the world remained gray and wet.

"There's always a but."

"But that's what drove them apart last time. She wanted to see the world, and he...didn't. Now he's supposedly had a complete change of heart? I don't buy it. I've done my best to convince her something's off, but she either can't see it or she doesn't want to." Reggie knew better than most what that was like. She'd turned a blind eye to all of Sam's faults, right up to the day he'd walked out on their marriage. Which, as it had turned out, was the best thing that could have ever happened to her.

"You think there's something he's not telling her." Chris cupped his lower jaw and slowly drew his fingers together.

"Yeah. I don't know what, but I'm afraid he'll convince Erin he's changed. I think that, even after all these years, she still loves him. There's a part of her that wants to give him a second chance. What if she does, and he breaks her heart again? The last time that happened, she took off, and I didn't see her for a couple of years. What's going to happen if he lets her down again? She and I are finally getting to know one another. Will I lose my sister completely this time?" The possibility was keeping her up at night.

"Hmmmm." He repeated the motion along his jaw.

Reggie stared at him expectantly. She drummed the fingers of one hand against the wet fabric of her jeans.

"I think," he said after she'd grown so antsy she'd begun to wonder if talking to him had been such a good idea after all. "I think you're really trying to deal with two problems."

Reggie felt her face scrunch so tightly her brows nearly touched. As far as she could see, there was only one problem. His name was R-o-n. "Care to explain?"

His boots made a wet, sloshing noise as Chris

shifted his feet. He held out one hand with the palm facing up. "There's Ron and Erin." He made the same motion with his other hand. "And then there's your reaction to Ron and Erin. I think it'll help if you keep those two things separate." He moved his hands up and down like a teeter-totter.

The concept puzzled her. She slowly turned it over in her mind. "I'm not sure I get where you're going with this," she admitted.

Chris's head barely bobbed. "You're worried about how it will affect you—and your friends— if Erin accepts Ron's job offer. And you're concerned that your own relationship with Erin might suffer if she gives Ron a second chance and things don't work out between them."

"That makes me sound like I'm only worried about myself." Trying not to sound as defensive as she felt, Reggie asked, "Wouldn't you be worried if we were talking about your sister and someone from her past?"

"If I had a sister or a brother, I would. You definitely have every right to be concerned." Chris nodded to himself. "Don't you think I worried about how my life would change when Connie died? At first, there was this overwhelming grief that she was gone. My heart broke for Hope, that my little girl would never know her mother. My next thoughts, though, were all about me. How could I work and raise a baby? Was my social life over? Would I ever get to hang out with friends or drink a beer on a Saturday night? Which was all dumb. What I should have been asking was, 'Am I ever going to sleep through the night again?'"

Reggie laughed. "Have you? Slept through the night?"

"Once in a while." He grinned. "I'll tell you one thing—I'll never take sleep for granted again." His expression smoothed. "Anyway, I understand. Of course, you want to know what it all means to you if Erin takes off with Ron. Or if he breaks her heart."

Reggie's shoulders softened as the tension that had gripped them began to ease. Chris understood, and he didn't blame her for feeling the way she did.

The man in the passenger seat cleared his throat. "I think the real question, though, is, 'What if he doesn't?'"

"What if he doesn't...what?" she asked. She studied Chris's squared-off jaw.

"What if he doesn't let her down? From what you said, Erin might still love this Ron guy. What if he's the love of her life and she doesn't take that second chance?" Chris stared through the fogged-up windows as if blue skies and sunshine were just out of sight. "Will she spend the rest of her life wondering if they could have made it work this time?"

Reggie caught her lower lip between her teeth. Were they still talking about Erin and Ron? She didn't think so. Leaning against the head-rest, she let a recurring daydream play against the backs of her eyelids. In her dream, she saw herself and Hope standing on the inn's front porch in a couple of years while Chris loped across the front yard toward them, a happiness that mirrored hers glowing on his face.

Was that the second chance Chris was talking about? Surprised by how much she wanted it to be, she shifted her position. In only a few short months, her divorce would be final. Once it was, she'd be free to move forward in her relationship with the handsome handyman who'd won a place in her heart.

For now, though, the rain had tapered off. It was time to go. She'd leave the trailer where it sat for a few days and let the bright Florida sun dry the unused bales of hay. Later this week, she and Chris could return to finish the maze. In the meantime, she had plenty of other work to keep her busy. Sometime this evening, she wanted to talk to Erin about second chances, too.

"Thanks." She sought Chris's blue eyes while she traced her fingers down his forearm. "You always say just the right thing."

"You're not so bad in the advice department yourself."

She gave his hand a squeeze before opening her door and swinging her feet to the running board. "I'll unhitch the trailer. You get the tools and such?"

"Sounds like a plan."

Splashing through puddles, she went about her business, content that, whatever the future held, she'd be ready for it when the time was right.

Eleven

Erin

Slowly, Erin rotated the green twig she held over the campfire. At the end, the outside of a marshmallow turned a golden brown. "It's almost done," she told Lily. "Are you ready?"

Lily held out a paper plate, where a square of chocolate sat in the middle of a graham cracker. "I can't wait!"

Squealing with excitement, the little girl bounced up and down on one of the logs some long-ago camper had arranged around a fire pit. The paper plate jiggled. Erin grabbed an edge just in time to keep everything from sliding into the dirt.

"Hold still, wiggle worm." She poked Lily in the ribs.

Wearing a goofy grin, Erin swung the

marshmallow out of the flames. With a cracker she pulled from the package, she scraped the puffy white confection onto the chocolate.

"Aaaaaah! This is going to be sooooo goooooood!" Lily's feet drummed the ground.

"Give it a couple of seconds to cool while the chocolate melts," Erin coached the ten-year-old who'd sworn she'd wanted to make s'mores "for her whole life."

Sitting on the other side of the fire, Megan plunged her own marshmallow into the flames. "I like mine burnt," she explained. The twelve-year old waited until the white outside turned black before she removed her stick from the fire. She blew on the now-charred treat until it cooled enough to handle. After licking her fingers, she pulled the burnt candy off the stick. Some of it stuck. Long strings of white goo dripped onto Megan's chin as she popped the marshmallow into her mouth.

"Mmmmmm," she murmured happily while she chewed.

"What do you think, Lily? Do you like s'mores?" Erin asked, though the chocolate smeared across the little girl's face made the question moot.

The child bobbed her head so quickly, the end of her braid brushed across her plate. Erin stifled a groan. She'd have to wash the mess out of Lily's hair before they turned in tonight. Otherwise, their tent would be crawling with ants by morning. Fortunately, in her quest to be ready for anything on this, her first camping trip in Topsail Hill Preserve, she'd stashed a couple of gallons of water in the back of the jeep.

"Can I have another one, please?" Lily licked her fingers.

"Yes, but just one more." Trusting his girls into her care for an overnight camping trip hadn't been easy for Zeke. The long list of instructions the single father had given Erin included limits on the amount of sugary treats Megan and Lily could have. Erin had pinkie-sworn to abide by the rules.

Which reminded her...

She glanced across the fire to Megan. The older girl had threaded several marshmallows onto her stick. How many did that make? Five? Six? Too many by all counts. "Last one, Megs," she said.

She thought she might get some pushback on the request, but Megan dutifully twisted the end of the bag of marshmallows and set it aside. She held her stick toward the flames.

A twig cracked behind them. Bushes rustled.

In an instant, Erin was on her feet, her body positioned between the girls and whoever, or whatever, had decided to pay them a visit. Another stick broke, and her heart rate shifted into overdrive. Something big was coming through the woods.

A bear? A wild hog?

Don't be ridiculous, she told herself. Wildlife wouldn't wander this close to a campsite filled with people. And they weren't alone. She could see their neighbors' campfire through the trees and beyond it, a well-constructed restroom. It was far more likely that Zeke had decided to check up on them.

Yeah, if that was true, why were the hairs on the back of her neck standing on end?

Suddenly, the whole idea of taking the girls camping in the Preserve didn't seem half as smart as it had before the sun went down. For all the good it would do, she held the green twig out like a sword. A bit of marshmallow gleamed whitely from the end of the stick.

"Erin?" Sounding a tiny bit concerned, Megan stood.

"Everything's okay, but Lily, why don't you move over by your sister for a minute." The more distance she could put between the girls and whatever was coming through the woods, the better.

A bush at the edge of the campsite shook.

Erin shot a glance at the jeep. Wary of the fire, she'd parked it twenty feet away. Now, with two young girls to protect and an uninvited guest bearing down on them, she wished she'd cut that distance in half.

Thinking quickly, she made a plan. If their visitor turned out to be a predator, whether it had two legs or four, she'd grab one of the flaming logs from the campfire and throw it at the interloper as hard as she could. Then, keeping the girls in front of her, she'd hustle them into the vehicle.

The leaves of the bush at the end of the campsite parted. Two hands—hands, not paws or claws—appeared in the gap. Erin allowed herself to take a breath, but she kept her guard up. Was their visitor a friend or foe?

A man's ruggedly handsome form emerged from the woods. He stepped into the clearing.

"Ron!" she gasped.

"Yeah, it's me," Ron plucked a leaf from the brim of his baseball cap. "Were you expecting someone else?"

"No one." That was the problem. She hadn't expected anyone. "I, um, I thought you might be a bear."

Ron's laughter rang out. The look on Erin's face must have conveyed her dismay because the sound died quickly. "Sorry," he said, chuckling. "I'm awfully sorry. I meant to be here earlier, but a couple who'd rented one of the canoes was late returning their boat to the concession stand. I thought it'd be easier if I just cut through the woods instead of going the long way around. I didn't mean to frighten you."

Now that the moment had passed, Erin felt her face heat. She shouldn't have reacted the way she had. She knew good and well that Florida's black bears weren't aggressive unless provoked. Even then, they were far more likely to climb a tree than take a swipe at a couple of marsh-mallow-eating pre-teens.

The girls! Oh, my goodness, were they scared?

Schooling her features, she adopted a breezy tone. "False alarm, girls. It's just my friend Ron. Come here and meet him." As Megan and Lily hurried to her side, she swung toward the man dressed in green khakis and a tan shirt with a Topsail Hill Preserve emblem on the pocket. "Ron, this is Megan and Lily. They volunteered to be my campout guinea pigs tonight. We were having some s'mores. Want to join us?"

"Just in time for dessert!" Rubbing his hands together, Ron stepped fully into the clearing. "What's a camping trip without s'mores? Megan, Lily, glad to meet you." He nodded to the older

219

girl. "Erin tells me you're pretty good with a paddle." When Megan beamed at the praise, he turned to Lily. "And you're quite the cook, I understand. Can you show me how to make a s'more?"

Grinning, Lily darted to the log where she'd abandoned their supplies. "First, you take a graham cracker…"

While Ron pretended he needed the lesson that Lily was only too happy to provide, Erin pulled Megan to her side. "It was silly of me to get scared like that. I know there's nothing in these woods that would hurt us." She took the bag of marshmallows Megan still clutched and held it open.

"You said we couldn't have any more." Megan eyed the bag.

"I think two more couldn't hurt." After the excitement of the last few minutes, not even Zeke would fault her for giving the girls extra treats. "Are you okay?"

Megan helped herself to a couple of the puffy candies before Erin had a chance to change her mind. Giggling, she bit into a marshmallow without bothering to toast it. "You should have seen yourself. What were you going to do if it was a bear? Tickle him to death with that little stick?"

"It's a good thing no one caught me on camera." Erin laughed, relieved that the older girl had found humor in the incident. "It would have ended up on one of those shows about funny home videos."

"I wish I'd thought of that." Megan's eyes sparkled.

Erin slung her arm around the girl. "Thanks for taking such good care of Lily. You're a wonderful big sister."

As she said the words, a pang of conscience struck her. She and Reggie had never had the kind of closeness Zeke's daughters shared. While she could blame the ten-year gap in their ages, the truth was, she could have tried harder to build a relationship with her little sister when they both were younger. That was one of the things she loved the most about moving to Sugar Sand Beach and opening the inn—it had given her the chance to really get to know Reggie.

Now, though, just as she and Reggie were growing closer, Ron had breezed back into her life. Her gaze shifted to the man who'd asked her to walk away from the commitments she'd made. From her friends. From her sister.

Was she really considering his offer? She shuddered.

"C'mon," she said, her arm still around

221

Megan's shoulders. "Let's sit with them for a little bit. We'll get Ron to tell us all a bedtime story before you girls turn in." Once upon a time, when she and Ron were traveling across Europe together, she used to love sitting at their campfire, listening to the stories he'd tell.

"No ghost stories," Megan whispered. "Lily won't be able to go to sleep."

"Got it." Erin hid a knowing smile. Megan might act like a bigger, braver older sister, but even twelve-year-olds had nightmares. "I'll make sure to warn him."

For the next half hour they sat watching the flames flicker while, one by one, they spun yarns. When it was her turn, Erin shared an experience she'd had while trekking in the Himalayas. Her guide—or Sherpa, she explained—had brought along a yak to carry their equipment and, one night, the long-haired cow had escaped its tether. The beast wandered into one of the tents, where its horns punched holes in the canvas. The walls collapsed around him. The frightened yak ran off, dragging the tent and leaving a trail of camping gear in its wake.

"Oh, the poor thing!" Megan giggled.

"Did you find him?" Lily asked.

"Oh, yeah. He tired out pretty quickly. My Sherpa rounded him up and brought him back to our camp. He never tried to get into a tent again."

"I bet he didn't!" Ron exclaimed while everyone had a good laugh.

Soon after, she left Ron tending the fire while she helped the girls get ready for bed. By the time she'd washed the goo out of Lily's hair and tucked Megan into the sleeping bag beside her little sister's, the pair could hardly keep their eyes open. Soft snores filled the tent before she zipped the flap closed.

She plopped down on the log a short distance away from Ron. "So you never explained how you ended up here tonight. How'd you even know we were in the Preserve?" At first she'd wondered if Zeke had asked him to check on the girls. She'd rejected that thought almost immediately. Zeke and Ron didn't even know each other.

"I can usually count on one or two boat rentals for every six or so overnight guests, so I like to know how many campers there are in the park." Ron stirred a stick through some of the ashes. "I saw your name on the list of reservations at the Ranger station. I hope you don't mind my dropping by."

"Not at all," she assured him, surprised by how much she meant it. There was something comforting about sharing responsibility for the girls with another adult. She paused before she added, "Well, you did startle me by coming out of the woods like you did. Zeke—he's the girls' father—he gave me a list of rules to follow. I'm pretty sure 'don't let my daughters get eaten by a bear' was right at the top."

If it wasn't, it should have been.

"You didn't honestly hear a couple of bushes rattle and think 'bear,' did you?"

"I had a run-in with a grizzly when I was backpacking across Alaska once," she explained. "Ever since then, I've been a little leery when it comes to six-hundred-pound bundles of fur." She'd been lucky. The brown bear had been more interested in the salmon he'd caught than her, but she'd never forgotten the sight of those massive jaws or the claws that had ripped into the fish.

The stick Ron had been using dropped into the fire. "A grizzly?"

She widened her eyes. "Just once, but that was enough, thank you very much."

"I'm sorry. I didn't know. I never would have..."

It certainly wasn't his fault she was a little phobic. "Don't worry. I lived to tell the tale. And I know black bears have an entirely different temperament, but I haven't been responsible for two young girls before. I might have overreacted a tad."

Ron's forefinger hovered a quarter of an inch above his thumb. "Maybe just a little." He grinned.

Ready to talk about something—anything— else, she posed a question she'd been meaning to ask ever since she'd learned Ron planned to spend more than a few days in Sugar Sand Beach. "Summer is your busiest season, isn't it? They don't need you in Houston?" She'd googled his company and learned it had grown substantially from the fishing charter business he'd begun while they were married. It now encompassed practically all outdoor sports activities.

"I've taken a huge step back from the day-to-day operations." Ron propped his elbows on his knees and clasped his hands together.

She nodded, trying to understand. "I guess this new venture involves a lot of planning. You'd need time to focus on that." Which still didn't explain why he was running a concession stand in Florida.

"Yeah, well. About that—" he started.

"Shhhh." She held up a hand. "I think I heard the kids."

Erin swung a look at the zippered closure on the tent. Sure enough, the pull tab slowly rose and the tent flap opened.

"Erin?" Megan's voice came from inside. Her long hair a messy bundle, she poked her head through the opening. "There's a mosquito in here."

Lily's face appeared below her big sister's. "It's too hot. I can't sleep. I want to go home."

Erin gulped. What was she supposed to do now? She glanced around, mentally cataloguing everything she'd need to do in order to leave in the middle of the night. She'd have to douse the fire and make sure it was completely out. That was step number one. A cook stove sat on a small table where she'd planned to fry bacon and eggs for breakfast. The lantern stood on a nearby stump. Folding chairs flanked the tent's entrance. The girls had emptied their bedrooms for the overnight excursion. Sleeping bags, air mattresses, pillows and duffle bags crowded the roomy, four-person tent.

She sighed. It'd take an hour or more to break down the campsite, stow the gear and get on the road. But what was the alternative? Force Megan and Lily to endure an uncomfortable night? If she did that, they'd probably never want to try camping again.

Ron's fingers on her arm startled her. She stilled, enjoying the touch. "What?"

"You take them home," Ron said softly. "I'll pack up all this stuff and drop it off at the inn."

Much as she appreciated the gesture, Erin shook her head. "I can't ask you to do that."

"You're not asking. I'm offering. Actually, I insist." Beneath his baseball cap, Ron's blue eyes bored into hers. "It's the least I can do after scaring everyone earlier."

Erin bit the inside of her cheek. She didn't want to owe Ron any favors. Still, as long as she was heading out anyway, it'd be nice to get the kids into their own beds before midnight.

"Errr-iin. There's mosquitoes!" Megan's whine was followed by the sharp slap of a hand on skin.

The slap tipped the scales.

"I'm coming." Her decision made, Erin jumped to her feet. Turning to Ron, she said, "You can break camp, but you don't have to haul it all to the inn. I'll come back and pick everything up."

Ron kicked sand onto the fire. "I'll be finished long before you can make the round trip. Dropping the stuff off makes more sense than sitting around here, letting the skeeters feast on me."

The logic of his argument left her little choice. Reluctantly agreeing, she sent the girls to her jeep. She glanced at Ron a final time. "Where's your truck?" she asked.

He aimed a thumb at the woods behind him. "Just the other side of that thicket. Less than a five-minute walk. I'll put the fire out and then go get it."

"I brought water." She pointed to the gallon containers she'd positioned near the pit. Her car doors slammed. The girls were ready to go. Before leaving, she thanked Ron one last time.

"Yep." He kicked more sand. "Keep your eyes peeled."

"For bears?"

"Nah. Deer," he said with a chuckle. "Drive safe."

Intending to do just that, she slipped behind the wheel of her Jeep and headed for home.

Ninety minutes later, the crunch of gravel gave way to the muffled quiet of dirt and grass beneath her tires as Erin pulled the jeep to a stop in front of the activity center. The neat stack of camping gear by the door told her Ron had already been to the house and gone. A yawn caught her off guard, the stress of the day catching up to her. For half a sec, she entertained the thought of catching forty winks before she hauled the tent and sleeping bags inside. Or maybe she'd just leave it where it was until morning and go on to bed.

She knew better, though, and stretched. Experience had taught her the folly of leaving food unattended. The scent of chocolate and marshmallows would draw critters who'd dig through the pile with sharp claws. Unless she wanted them to ruin everything, she needed to move the equipment and supplies inside.

Moving quietly lest she wake the sleeping household, she made quick work of the job. Tired, she didn't notice the truck parked under a nearby tree until she'd finished and was sliding the barn door closed. She smiled at the sweetness of the idea that Ron had waited around to make sure she got home safe. At the same time, it struck her as odd that he hadn't insisted on helping her stow the camping gear.

Intent on satisfying her curiosity, she crossed to the truck. Warmth spread through her chest when she spotted Ron asleep behind the wheel. He must have nodded off while he waited for her because he sat upright with his head pressed against the window, his ball cap askew. She tapped lightly on the glass so she wouldn't startle him. He roused like someone who'd only dozed off minutes earlier and motioned for her to get in. Her own fatigue banished for the moment, she rounded the bumper.

"Hey, sleepyhead," she murmured as she stepped from the running board and slid onto the passenger's seat. When they were married, she'd been amazed by his ability to go from wide awake to snoring in thirty seconds flat. Apparently, he still did. "You know the ability to fall asleep quickly is a gift, right?"

"I don't think about it much, but I guess you're right." Ron rubbed a hand over his eyes. "You still have trouble settling down at night?"

"Not so much now that I'm here." It was warm in the truck. Ron's unique scent, once as familiar to her as the back of her hand, filled the air. She took a deep breath while she gestured at the inn and beyond. Until recently, she'd often tossed and turned for twenty minutes or more before she nodded off. "Thanks for staying," she said, shifting on the seat to face him. "You didn't have to."

"You've got some nice stuff. I didn't want anyone to steal it. Then again, you always did insist on top of the line." Ron ran a hand through his tousled hair and resettled his hat. "You like that portable shower? I've been meaning to get one of those."

"I brought it with us this time in case the girls wanted to see what it was like to 'rough it,' but it sure came in handy when I was in Brazil three years ago." Swimming in the Amazon or its tributaries was dangerous. From caiman as large as the biggest alligators to the tiny, fabled candiru, all kinds of threats existed in the rivers. She had loved travel as much as the next person—okay, more, actually—but that didn't mean she took foolish chances.

"Speaking of the girls, Megan and Lily sure are cute. How'd you end up with them tonight?" Ron asked.

She hesitated, not sure how much he knew about her friends' lives or whether their relationships were any of his business. Deciding to err on the side of discretion, she kept Nina's name out of it when she answered, "I've been hoping to have a trial run for the overnight camping trips I want to offer at the inn. When the girls turned up their noses at the idea of another night of putt-putt golf with their dad and the woman he's seeing, I invited them to come with me." She smiled. The offer had had the twin benefit of giving the contractor and the chef a rare evening alone together.

"You don't have to be cagey, Erin. I know Zeke and Nina are seeing each other." When she wordlessly tilted her head to ask how, he shrugged. "Sugar Sand Beach has an awesome grapevine. Plus, working at the Preserve, I hear things." He shrugged.

She just bet he did. Ron had always been a good listener, the kind of person people naturally confided in. But if a relative stranger like him had heard about Zeke and Nina, it was a good bet that everyone else in town had, too. Erin would have to warn Nina about how fast word spread in Sugar Sand Beach. Not that the chef would mind if it got around that she was seeing Zeke. After all, neither of them had tried to keep their relationship under wraps. But knowing how much her friend valued her privacy, a word to the wise was in order. If for no other reason, in case things with Zeke ended badly. For that matter, it wouldn't hurt to remind Michelle and Reggie how fast the rumor mill churned around here.

"You're good with them, with Megan and Lily, I mean."

Ron's voice derailed her train of thought. She was only too happy to refocus it. "They've spent a good bit of time with us this summer. Megan likes to get out on the water, so I've been giving her kayak lessons. Lily wants to be a chef when she grows up. She idolizes Nina."

Staring straight ahead, Ron asked, "You ever wonder what our lives would be like now if we hadn't split up? Would we still be living in my dad's old house? Would we have kids? I used to picture us with a baby sometimes, but I never asked whether you even wanted one. Did you?"

She blinked as the conversation swerved into uncharted territory. Sure, her biological clock had chimed a time or two. What woman's didn't? But other than Ron, she'd never loved any man enough to want to make a baby.

With Ron, though?

Maybe...if their marriage had held together for longer than a nanosecond. But it hadn't, and she didn't see much sense in rehashing a past they couldn't change. Rather than answer, she turned the tables on him.

"How about you?" The night they'd had pie at the diner he'd told her he'd never married. But these days families came in all shapes and sizes. "No kids?" she asked.

"Nah." Ron shrugged.

"Why not?" Though she tried to bite back the words, the question escaped before she had a chance to stop it.

"To be honest," he said quietly, "I never found anyone who quite measured up to you."

Whoa! How was she supposed to respond to that?

Confessing that she felt the same about him wasn't a good idea. Not when he was leaving soon and she wasn't going with him.

She wasn't going with him, was she?

The urge to throw her lot in with Ron's, accept his job offer and see whether or not they could rekindle their love for one another…Well, she'd be lying if she said the idea didn't bubble within her. Was giving him a second chance really so bad?

Her breath labored. Tears dampened her eyes. Chastising herself, she brushed them away with the backs of her hands. She was tired, that's all. She always did get emotional when she was tired. The long day and even longer night had simply worn her down.

"I'm beat," she admitted. "I'd better call it a night."

"Yeah. All right." Ron's leather seat creaked as he leaned close enough to press a chaste kiss to her cheek. "Good night, Erin. Get some sleep."

"I will," she promised as she climbed down out of the big truck.

But an hour later, she lay listening to her sister's slow and easy breathing while the pros and cons of leaving with Ron crowded her mind, each one vying for first place. Her thoughts grew so jumbled, she gave up on sleep and stared at the ceiling, the tips of her fingers pressed against the spot where Ron's lips had brushed her skin.

Her hand wrapped around one of the mismatched mugs from the cupboard, Erin nursed a second cup of coffee at the tiny table in the apartment's small kitchen. Through a gap in the curtains, she noted that the eastern sky had turned a lighter shade of black. Before too much longer, the sun would pop over the horizon and begin its daily trek toward the west. By the time it sank and everything turned dark again, she had a decision to make. A daunting task on the best of days. Facing it after a sleepless night wasn't going to make it any easier. Nor was the headache that raged inside her head like a caged beast.

She had to do it, though. Had to decide. Although Ron said he'd wait a couple of months for her answer, she couldn't leave Michelle, Nina or Reggie dangling that long. For one thing, there was the partnership agreement to consider. In just a matter of days, Michelle intended to solidify their loose arrangement by giving each of them an equal say in the Sugar Sand Inn. Legally. With signatures and everything. Much as she appreciated her friend's generosity, Erin couldn't accept her share of the property. Not unless she was going to stick around to help manage the place.

She massaged her throbbing temples with the fingers of her free hand and prayed she'd left some aspirin in the medicine cabinet. If not, she'd just have to endure the jackhammer tearing up her head because she was not going to the main house to get some. Not now. Not until she'd decided whether she was staying in Sugar Sand Beach or jetting off with Ron to hobnob with the rich and famous.

And maybe, just maybe, rekindle the love they'd once shared.

Her coffee had grown cold. Abandoning it, she crossed to the window, where she pushed the curtain aside. The pros and cons of accepting Ron's job offer swirled through her mind, making her head hurt worse than ever.

She peered into the darkness at the house she

and her friends had worked so hard to transform from a crumbling edifice into a beautiful home. Thanks to Michelle's skills at organizing and decorating, Nina's incredible talent in the kitchen, Reggie's hard work in the garden, and her own contributions, they were only weeks away from opening a first-class inn and cafe. Already word had spread. Reservations were flooding in through the website.

Her focus drifted to the old tool shed next door, the hub for all the activities she'd planned for the inn's guests and visitors. She'd willingly added her personal collection of kayaks, canoes and equipment to the inn's assets. Though she'd hung onto the cottage in Key West, she'd poured every other dime she owned into making their dreams for the Sugar Sand Inn and Cafe come true. If she left, she could kiss all of that goodbye. The money. The boats. Everything. Which was bad enough, but money was, after all, only money.

Friendships, though, that was the real kicker. She'd made a commitment to her new life here in Sugar Sand Beach. To her friends. To her sister. They were all counting on her. She refused to fool herself into thinking she could walk away from those promises without wrecking her friendships with Nina and Michelle, without losing her newfound closeness with Reggie. By leaving, she'd be doing irreparable damage to those relationships.

And for what?

For a second chance at love? For a future with Ron? Was the possibility that they'd make a go of it this time worth all she'd lose?

They'd been in love once. Deeply. Completely. After they'd parted, she'd hidden her love for Ron so well that not even her best friends knew it was there. But it had never died. Not completely. And she'd never forgotten him. In the twenty years they'd been apart, she hadn't woken once without looking for the indentation of his head on the pillow beside hers. Without yearning for the feel of his arms around her. She'd even missed the sound of the snores that, for an all too brief period of time, had lulled her to sleep each night.

If there was a chance, however remote, that she could have all of that again, didn't she owe it to herself to try? No matter what the cost?

Her head throbbed.

The rattle of a doorknob on the other side of the apartment made her turn away from the window and her thoughts. Dressed for the day in shorts and a loose T-shirt, her strawberry-blond curls tamed into a sleek ponytail, Reggie emerged from the bedroom.

"You're home. I didn't expect you until noon." She glanced over her shoulder. "Why'd you close the door?" she asked, obviously puzzled by the change in plans.

"Megan and Lily lasted less than an hour after they turned in last night before they'd had enough. After I dropped them off, I came on back here. But I got up early and didn't want to wake you." Mentioning Ron's visit or the fact that she'd never actually gone to sleep would only prolong the conversation that was making her headache worse than it had been.

"Oh, that's too bad. I was hoping they'd have a good time."

"They enjoyed themselves up to a point. We cooked hot dogs and made s'mores. What's not to love about that, right?" The girls had actually lasted longer than she'd thought they would.

"Right. I'm headed over to the house for breakfast. Then out to the garden for a while." Reggie danced on her tippy-toes before dashing into the bathroom.

The toilet flushed a few minutes later. The sound of water in the sink cut off seconds before the redhead stepped into the short hallway. "You coming?" she asked.

Erin ran a hand over the ratty sweatshirt she'd pulled on over her sleep pants. "I'm not hungry. You go on ahead." She felt her sister's eyes study her.

"What's on your agenda?" Reggie's footsteps toward the door slowed.

"I just dumped all the camping gear in the center when I got home last night. I'll need to tidy up a bit. Then I thought I'd work on getting a little more settled in here." She'd been too busy to unpack her boxes in the weeks since she and Reggie had moved into the apartment. Sorting through them now would give her a chance to decide what she needed to put in storage and what she should take with her when she left. If she left, that was.

"You want me to bring you anything? Coffee? Toast?"

"No, thanks." Despite the unrelenting pain in her temples, she managed a smile. "I'm good."

Reggie weighed this for a second before she lifted one shoulder in an acquiescent shrug. "Okay, see you later."

After she watched her sister mount the back steps into the main house, Erin used the facilities where—praise be!—she found a bottle of aspirin in the medicine cabinet. She downed two tablets with the dregs of her coffee. By the time she changed clothes and ran a comb through her hair, the pounding in her head had subsided enough that she felt up to tackling a little work.

Thanks to the great job Ron had done with the camping gear the night before, setting things to rights in the center took less effort than she expected. In no time at all she stood in front of the half-dozen boxes she'd moved from place to place since her arrival in Sugar Sand Beach.

"If I haven't used this stuff in six months, do I really need it?" she asked. She'd always traveled light. The urge to simply haul the unopened boxes to the curb surged through her. Remembering, though, that one of them held photograph albums, she resigned herself to sorting through each and every one.

She hit pay dirt in the second box. On top of the winter sweaters she'd never needed in Key West, she unearthed a tattered world map. Beside it lay a box of pushpins, the same pins she'd used to tack the map to the back of her bedroom door in the cottage. Carefully, she unfolded the paper on her bed. She ran one hand over it, smoothing the torn edges, feeling the tiny bumps and holes that marked all the places she'd traveled.

Each year, as the tourist season drew to a close in Key West, she'd treated herself to an excellent seafood dinner and a bottle of the best wine she could afford. Then, when everything swayed just a bit, she'd stand on the other side of the room and throw darts at the map until she managed to hit it. Wherever the arrow struck, that's where she'd spend the next six to eight weeks. Absorbing the culture, seeing the sights, getting to know the people as well as she could. In fair weather or foul, feast or famine, she'd stay wherever the dart had taken her until Alaska's spring thaw. Then, she'd throw her duffle bag over her shoulder and head north to Seward, where she'd spend the summer guiding tourists on kayak trips.

The borders of the countries blurred. She rubbed her eyes and was surprised when her fingers came away wet. The map, planes, trains and automobiles had been second nature to her, her routine for twenty years. If she hadn't loved every minute of it—and who did?—she could honestly say that she'd enjoyed most of them.

The last few years, though, not so much.

She no longer thrived on the challenge of making herself understood in a country where no one spoke English. She'd already hiked the Silk Road and visited the monasteries of Sanahin and Haghpat. She didn't need to do it again. Instead, she wanted to walk into a Starbucks, order a Grande Mocha Latte and know that was exactly what she'd get and how much she'd have to pay for it. At the end of the day, she no longer had any interest in spreading her bedroll over hard ground. She wanted a bed and a mattress and, whenever possible, soft linens with an 800 thread count.

But if she accepted Ron's offer, she'd be signing up to do it all over again. Maybe not the bedroll—he had promised luxurious accommodations, after all. But certainly the rest of it. Dealing with language barriers and going on five-day hikes and suddenly finding herself on the wrong side of a border during a military coup.

Yeah, she'd pass, thanks.

That wasn't the life she wanted anymore. Ten years ago, she would have jumped at the chance to jaunt around the world with Ron. Even five years ago, she might have considered it. But she'd chosen a different path now. One where seeing the seven wonders of the world wasn't nearly as important as the relationships she shared with Michelle, Nina and Reggie. As much as it would break her heart to watch Ron leave, she couldn't risk what she'd built here in Sugar Sand Beach for the chance that, maybe, she and Ron would have a second chance at love.

Her decision made, she folded the map into quarters and returned it to the box of sweaters.

The pack of darts and the push pins went in next. Carefully, she taped the flaps closed. Grabbing a permanent marker, she wrote 'Donate' in bold strokes across the top. She shoved the box aside and took the next one from the stack. As she did, she brushed a hand through her hair and smiled.

The headache that had plagued her all morning had finally lifted.

Twelve

Michelle

Not sure whether she should knock or simply barge on in, Michelle rapped lightly on the door to Erin and Reggie's apartment. She gave the knob a tentative twist. It wasn't locked.

"It's Michelle," she called, opening the door just a crack. She kept her voice low in case Erin had gone back to bed. That's what she would have done, how she treated the occasional headache—lights off, flat on her back, something wet and cold pressed to her forehead. A pack of peas from the freezer would do the trick in a pinch.

When no one answered, Michelle gave the door another push. She peered inside, surprised to see the curtains wide open, lights blazing. The fruity scent of shampoo and conditioner drifted in the air.

"Erin?" She called louder this time. "Reggie said you had a headache so Nina sent over some peppermint tea."

"How sweet! I'll be right there."

Erin appeared briefly in the doorway to the bedroom. Before she ducked out of sight again, Michelle gave her friend a quick once-over. Clean shorts. Clean T-shirt. Hair freshly washed and turbaned in a towel. Erin certainly didn't look like someone who was dealing with a migraine.

"How'd she know I had a headache?" Erin strode out from the bedroom running a comb through her damp hair.

"She said your forehead was all scrunched up. A sure sign." Michelle placed the mug of tea on the small table.

"She knows me too well." Finished with the comb, Erin tucked it into a back pocket. "Here, have a seat. Can I get you some coffee? Water? Or do you want some of this?" She lifted the lid on the to-go cup and sniffed. "Mmmmm. Yummy."

"No, thanks." Michelle relocated a stack of photo albums from the lone guest chair to the coffee table. "You look pretty good for someone who's under the weather. What's going on?"

"Long night." Erin sighed. She straddled one of the kitchen chairs. "I'll spare you the details and hit the highlights. The girls loved the whole camping experience. Hot dogs. S'mores. Everything but sleeping in the tent. Ron showed up. The mosquitoes were fierce. I think Megan would have stayed, but Lily couldn't sleep. I brought them both home early. But then I couldn't sleep so…headache."

"Whoops! Roll that back a bit." Erin had tried to slip that part about Ron past her, but she'd caught it. Didn't entertaining an ex while taking care of Zeke's daughters break the no-boyfriend rule of babysitting? "What was that about Ron? Were you expecting him?" Michelle stared at the blonde.

"Nope. Total surprise." Erin grinned sheepishly. "Actually, I was planning to gloss over that part."

Michelle pinned her with the "mom look" she'd perfected in dealing with Ashley and Aaron. Like the twins, her friend couldn't hold up under the scrutiny for long.

"He dropped by to check on us after someone at the ranger station told him we were there," Erin confessed. "He was surprisingly good with the girls. Lily 'taught' him how to make s'mores," she said, using air quotes.

"Of course she did." That sounded innocent enough. With an encouraging smile, Michelle urged Erin to go on.

"After I tucked Megan and Lily in for the night, he and I talked for a little bit. About fifteen minutes later, the girls said they wanted to go home. Ron actually stayed and broke camp so I could take care of them. He was waiting for me when I got back here."

Michelle's breath caught. Though Erin had tried to hide it, over the years Ron's name had come up often enough that Michelle knew her friend had never gotten over him. She couldn't help but wonder if this new venture he'd proposed wasn't his way of trying to win back Erin's heart. This time, he'd offered to give her the one thing she'd asked for when they were married. But if Erin left with him, would he keep his promise? If he didn't, it would leave Erin in pieces. Was she willing to take that chance? Michelle waited.

"He, um —" Erin stared at the floor. "He told me I was the reason he'd never remarried. That he'd never found anyone he loved like he loved me." She scuffed a sneakered foot across the linoleum. "The thing is, I feel the same way about him, but..."

"But?" Michelle's entire body stilled.

"But it's not going to work out." Sadness welled in Erin's eyes.

"Are you sure? If you love each other..." Michelle's voice trailed off when Erin shook her head.

"Our goals have flip-flopped." Erin held her hand level with the floor before turning it palm-side-up. "We're not in our twenties anymore. We want different things. Now he wants nothing more than to see the world, and that's the last thing I want to do. I've been there, done that, and have far too many T-shirts to prove it." She plucked at the picture of a charging rhinoceros on the one she wore. "Ironic, right?"

"So." Michelle paused. "You're not leaving?" She needed to hear Erin say the words.

"I'm not going anywhere. I can't ask Ron to give up his hopes or his dreams. But I can't go with him. I don't want to." Erin sipped her tea and set the cup on the table. "You know," she said, her nose wrinkling, "that stuff would be a lot better with some sugar or honey. The smell makes me think of peppermint patties. Or those little candies you get at restaurants sometimes. You know, the red-and-white ones that melt in your mouth. But then you take a sip and...yuck."

Michelle chuckled. "I've always thought the same thing. Nina says sweeteners of any kind defeat the purpose, though."

"Let Nina drink it, then." Erin pushed the cup aside. Twisting, she stretched both arms above her head. When her hands landed on the back of the chair, she sobered. "This wasn't an easy decision to make. I wrestled with it all night." She shook her head. "To be honest, I've been struggling with it ever since he showed up here. Now that I've made the decision, though, I know it's the right one." She pressed a hand over her heart. "It feels right."

"I guess that means I can tell Dave we're still on for Friday night?" Michelle hated to ask, but she needed the answer.

"Yes. Definitely. Nothing's changed."

Michelle let go of the breath she'd been holding. She hadn't brought it up because she didn't want to put even more pressure on Erin, but she'd had a lot riding on the decision her friend had reached. If Erin had decided to jet off to Timbuktu with Ron, she'd have needed to restructure the whole partnership agreement. And then there was the not-so-little question of whether or not she, Nina and Reggie could make the Sugar Sand Inn and Cafe a success without Erin's help. Relief whispered through her.

Though she'd never interfere with true love, she had to admit, she couldn't be happier that Erin had decided to stay.

Michelle nudged one corner of the blue binder until the edges aligned with the end of the dining room table. They'd stored the immense table and matching chairs in the turret during the renovations. For tonight's signing, she'd asked Chris to bring it into the main parlor. Silently, she checked the other six binders, the pens and the water glasses spaced at regular intervals along the mahogany surface. One each for Erin, Nina, Reggie and herself. Three more for Dave, his paralegal and Mark the attorney, who'd be handling all her legal work after tonight. Satisfied that everything was as perfect as she could make it, she slipped her shaking hands into the pockets of her favorite A-line dress.

"All set?" Dave's voice whispered for her ears alone.

"I—I'm not sure." It wasn't every day that she gave away a large portion of her net worth. She ran one finger of her right hand along the inside seam of her pocket.

"You have nothing to worry about. The contracts include every provision you asked for. Unless you've changed your mind?" He let the question hang in the air between them.

"No. Not me. But I do worry about the others. Erin says she's made her choice. But love is a wild card. What if she decides she can't live without Ron? What if Sam reneges on his promises and tries to claim half of Reggie's share? Or if Nina doesn't like the way we structured the cafe as part of the property?" She slipped her hand from her pocket to worry a fingernail between her teeth.

"Now, now. None of that." Dave tenderly tugged her fingers into his warm grip. "Erin's as levelheaded as they come. If she told you she was staying put, you can take that to the bank. I drew up the papers that Sam signed relinquishing all his claims to Reggie's assets; he wouldn't have legal standing if he decided to challenge the agreement. As an attorney, he knows that. As for Nina, you discussed all of this with her, didn't you?"

"Yes," Michelle whispered. She closed her eyes for a brief second while Dave's soothing voice calmed her jangled nerves. He was right. She couldn't predict the future, but she had reviewed the details of the joint venture with the rest of the girls, including Nina. They'd approved every single line.

"Let's get started, then. I don't think we'll hit any snags, but if we do, we can reschedule this for another night."

Michelle gave Dave's hand a grateful squeeze. Taking a big gulp of air, she looked about the room. Reggie's deep tan contrasted beautifully with the sleeveless white top and loose silk pants she'd worn this evening. The young woman stood at the buffet, where she appeared to be contemplating the selection of appetizers Nina's assistants had prepared. Nina hovered nearby, looking elegant in a black satin, V-neck top over wide-legged trousers. For once, Erin hadn't chosen something exotic from the outfits she'd collected in her travels. But she'd never be a Plain Jane. While she stood on the far side of the room, quietly chatting with Dave's paralegal CoraBeth, light reflected from the sequins that embellished the cream-colored tunic Erin had paired with dressy slacks.

"I guess we might as well get started," Michelle said. She cleared her throat. The sound wasn't very loud, but it immediately drew the attention of every person in the room. She moistened her lips and plunged into the short speech she'd rehearsed.

"Thank you all for coming here tonight. I…" She stopped in mid-sentence.

What was she doing?

She didn't need to give a fancy speech. Not for her friends. Certainly not for Dave and his staff. She coughed quietly and started over.

"Erin," she said, meeting her best friend's eyes, "you've been my rock when I needed one." She let her gaze travel to the woman in black. "Nina, you've kept my body fed and my soul nourished." At the chef's brief nod, she moved on to the youngest member of their group. "Reggie, you understood that I needed a bridge between my new life in Florida and the one I left behind in Virginia." She inclined her head toward the front door and the rose bushes that flanked it. Addressing the group again, she said, "Those are just a few of the reasons we've been friends since the day we met. And, after tonight, we'll be business partners—and friends—for the rest of our lives. What do you think? Shall we sign these papers and make it official?"

"Here, here!" Reggie tapped the rim of her water glass against her plate. Leaving her still-empty dish on one of the occasional tables, she chose a chair in front of one of the blue binders.

Erin sat beside her sister while Nina crossed to the other side of the table. Michelle slipped in beside Nina, leaving Dave and CoraBeth to take their seats at the head of the table, while Mark sat opposite his boss at the other end.

Dave pulled a pair of reading glasses from an inside pocket of his suit jacket. "We're here for a final review of, and to sign, the partnership agreement that will make each of you equal partners in the Sugar Sand Inn and Cafe." He clicked the end of his pen. "We have a lot of ground to cover, so, if you wouldn't mind, please jot any questions on the notepads we've provided and we'll answer them at the end." Opening his blue binder, he pointed to the date and the names at the top of the first page. "Assuming everything above is correct, I direct you to the first paragraph, which reads: The parties hereto hereby form, pursuant to the Florida Business Organization Code..."

As Dave continued, Michelle carefully checked for inconsistencies between this document and the one she'd been over so often in the last three months that she'd practically committed it to memory. Every once in a while, she looked at the others. She wasn't at all surprised when Reggie's eyes glazed over by the end of the second page. Beside her, an intently focused Erin traced Dave's every word with her pen, stopping only for the occasional sip of water. Meanwhile, Nina scribbled a note when they reached the section that detailed the decision-making processes for the cafe. After that, she flipped pages without bothering to read them. Not that Michelle blamed her. Although Dave had used plain language wherever possible, a certain amount of mind-boggling legalese had been unavoidable.

It took about an hour before Dave finally closed his binder, scanned the room and asked, "Any questions?"

"I have one," Erin said without preamble. Rather than addressing Dave, though, she aimed her hazel eyes straight at Michelle.

"Really, Michelle?" Erin asked. "Do you really want to give us each a quarter of all this?" In a sweeping gesture, she indicated the house and the land beyond it. "I know we've all invested whatever we had to make the inn and cafe a success, but this gift seems out of proportion to our contributions. So I have to ask, is this really what you want to do? 'Cause if you have any doubts at all, we should call this whole thing off."

"Absolutely," Reggie chimed in, her agreement obvious.

"Definitely." Nina nodded. "I know you want to make sure we recoup our initial investment, but can't we find a way to do that while still letting you hold onto the inheritance your birth mother left you? I mean, the money I kicked in was nowhere near what the land alone is worth. With the house and the other buildings, we've got to be talking—"

"Millions," Reggie whispered.

Michelle's heart melted. Tears stung her eyes. She had no doubt that with one word, one murmur of dissent, her friends would walk away from the gift she intended to give them. That's what made their relationship so special, and it was why she was more certain than ever that forming the partnership was the right thing to do.

Her emotions ran so deep that her voice took on a thready quality as she said, "You're the best friends a girl could ever want. You know that, right? This partnership isn't about the money you put in. It's about us, our friendship. When I needed you, you were right by my side. It was your idea to transform this house into an inn. To open a cafe." Acknowledging the contributions that were worth far more than money, she nodded to each of them in turn. "We've all worked hard to make this dream come true. And yes, I'm certain I want to protect your interests, as well as mine, by forming this partnership."

Erin brushed the corners of her eyes with the tips of her fingers. "Okay, then. As long as you're sure." She sniffled.

"I am," Michelle said, her voice firming. She hadn't been this certain of anything since the day Allen asked her to marry him.

Erin glanced at Dave. "That's all I wanted to know. Everything else is pretty straightforward."

The attorney tapped one finger on his blue binder. "Anyone else?"

"I have a question...for Erin."

Michelle blinked as Reggie shifted in her chair so she could see her sister's face more clearly. "You've always been a wanderer. But this"—she tapped her copy of the contract—"this means you're going to have to stay put. It's going to take all four of us to succeed. We need you to promise you won't disappear. Can you do that?"

Erin's composure wobbled. She slid her hand the short distance across the surface of the table until her fingers touched Reggie's. "I can. I do."

That was enough for Michelle, but Reggie wasn't willing to let it go. "And Ron? What about him?" she demanded.

"I spoke with him last night, as a matter of fact." Erin's features firmed. "I turned down his job offer. I told him he should move on to the next person on his list. That this was my final answer." A smile broke across her face at the reference to a popular game show.

"I'm so glad." Reggie's breath shuddered. Tears sparkled in her eyes as she leaned in to embrace her sister. Both of them pulled tissues from the box in the middle of the table when Erin returned the hug just as warmly.

"Now that that's over." Nina used an airy tone even as she blotted her own eyes. "It's my turn."

Michelle tensed. Did the chef want more control over the day-to-day operations of the cafe? A different profit-sharing structure?

"I want to know about Aaron and Ashley. Are they okay with this?" She tapped the top of her binder with neatly trimmed fingernails.

Tension flowed out of Michelle like air escaping a balloon. She'd thought her friends couldn't surprise her any more than they already had. Evidently, she was wrong about that. Their concern for her children made her feel ashamed that she'd ever questioned whether establishing the partnership was the right move to make. Her determination greater than ever before, she assured her friends that the twins were fine with her decision.

"I talked it over with them when they came

down last month. They understand that eventually they'll inherit my share of the inn." She turned a wicked smile on Erin and Reggie and, last but not least, Nina. "Sorry about that, but you'll have to deal with them on your own when I'm gone."

Laughter rippled about the table as the mood in the room lightened. After that, they sped through the rest of the process. Once everyone else had signed their names on the lines Dave had indicated with color-coded stickies, Michelle stepped forward. Smiling for the camera Mark held, she was glad when her hand didn't tremble, not even a little bit, as she added the final signature that made the document legally binding.

At a signal from Nina, Viola and Ethan emerged from the kitchen. Viola carried a dome-shaped cake so beautifully decorated, Michelle hated to cut into it. She did, though, and they all celebrated with slices of the rich chocolate-and-raspberry confection, which they washed down with champagne they took from Ethan's tray.

Dave was the last of their guests to leave when the evening drew to a close. Wanting a private moment with the attorney, Michelle walked with him to the door. "Thank you," she said. "I couldn't have done this without you."

Dave clasped her hands between his. His voice rang with sincerity as he said, "I was glad to help." A smile shaped his full lips. "But I'm even happier that you'll no longer be my client. I'm looking forward to our evening tomorrow."

A rush of heady excitement shimmied from the top of Michelle's head to her toes.

"I'll pick you up at six," he continued. "We'll have an early dinner on our way to the theater."

"Perfect," Michelle whispered. "I can't wait."

Gosh, I hope I don't ruin the heels of these new shoes, Michelle thought as she picked her way up the graveled walkway. Someone—probably Nina—had left a light burning in the foyer. Other than that, the house was a dark outline against the moonlit sky.

One of her heels plunged a little deeper into the dirt beneath the stones. She wobbled.

Or I could fall flat on my face. Wouldn't that be a nice ending to a special night?

She wished she could stop and kick off her shoes. With her luck, though, sharp stones would only end up slicing open the bottoms of her feet. Next time—if there was a next time—she'd wear flats. But the state of the inn's walkway, and for that matter, the parking pad, was something to consider for their guests. She should talk to Reggie about replacing the gravel with concrete. Or pavers. Yeah, pavers. Those would look nice.

A hint of Dave's cologne—spicy, masculine—wafted in the air. She drank it in. A sudden awareness of the man at her side filled her. Her face heated.

What was she doing, thinking about pavers and concrete and shoes, of all things, when she should be thinking about Dave?

He'd been...wonderful. The entire night had, in fact, been every bit as perfect as she'd hoped it would be. The man himself had been full of surprises, beginning with the car and driver he'd hired for the evening. Being able to share a drink or two at dinner, a glass of wine at the theater was just one of the many details he'd so thoughtfully considered.

She'd always admired the way Dave dressed, but the suit he'd selected for tonight's outing was something else. The salted strands of his dark hair looked even more distinguished—as if that were possible—against the charcoal gray that had been tailored to showcase the wide set of his shoulders.

The restaurant he'd selected was nothing

short of amazing. Located between Sugar Sand Beach and Destin, the intimate little bistro offered seating spaced far enough apart that the murmur of conversation at one table didn't carry as far as the next. Overhead beams and twinkle lights woven into sprays of dried thistle added to the romantic atmosphere.

Because neither of them wanted to miss curtain time, he'd taken the liberty of ordering ahead. They'd shared an appetizer of blackened brie, which they spread on tiny wedges of toasted walnut bread. The juxtaposition of the spicy outer crust with the cool, creamy cheese and the sweet toast made every one of her taste buds sit up and take notice. Which had been just right for the beet salad she'd requested instead of the delicious-looking chopped one Dave had ordered.

Humor had sparkled in his eyes at her choice. "Really? Beets?"

She'd nearly melted under his teasing gaze. It had taken her a full minute to form an answer. "Nina is an adventurous chef," she'd told him, "but she absolutely hates beets. Won't allow them in the house. I, on the other hand, love them. But I only eat them when I'm out—it's a small price to pay for keeping her happy."

Conversation had flowed easily between

them for the rest of the meal while candles flickered and the hushed voices of the other diners faded into the background. She could have lingered all night at their table, feasting on the plump scallops that had been seared to perfection and, most of all, enjoying Dave's company. As it was, the two hours they'd spent at the restaurant had flown by so quickly, she'd regretted it when it was time to leave for the play.

Which had been another altogether delightful surprise. Movie theater seating had surrounded the round stage where a dedicated troupe of local actors performed. They'd been so talented, she'd gotten caught up in the antics of mild-mannered Elwood Dowd and his six-foot invisible friend. As much as she enjoyed the show, though, she'd retained an awareness of Dave's fingers threaded through hers, the subtle scent of masculinity and heat that flavored the air around him. She supposed her only true regret of the night had come when she'd had to let go of his hand for the final curtain call and the thundering ovation that followed.

"I had a wonderful time tonight," she said as they reached the front steps.

"It was fun, wasn't it?" His hand at her elbow guided her up the stairs. "Um, Nicholas Sparks is giving a reading at the bookstore in Destin tomorrow. Want to go? Afterwards, you could come to the house. I'll grill steaks."

Her inner alarm sounded. A second date on the same weekend? Too much, too soon. And besides, Nicholas Sparks? "Do you like his books?" she asked.

Dave's feet shuffled on the porch's wooden boards. "To be honest, I haven't read any of his work. I thought you might like him."

That was just like Dave, consistently putting her wants and needs before his own. Uncertainty flooded her. How did she turn him down without hurting his feelings? "That's an incredibly sweet offer," she began. He stilled when she placed her hand on his forearm.

"But you're not interested, are you?"

Her insides melted a bit at the note of self-doubt that had crept into his voice. She moved her hand from his forearm to his chest. Through the soft wool of his jacket, she felt the comforting beat of his heart.

"Not in Nicholas Sparks," she said. "You, however. I'm very much interested in you. I just...need to take things slow. Rain check?"

The smile that softened Dave's features told her he'd give her the space she needed. "I can wait," he said, confirming her thoughts. "As long as it's not too long."

"How about later this month?" At his downcast expression, she hurried to explain. "With the soft opening of the cafe next week and the big grand opening of the inn a few days later, I have a million things going through my head at once. Even tonight, I couldn't help but notice how the gravel dug into my heels. That started me down the road of alternatives—like concrete walkways or pavers. Which was not what I wanted to be thinking of when I was with you."

He took both of her hands in his. "I'm good with taking things one step at a time. As long as we're taking those steps together."

She smiled up at him, committing the lines of his face to her memory. "You're a good man, Dave Rollins."

At that, he moved almost imperceptibly closer.

A sudden nervousness passed through her. She'd loved her husband and her marriage so much that cheating had never crossed her mind. Not that she hadn't had plenty of opportunities. But a chilly attitude had discouraged the guys who'd tried to get a little too friendly over the years. So it had been a long time—a quarter of a century or more—since she'd kissed a man who wasn't her husband.

She wasn't sure what to do. How did she let

Dave know she even wanted him to kiss her? Where did she put her hands? Did she keep her lips pressed tightly together? And where was the fun in that?

She needn't have worried. Dave moved close enough that the width of his shoulders blocked the light. The scent of his cologne, of him, enveloped her. He cupped her chin in the palm of his hand, his long fingers caressing her jaw. The motion felt so right—so good—that she moved in sync with him when he tipped her face toward his. The press of his lips against hers felt like the most natural thing in the world.

If, that was, she considered the bright burst of yearning it ignited natural. No one was more surprised than she was when she did.

All too soon, the kiss ended, their lips parted. It was only then that she noticed she'd twined her hands around his neck. Not in the least bit embarrassed by that find, she ran her fingers lightly down the soft wool of his jacket.

"You think, next time, we can try that again, too?" she asked, her voice husky with desire.

Dave's eyes caught the light, and he smiled. "Just try and stop us," he said playfully.

He saw her safely inside before, whistling a Jack Brooks song from the play they'd seen, he retraced his steps to the car that idled in the parking area. Michelle stood at the door and watched the town car's taillights disappear before she headed to the kitchen for a glass of water. The moment she crossed the threshold, however, lights blazed. She scanned the room, noting the three eager faces that beamed up at her from around the table in the breakfast nook.

"Awww, you waited up for me? You didn't have to do that," she protested, although she was suddenly very glad they had. Their presence reminded her of the nights she'd sat waiting for Ashley and Aaron to come home from their dates and how they'd talk into the wee hours.

"We couldn't wait till morning to find out how it went with Dave," Nina explained.

"Yeah, did he kiss you?" Reggie asked, demanding details. "Did you kiss him back?"

Erin patted the seat beside her. "Sit down, and tell us everything."

And, with a fresh awareness of how lucky she was to have such wonderful friends, she did exactly that.

Thirteen

Nina

"Two scrambled. Grits, bacon, biscuits. One ham and cheese cass. Hash browns, toast." Finished with her rapid-fire delivery, Gwen tore the order off her pad and slipped it under a metal bar on the counter.

Viola turned away from the Aga range to glance at the paper. "Ethan, toast and biscuits," she called. Grabbing two eggs from a nearby carton, she one-handedly cracked them into a bowl. "Chef, ham and cheese."

"Got it." At the long end of the kitchen counter and just out of their guests' view, Nina wiped her forehead on the sleeve of her fitted, white jacket. Shouldn't the rush be slowing down by now? By her count, she'd put the finishing touches on at least forty plates, twice

269

the number of invitations she'd issued for the soft opening.

"Table four sends their compliments, Chef." Gwen checked the order slips at Nina's station and slid plates of eggs Benedict and waffles onto her serving tray. "Table six asked if they could have a word."

"Was there a problem?" Her hand hovering over a bin of parsley sprigs, Nina stilled. So far, she'd heard nothing but compliments. She'd hoped to keep it that way.

"Not that I'm aware of, Chef. I think she just wants to say hello. Maggie somebody."

Nina's breath eased. Gwen lived in nearby Miramar Beach and probably wasn't on a first-name basis with everyone in Sugar Sand. Waitressing at the cafe would change that over time but, for now, she filled in the blanks for the brunette. "Maggie Henson. Mayor of Sugar Sand Beach. Tell her I'll be out in a minute."

As busy as they'd been since the doors opened at eight this morning, she hated to leave her station. If it had been anyone else, she might have stayed put. But Maggie was Maggie, a dear friend as well as a strong advocate for the inn and the cafe.

Nina finished adorning a plate of yummy-looking scrambled eggs with a few springs of parsley. She set the dish beneath the warming lights.

"And Chef?"

"Yes." Nina checked the next order. She added a dollop of whipped cream to the half stack of golden brown pancakes and reached for a squeeze bottle filled with raspberry sauce.

"It's awfully busy out there. I'm falling behind. If it's going to stay like this, you really need to hire a second waitress."

Once more Nina halted in the middle of a task. Lowering the sauce she'd intended to drizzle over the whipped cream, she blinked. The dining room should be practically empty by now, shouldn't it? She hadn't been too shocked when all twenty-four tables had filled within the first five minutes. She hadn't specified the number of guests in each party, after all, and she'd expected a few extras to show up. But the entire staff had been moving at warp speed ever since. Now that she'd stopped long enough to think about it, she realized that the initial crowd had all been served their food an hour ago.

Who else had known about the soft opening?

"Let's get those plates out before the food gets cold," she said, dismissing the waitress with a smile that hid a niggle of concern. She whipped off her apron.

"Viola, you're in charge," she called as she strode purposefully toward the dining area. Before reaching it, she paused long enough to check her image in the mirror she'd hung out of the sight of her customers. She smoothed a runaway strand of hair into the sleek chignon, then, satisfied that she at least looked the part of a cool, calm, collected chef, she plastered a warm, welcoming smile over a mounting sense of unease.

An unease that threatened to turn into full-fledged panic when she got her first glimpse of the packed dining room. Every seat in the place was taken. At a four-top in the corner, someone had even scrounged up extra chairs to accommodate six guests who sat hip-to-hip around the table. She gulped. She hadn't planned on feeding every citizen of Sugar Sand Beach this morning, but it sure looked like that was exactly what was happening.

Determined to do her best, she made a beeline for Maggie's table, where she welcomed the mayor to the cafe's opening. "I'm glad you made it. I thought you might be too busy to come."

"I wouldn't miss this, and it was so worth it. Every morsel was absolutely delicious, and the service was excellent." Maggie blotted her lips with her napkin. "I'm going to have to up my game at the Diner or you'll put me out of business."

"You don't have a thing to worry about," Nina assured the mayor. The cafe's limited hours would help Maggie's Diner keep its first-place status in a town with only two restaurants.

Maggie placed a three-dollar tip beside her dishes. "I guess I'd better leave and let someone else have this table. There were people waiting when I came in. Besides, I need to check the weather reports before I go to work."

What was there to check? The weather hadn't changed. It was hot and steamy. From what Nina had heard, that was typical for September in Florida. She would have said as much to Maggie, but the busboy hovered nearby, waiting to clear and reset the mayor's table. Nina signaled him over and gave the still-full dining room another glance. The crowded tables spurred her into action. She lingered only long enough to wave and smile at the rest of the guests before she ducked back into the kitchen.

At the hand-washing station, she whispered to Viola, "It's a madhouse out there. I'm afraid we're going to run out of food." Yesterday, they'd prepped twice as much as she thought they'd possibly need for the first day. It didn't look like that would be enough. "How are we doing on supplies?"

"Fine, Chef. We have plenty of bacon, sausage and eggs. Ethan was runnin' low on biscuits, so I took a tray from the fridge. They're in the oven now, along with another pan of casserole— sausage this time."

Nina nodded. She'd intended to save the extras for the next day, but if they had to make another batch or two this afternoon, so be it.

"Ethan, how are you doing with waffles and toast?" She turned her attention to the young prep cook.

"All good, Chef. I'm working through my third pitcher of batter now. There's two more in the cooler. We're running a little low on sourdough bread, but we have plenty of whole wheat, white, and rye."

Nina mentally added to her shopping list as, wearing black pants and matching white shirts, Reggie and Erin burst through the back door into the kitchen.

"Hey, Chef," Reggie called. "Michelle sent us. She has ten more parties waiting for tables, and people are still arriving. She said to tell you someone posted their invitation on the bulletin board at the community center."

"Oh." Nina let out a long, slow sigh. "I guess

that explains the turnout." So much for her idea of easing into normal operations. Once the announcement went public, word had, no doubt, spread like icing on a cake from one end of Sugar Sand Beach to the other. She folded her hands at her waist. "Well, I guess we'd better get these people fed."

"We're here to help if you need us," Erin said. "Ron showed up. I guess he thought I'd get him a table. He thought wrong. I recruited him to direct traffic out front." She grinned. Her announcement that she was staying put in Sugar Sand Beach had not yielded the expected results. Instead of moving on to the next candidate on his list, Ron had insisted on finishing out his contract with the Park Service. All through September, he'd found one excuse after another to see Erin. In return, she sat beside him at church on Sundays and had even invited him to a casual cookout at the inn last weekend.

"Chris took a bunch of folding chairs out to the porch so people wouldn't have to stand while they waited for their tables. Now where do you want us?" Reggie asked.

Nina's eyes filled. In the ten minutes she'd been in the dining area, orders had stacked up like hotcakes at her station. "Either of you have any experience as a waitress? Poor Gwen is overwhelmed." When Erin said she did, Nina handed her an order pad and a pencil.

"Reggie, that means you're on dish duty." She nodded to the stacks of dishes, glasses and cutlery beside the sink. Viola and Ethan were supposed to load the dishwasher whenever there was a lull, but there'd been no letup.

"Wash your hands," she told them both. "Grab aprons. Use hairnets—there's a box of them on the shelf over the apron rack."

"Yes, Chef," the two sisters said in unison.

The next two hours passed in a blur of beautifully plated dishes. By the time Michelle popped into the kitchen to announce she'd shown the last guests to their tables, Viola reported that they'd completely run out of biscuits and only a few drops of Hollandaise sauce remained. Another thirty minutes sped by before Gwen said only a handful of people lingered over coffee in the dining area. Not long after that, the busboy, Dax, propped himself against a bare patch of wall, his dish tote empty.

"Whew! I can't believe we did it." At her station, Nina placed her hands over her lower back and stretched. Instead of the forty or so plates she'd expected to prepare this morning, they'd served over a hundred guests. She turned to face Viola and Ethan.

"You. Were. Amazing," she said, knowing her eyes glistened with heartfelt thanks. Next, she spoke to Gwen and Dax. "We couldn't have done this without you." Continuing to dole out praise, she glanced at Reggie, Erin and Michelle. "Thanks for pitching in. It made a huge difference."

Viola cleared her throat. "Great job, Chef!" She clapped her hands, a move that triggered a round of applause.

Nina wiped her eyes. "I can't tell you what this means to me," she said after the room quieted. "A lifetime of planning went into this day. Things didn't go quite the way I thought they would." Her voice wavered the tiniest bit. She'd hoped to work through a few hiccups during their soft opening. Instead, they'd been in high gear ever since the doors opened. Come to think of it, maybe that was one of the hiccups she needed to address. "Take an hour—you deserve it." She glanced at the clock. "We'll meet back here at one to clean up and prep for tomorrow."

As the others fanned out, Michelle crooked her finger, beckoning her. "Come here. There's something you need to see."

"What?" Nina pulled two empty squeeze bottles from the line of sauces at her station. She set them on the counter.

"You have to see this to believe it." Michelle's smile spoke of secrets.

Her curiosity overcoming her need to get a head start on prepping for another busy day, Nina followed Michelle as far as the entrance to the dining area. There, her gaze landed on a table in the far corner, where Maggie's Uncle Jack sat with Ruth Bees. As she watched, a coquettish Ruth giggled at something the older gentleman said.

"Well, I'll be," Nina whispered. "I thought those two hated each other." During Senior Days at the Inn, Ruth and Jack had turned trading pointed barbs into an art form.

"That's what everyone thinks," Michelle said, smiling to herself as Jack slowly got to his feet. Gently, he held out an arm and, treating the elderly woman as if she were made of bone china, escorted Ruth out of the room.

"Aw, they're sweet on each other," Nina observed. "Do you think Maggie knows?"

"There's not much that gets past Maggie," Michelle answered.

"True." Nina's eyes narrowed. "Speaking of which, she made an odd comment while she was here earlier."

"Oh?" Michelle's brows rose with interest. "What'd she say?"

"She said she wanted to watch the weather reports before she went to the diner. Are we supposed to get some rain this afternoon?" After the hectic morning, she would probably need to make a resupply run to the big box store in Destin. Bad weather would only slow her down.

"It wouldn't surprise me." Thunderstorms frequently boiled up out of the Gulf in the late afternoon. "But I did overhear a couple of people talking about a tropical storm down on the other side of Cuba. Someone said it might turn into a hurricane by the middle of the week."

"Huh." Nina shook her head. "Cuba? I'd hate to be there." She shivered at the thought of being stuck on the tiny island when one of the strong storms hit.

"You and me both," Michelle agreed. "It seems odd to be concerned about a storm that's so far away, but you know how people love to talk about the weather." She shrugged the topic aside. "Must be a slow news week."

Relief washed through Nina. "As long as it's nothing for us to worry about. I have enough on my plate as it is." She ran a hand down the front of her jacket. "If we stay this busy after next week's grand opening, I'm going to need to hire an additional waitress and a busser. Maybe even another prep cook."

"Let's see how it goes, but I don't think you'll have much choice. It's either that or limit the number of guests we seat each day." Michelle squared her shoulders. "Speaking of the open house, I still have a few last-minute details to take care of this afternoon. I'd better get busy."

"Yeah, me, too."

But as Michelle headed for her office, Nina stared quietly into the dining room. She overlooked the crumpled napkins and empty coffee cups that littered several of the tables. Instead, she chose to picture the room as she had seen it earlier today—filled with happy customers enjoying the food she'd prepared for them. There'd been times in her life when she'd thought this day would never come. Now that it had, she drank in the moment.

Gradually, she became aware of the chatter of voices coming from the sun porch. Cushions creaked and feet shuffled as Viola and the rest of the staff trailed into the kitchen at the end of their break. Nina stirred. She took one last glance at the dining room before her gaze drifted to one of the windows. Beyond the glass, puffy white clouds floated in the brilliant blue sky of another perfect Florida day.

Fourteen

Reggie

"Hey, Jimbo. You took time away from the garage to come see us this morning? That was nice of you." Reggie consulted the seating chart on the hostess stand. Not that she needed to. Most of the tables were vacant, a far cry from yesterday's crush.

"Not much business today. Ever'body's busy, I reckon." Jimbo's thick Southern drawl rolled between his lips. He hooked his thumbs around the straps of his overalls. "You got any of that there breakfast casserole I heard so much about yesterday? Got me a hankerin' for some."

"We do." Reggie nodded. By the time the last customer had been served the day before, only a few egg curds had clung to the sides of the second pan Nina had pulled from the oven.

Determined not to run out of the dish that was proving to be so popular, today the chef had prepared twice as much. But here it was, midmorning already, and Reggie doubted they'd even gone through the first casserole dish.

Deciding to give Jimbo a seat with a view, she used an erasable marker to put an X over a table by a window. "Are you meeting anyone?" she asked, hoping for at least one more customer.

When Jimbo said he was "all by his lonesome," she swallowed her disappointment. She picked up a menu and took a set of silverware wrapped in a napkin from the bin in the hostess station. "Right this way," she said, guiding him through the sparsely filled room to table five. She placed his menu and cutlery within reach. "Can I get you some coffee?"

"Had some already. Doc says I can only have one cup a day." Grousing about his doctor, Jimbo sank onto his chair.

"Gwen will be with you in a minute. In the meantime, you just sit there and enjoy the view. It's such a pretty day." A break in the oppressive humidity had come as a pleasant surprise when she'd stepped outside this morning.

"It won't stay like this." Without bothering to look at the clear, blue skies, Jimbo pulled his cell phone out of the bib pocket of his overalls.

Staring intently at the device, he flicked through several screens.

How odd, Reggie thought, as she wove between the tables on her way back to the hostess stand where she'd taken Michelle's place. Yesterday, chatty customers had crowded the room, their conversations filling the background with a not unpleasant buzz punctuated by occasional laughter. Michelle said she hadn't received a single complaint from the people who'd lingered on the porch for up to an hour while they waited to be seated.

Today, though, the cafe had an entirely different vibe. Reggie had shown less than a dozen parties to their tables. Most of them had eaten quickly and hurried out the door. Had the crowds the day before scared everyone else off? She supposed that was possible. It didn't, however, explain the subdued atmosphere, where customers spoke in hushed tones and held on to their cell phones like drowning men clung to life preservers. They asked for ketchup, hot sauce or more cream in tones that bordered on impatience. Even the unflappable Jimbo seemed uncharacteristically grumpy.

Reggie peeked into the front parlor. No one waited for her on the plush chairs. Just in case someone thought they were supposed to sit on the front porch, she checked outside. Her heart sank a little more. She knew Nina had expected at least a few repeat customers. So far, though, there hadn't been a single one.

Why was that? Not the food. Each dish lived up to Nina's exacting standards. Not the cost. Every item on the menu was attractively priced. The location, the service, the cleanliness—those were all non-issues. So why had people turned out in droves yesterday but ghosted the cafe today?

Her thoughts turned as fitful as the breeze that stirred the sea grass. Leaning on the railing, she took a minute to sort them out. But not even the dry air that, for once, didn't slick her skin with moisture or turn her hair into a mass of ringlets could lift her spirits.

Spotting Chris's familiar truck on the graveled driveway, though, that banished her gloomy thoughts. In their place, a bright happiness bubbled in her chest. Along with it came a fresh awareness of how badly she'd fallen for the rugged handyman with the boy-next-door looks.

Did he feel the same way?

Suddenly self-conscious, she untied and re-tied the bow on the dark green apron Nina had insisted she wear whenever she worked in the cafe.

But something was wrong.

She knew it the instant Chris braked to a stop in the parking area and hustled out of his vehicle. Rushed, agitated strides replaced his normally unhurried movements. Instead of his usual smile, he practically glowered.

Had something happened to Hope?

Reggie bolted toward him. They met him halfway up the path.

"Is everything all right? I didn't expect to see you here today," she asked, her voice freighted with worry. She searched his face but didn't recognize the emotion that played across his features. Her stomach somersaulted.

"I came to hang the shutters. You want me to, don't you?" Chris's frown deepened when he swept a quick look over the porch. "Why haven't you moved any of this stuff inside yet?"

Hang the shutters? Move the porch furniture? Had he lost his mind?

They were in the middle of the most important week since their arrival in Sugar Sand Beach. The soft opening of the cafe paved the way for the open house this weekend, which led straight into the arrival of the inn's first paying guests on Monday. Turning the house into a darkened tomb was the last thing anyone wanted to do. She twisted her apron strings. "Why would we do any of that?"

"Because of Ursula."

Reggie's chest tightened. Someone had whispered that name in the cafe this morning. She ventured a cautious, "Ursula who?"

"Not a who. A what," Chris corrected. He stared down at her in what she could only call dumbfounded disbelief. "No one told you about the hurricane?" he asked. When Reggie only shook her head, his eyes widened. "Ursula is predicted to make landfall somewhere between Tallahassee and New Orleans early Thursday."

Today is Tuesday.

Reggie swallowed, hard. Suddenly weak at the knees, she wished she'd stayed on the porch, where there were chairs she could collapse onto if her legs gave out. She tried to argue. "That can't be right. We checked the weather reports yesterday. There's a tropical storm down around Cuba. But that's over a thousand miles from here."

"There *was* a tropical storm. Now it's a hurricane. Her name is Ursula. She's big, and she's fast. We need to secure the house and get out of her way."

Surely, Chris wasn't the only one in town who watched the news. Why hadn't Gwen or Dax said something about a hurricane? Reggie shook her head. None of this made any sense.

"You'd think someone would have mentioned it if a hurricane was bearing down on us."

"It wasn't, though," Chris explained. "No one considered Ursula much of a threat. The early reports predicted that she'd fizzle out. Storms do that sometimes. But everything changed when the latest hurricane advisory was issued just a little while ago—at ten. Instead of dying down, she's picked up speed and strength. She's growing more powerful by the hour. At this rate, she'll be a Cat 4 by the time she makes landfall. One of the projected paths says that's right here." Chris pointed at the ground beneath his feet.

Reggie glanced over her shoulder at the inn. "Um, about that…Nina's in the middle of the breakfast service, and we have a big open house scheduled for Sunday."

"Whatever plans you have, they're on hold until we see where this hurricane actually hits and how much damage she does." Chris clapped his hands. The sound echoed across the yard like a starting gun. "Now, we need to start bringing everything that isn't nailed down inside. Put it in the house, the garage, the shed. Wherever you can find room. And the shutters. I need to start hanging them now. It's a two-day job for one person. With your help, I might be able to cut that time in half."

"But we're in the middle of the breakfast service!" Impatient, Reggie tapped her foot.

Chris issued a long-suffering sigh. "Let's go talk to Erin, Nina and Michelle. Everybody's going to need to pitch in."

"Erin went for a run," Reggie said, powerless against the shakiness in her voice.

The next thing she knew she was in Chris's arms, her head resting against his shoulder while he murmured comforting words in her ear.

"It's okay. Everything's going to be okay. Our lives, that's what's important. We'll board up and get out of the hurricane's path."

He pressed her close long enough for her heart rate to return to normal. Moving his hands to her shoulders, he held her at arm's length. His blue eyes bore into hers.

"But we can't dawdle. We need to get busy."

Bolstered by Chris's strength, Reggie straightened. Kicking herself for not finding out earlier, she asked, "Where's Hope?"

"Home," Chris said as if it were the most normal of days. "I boarded up my house first. And Mrs. Bees's. Mom's trying to keep Hope awake so she'll sleep in the car. They'll leave for my aunt's condo in Jacksonville later this evening. I'll follow as soon as we finish here."

There was so much wrong with that plan,

Reggie didn't know where to begin. She gave it her best shot. "You should go with Hope and your mom."

"The sooner we get started, the sooner we can all get on the road."

Arguing would waste time that was already in precious supply. She took Chris by the hand. "Let's find Nina, then."

Considering the dearth of customers this morning, Reggie expected to walk into a quiet kitchen. Not a deadly quiet one. Or one where Viola looked like she was on the verge of tears. Reggie certainly hadn't expected to see the normally confident Nina looking pale, with an equally lost Michelle standing beside her. Gwen and Dax huddled in one corner, where the waitress muttered, "It could still turn. It could still turn," like a needle skipping over a scratch on a vinyl record.

Reggie moved directly to her friends' side and took their hands. They were as cold as a frozen margarita. "I guess you've heard about the hurricane?"

"I got an alert," came Michelle's breathless reply. She held up her cell phone.

"Zeke called," Nina said in a flat voice. "He says we need to get ready for a major blow. I—I don't know what that means exactly."

All eyes turned toward Chris when he cleared his throat. "It means you need to close the cafe, send anybody still out there home." He gestured toward the dining area, where scattered customers finished their breakfasts. "And get everything in here put away. Everyone needs to pack an overnight bag—take as much as you need for a week."

Someone gasped. Reggie thought it might have been her.

Chris held up a hand. "You might not be gone that long. This could all blow over. In which case, we'll be back by Friday. Or if the damage is severe, you could be gone a lot longer. It's better to be overprepared than under." His attention shifted to Michelle. "Start calling hotels to make reservations. A lot of people are gonna be trying to get out of the hurricane's path. Places are gonna fill up fast, so it might take you a while to find rooms. Not anything farther west than Gainesville. Look south and east from there."

"I'm on it," Michelle said. "I just need a head count so I know how many rooms to get." Her gaze swept the kitchen. "You're all welcome to come with us. Gwen?"

"No, thanks. We always go to my aunt's place in Alabama." The waitress untied her apron strings. "Chef, if you don't mind, I'm going to head on home."

While Reggie pondered Gwen's use of the word "always," Nina nodded. "Of course," she said. "Check in with me when you're back and everything is safe."

Michelle turned to Dax. "What about you, hon?"

"My folks have a hunting cabin in north Georgia. That's where we usually go." He, too, removed his apron. "I'd better take off. Dad's going to expect me to help him board up the windows."

"Sheesh," Reggie whispered. Words like "usually" and "always" made her want to ask how often this kind of thing happened.

Nina made shooing motions with her hands. "Stay safe, Dax." She glanced at Viola. "You and Charlie want to come with us? You, too, Ethan?"

"I'm going to call Charlie right now, and I'll let you know," Viola answered. "Then I need to round up Malcolm and Dimella. They had school today, believe it or not. Dimella ain't gonna like this one bit. She made the lacrosse team. They have their first game Friday night."

"We had a busy weekend ahead, too," Reggie pointed out. The words were barely out of her mouth before she regretted saying them. "Sorry," she said softly.

"Dimella might still make her game, and all the plans for the inn could still go forward. Ursula could turn or weaken or do a hundred different things," Chris soothed.

"Or she could slam right into us, like what happened to Mexico Beach a couple of years ago." Ethan's eyes glowed with a mix of excitement and fear.

Reggie's breath stuttered. Blood pounded in her ears. Hurricane Michael had devastated the area when it roared ashore as a Cat 5. She shot Chris a pleading look.

He tsked. Shaking his head, he addressed the prep cook. "Now let's not get everybody riled up."

To the rest of them, he said, "There's only three things we can do." He held up his fingers one by one. "Prepare the best we can. Watch the weather reports. And get out of Dodge." He dusted his hands on his jeans. "I'm going to get started on those shutters."

A red-faced Ethan scuffed his foot against the floor. "I'd like to help." He turned a searching look on Nina. "Unless you need me in the kitchen, Chef?"

"I can handle things in here," Nina assured him. "But what about you? Don't you need to go home?"

"Nah. My brothers prob'ly done boarded up the fish camp. It's on stilts. We'll ride out the storm there. Like we always do. I can stick around here as long as you need me."

Reggie let her focus drift from person to person. Because she'd been filling in as the cafe's hostess, she hadn't spoken to Erin this morning. "Does anyone know what time Erin left for her run?" Her sister could be gone for hours.

She no sooner asked the question than they all heard the very welcome sound of someone coming into the house through the back door. Footsteps hurried across the sun porch. Three seconds later, Erin stood in the doorway...and she wasn't alone. Her voice rose. "Hey! Have you heard the news? We need to—"

Seeing the confab taking place in the middle of the kitchen, Erin skidded to a halt so quickly that Ron nearly bumped into her. "You've heard about the hurricane?"

"Erin!" Reggie cried as relief swept through her. "I was just going to come looking for you."

"Ron and I had planned a long run this morning. He heard about the hurricane, so we came straight back."

Reggie was so glad to see her sister that she could have kissed Ron for bringing her home.

"So is it true? We have to evacuate?" Erin asked.

Reggie glanced at Chris. The man stood, solid and stable, a source of strength. She drew from it and nodded. "We were just going over what we need to do to get out of here."

Chris cocked his head in Ron's direction. "Ethan's going to help, but I could use another pair of hands. We have a lot of shutters to hang."

Ron didn't hesitate. "I'm here. Whatever you need."

"Zeke's on his way, too," Nina said. "Connie has the girls. They're already on their way to Galveston, where her parents live."

Like a mother hen who'd accounted for all her chicks, Reggie grew more determined. The exterior of the house was her job, and she was ready to tackle it. She nodded to Chris.

"Chris, you and Ethan and Ron and Zeke— when he gets here—y'all work on the shutters. With all four of you, I'm sure you'll finish today. I'll move the tractor around behind the gardeners' cottage. It should be sheltered back there. Then I'll want to harvest everything I can from the garden and start picking up anything loose in the yard."

When Chris nodded his approval, she turned

to her sister. "Erin, the activity center has concrete block walls, a sturdy roof and a solid door. The kayaks and canoes should be as safe in there as they will be anywhere else. Once you're satisfied with all that, start bringing the porch furniture into the front parlor."

Erin's head bobbed. "Will do."

Nina volunteered to hang the closed sign on the gate out front and provide lunch for everyone. "I'll need to clean out the fridge before we leave. I'll freeze what I can. The rest, I'll pack in a cooler to take with us, so make sure to leave space for it in the car. Wherever we end up, I imagine restaurants will be crowded with people just like us. People who are trying to get out of harm's way." Her voice thinned, and she visibly fought for control. "After that, I'll get Mr. Pibbs and me ready to travel."

Michelle slipped a hand around Nina's waist. "Mr. Pibbs. Thanks for reminding me. I'll make sure they allow pets wherever we stay."

Heavy and hurried, another set of footsteps sounded from the back porch. Seconds later, Zeke appeared in the doorway. The contractor crossed the kitchen in three long strides that took him to straight to Nina. Pulling her to him, he kissed the top of her head. "I know this isn't the opening you wanted. I'm sorry."

Nina sniffled. "This isn't what any of us wanted, but it's the hand we've been dealt. Now we'd better get cracking. None of us wants to be sitting here when that storm comes ashore."

Speaking of hands.

Reggie reminded herself to raid the buffet in the main parlor. She'd make sure to bring along several decks of cards and a few board games for the hotel. The next couple of nights were going to be rough, and she had a feeling no one was going to get much sleep.

Fifteen

Erin

"I'll see your two cents and raise you a nickel." Holding her cards against her chest, Reggie separated seven pennies from her stash and slid them into the pot.

"Too rich for me." Chris threw his cards facedown on the table.

Pretending to struggle with the decision to stay in or not, Erin watched for Reggie's tell. On those rare occasions when they'd played Go Fish as kids, Reggie had rubbed one finger over her left eyebrow whenever she made a book. Erin had seen her sister repeat the motion during one of the Senior Days last month when she'd had a high-scoring word in Scrabble. This time, however, Reggie's fingers didn't so much as twitch.

"I'll see your nickel and raise you a dime," Erin said. She slid fifteen cents across the table. The bet was a sure thing.

"Whoa. Glad I got out when I did." The game was five-card, and Zeke had folded early on.

"I'll call." Reggie added a final dime to the pile of loose change in the center of the table.

Certain she had the winning hand, Erin showed her cards. "Two pair. Fives and Jacks," she said triumphantly. She started to scoop up the pot.

"Not so fast, sister." Reggie's smile widened into a grin. One at a time, she placed her cards on the table. "Full house!"

Erin stared at the trio of tens and the pair of sixes. Her eyes widened in disbelief. "But you didn't rub your eyebrow," she protested. "Not even once!"

"Ho, ho, ho!" Zeke smirked. "She got ya!"

"I don't do that anymore, thanks to Chris." Obviously happy with herself, Reggie high-fived the man seated next to her. Her face softened as, without breaking eye contact with him, she explained, "The first time we played cards together, he caught me tracing my eyebrow. Unlike you, *he* didn't use it to his advantage. He pointed it out."

"Good one, Reggie." Erin shook her head and

laughed. The contagious sound spread quickly as they all enjoyed the chance to relieve a little of the tension they'd been living with for the past forty-eight hours. Sitting on the couch in the misnamed suite that was actually one large room, Michelle looked up from the book she was reading long enough to join in, although Erin was pretty sure her friend didn't have any idea what they were laughing about.

Zeke pushed back the chair he'd rolled down the hall from his own room. "I'm going to get a soda. Nina, you want anything?"

Nina, the only one who'd remained quiet and subdued, stared at the TV screen. She absently ran a hand down Mr. Pibbs's back. "No, thanks," she said softly.

A few seconds later, ice and water sloshed as Zeke plucked a cola from the cooler in the corner of the room. "Probably ought to get some more ice," he said. Picking up the nearby plastic container, he dipped out a bucketful of water and dumped it in the sink. Repeating the process, he made enough room for additional ice.

"I'll come with you," Chris offered. He pushed away from the oblong table that was attached to the wall. "I need to stretch my legs. I probably ought to check on Mom and Hope, too." As it had turned out, some kind of stomach virus had been making the rounds at his aunt's condominium complex. Rather than risk dealing with a sick child in the aftermath of the hurricane, he'd loaded his mom and the baby into his truck. They'd joined Erin and the others in a caravan to a nondescript hotel midway between Lake City and Jacksonville. The closest town boasted a Starbucks and a Walmart. He'd visited both yesterday. They all had.

"Don't be long," Nina whispered. "It's almost five."

Immediately, the tension in the room ratcheted up a notch. The National Hurricane Center issued storm advisories at regular, six-hour intervals which, now that they'd traveled into the Eastern time zone, meant five and eleven. According to last night's update, Ursula had stalled off the coast. No one knew why, but everyone had a theory. One forecaster claimed that, as Ursula had churned the waters of the Gulf, the temperatures below the surface had cooled enough to slow and weaken the storm. Another theorized that a butterfly in Taiwan had flapped its wings hard enough to send a high-pressure zone dropping down from Canada. Whatever the reason, that advisory had held out the first little bit of hope that the hurricane would lose strength or turn. If it didn't, Ursula's

150 mile an hour winds would slam into Sugar Sand Beach this morning, with catastrophic results.

No wonder they'd played cards all night, Erin thought. The uncertainty had prevented any of them from going to sleep. Would Hurricane Ursula wreak destruction? Or would she fizzle? If she roared ashore at full strength, the first place she hit would bear the brunt of her fury. Would that be Sugar Sand Beach? Or would she wobble to the east or west? What would happen to the house that sat alone on a bluff overlooking the Gulf?

Her eyes felt gritty after twenty-four hours with no sleep. She rubbed them, but it didn't help. Not for the first time, she wished she'd followed Chris's mom's example. The woman had poured herself a healthy glass of wine and climbed into the bed next to the baby's crib shortly after Hope drifted off clutching her beloved Binky.

"I'm surprised Ron didn't come with us," Reggie said as the door closed quietly behind Zeke and Chris.

"Yeah, I was, too." Actually, shocked was a more accurate word. "I'm worried about him," she admitted. She had expected Ron to join their not-so-merry little band of evacuees. Especially after he'd spent all day Tuesday helping Chris and Zeke and Ethan with the shutters. The task was a monumental undertaking that involved fitting corrugated aluminum sheets into specially designed tracks on all the windows and doors. Once the shutters were up, the men had used electric drills to secure them in place with sidewalk bolts and wing nuts. They'd worked from the ground up, and everyone had cheered when, with a final zip-zip-zip, Chris had tightened the last bolt just before sundown.

Ron had waited until then to tell her he'd volunteered to ride out the storm at a local shelter, hunkering down with first responders and others who, for various reasons, couldn't leave the area. Watching him drive off, knowing he planned to stay in the hurricane's path, had been one of the most difficult things she'd ever done. She was pretty sure that was when she'd realized that, for the second time, she'd fallen head over heels in love with the man.

So, what was she going to do about it?

Nothing right now, she told herself as Chris and Zeke returned bearing ice and bags of potato chips from the vending machine down the hall.

"How are Hope and your mom?" Reggie asked the moment Chris stepped into the room.

"Still dead to the world." He sat beside her and picked up the deck of cards.

"Must be nice." Using one finger, Michelle marked her place in her book. "I don't think I can get to sleep until we know what's happening at home."

Erin twisted toward her friend. "Have you heard from Dave?"

Michelle held up her phone. "We've been texting." She gave a short laugh. "Evidently, his pacing has driven Sara nuts. She told him she'd kick him out into the storm if he didn't stop." The caring father had opted to stay with his daughter in Tallahassee.

A blue Breaking News banner appeared on the television screen.

"Hush. It's time." Clutching Mr. Pibbs to her chest, Nina pointed the remote at the TV and turned up the volume.

On the screen, a woman in a snug-fitting orange dress read from a teleprompter. "Hurricane Ursula has moved ashore east of Destin, Florida. Even before it made landfall, the storm was downgraded from a Category Four to a Category One hurricane, after it weakened considerably over the past six hours. Top winds have fallen from a high of 150 miles per hour to seventy-five, with gusts up to ninety-five. There are strong indications that the wind speeds will drop even more and that, by our next bulletin in six hours, it will weaken into a tropical storm." The woman looked offstage. "Well, Marty, that's a major change in such a short period of time. What more can you tell us about Hurricane Ursula?"

The camera panned left. The focus zoomed in on a man with slicked-down hair who sat behind a wide desk. Colorful maps showing the hurricane's predicted path filled the otherwise blank space behind him.

"Thank you, Carla," Marty said. "I have to say, I've never seen a storm lose so much strength so quickly…and I've been in the weather business for over twenty years." The anchor flipped to the next page in his script and looked up. Obviously aware that he was staring straight into the living rooms of his viewing audience, he said, "If this report holds true, it's definitely good news for Florida's Panhandle area. But remember, folks, Hurricane Ursula may not be a Cat 5, but it's still a powerful storm. Even at seventy-five miles per hour, winds at those speeds can rip siding off houses and uproot trees. Plus, we're predicting up to a foot of rain that will result in localized flooding. Whether the storm continues to weaken or regains strength, dangerous lightning will…"

Nina turned away from the television. "Is it my imagination, or does he sound disappointed?"

"A Cat 5 hurricane making landfall is big news. Good ol' Marty was probably counting on that to boost his ratings," Zeke opined.

"Yes, but what does that all mean? Is Ursula still a threat?" Reggie worried a fingernail between her front teeth. "When can we go home?"

"Let's switch to another station and see what they have to say," Chris suggested.

They checked the stories on three different networks. Each repeated some version of Carla and Marty's reports, although most of the others were a whole lot happier about Ursula's downgraded status.

Chris idly shuffled the cards. "If the storm's already made landfall, like they said it has—" He looked to Zeke.

"It's gonna die down real fast once it starts moving over land—" Zeke added.

"Then we ought to be able to head out at first light tomorrow," Chris finished.

Zeke batted the conversational ball. "We might run into some rain squalls, but what's left of the storm is headed northeast, so we won't be driving straight into it."

The cards made a soft *thrrrpt* as, his fingers arched, Chris shuffled the deck. "Traffic will be a bear, though. Bumper to bumper, most likely. Could take eight hours or more to get home."

Raising his eyebrows and tilting his head to one side, Zeke said, "We could get a jump on it and leave this afternoon."

"That gets my vote," Reggie said.

"I'm worried about all the food in the freezer. What if it all defrosted? Whatever gets us back home the quickest, that's what I want to do." Nina settled Mr. Pibbs on her lap and resumed petting him.

"That works for me, too," Erin said, though she suspected they'd all be more comfortable staying at the hotel rather than going back to the storm-ravaged coast. At the very least, they'd be dealing with power outages and downed trees. If the house was even still standing, that was.

She grabbed her cell phone. "I'm going to check in with Ron and see how things are going there." Leaving the rest of them to determine the exact time of departure, she headed down the hall to the room she shared with Reggie.

Ron answered on the second ring. "Erin?"

She expelled a shaky breath. Overloaded circuits had played havoc with cell service for the last twenty-four hours. She hadn't been certain her call would go through. She steadied herself. "Have you heard the news? Hurricane Ursula has been downgraded to a Category 1 storm."

"What's that?" Ron asked over a roaring sound. "I can't hear you. We're getting hit pretty hard right now. They say the storm is right on top of us."

Erin raised her voice until she was practically shouting. "I said, Ursula's been downgraded to a Cat 1. We're coming home later today."

A tremendous grinding noise came through the speaker. It was immediately followed by absolute silence.

"Ron?" Erin lowered the phone. She stared at the screen for a long second before she pressed it against her ear again. "Ron?" she asked hopefully.

Nothing. The call had disconnected.

Her heart stuttered.

"Try him again." Erin clenched the steering wheel with the same white-knuckled grip she'd held it in ever since they'd driven out of the hotel parking lot six hours earlier. Despite Chris and Zeke's hope that they could get ahead of the crush of people flooding back to the coast like an outgoing tide, traffic on I-10 had been heavy. It had only worsened after she'd followed Zeke's truck down the ramp that led onto State Road 331. The promised shortcut had taken them across the Choctawhatchee Causeway, where whitecaps danced in the normally placid bay. Erin had been afraid that Reggie might balk at crossing the three miles of open water, but her sister had done an admirable job of staying calm. Possibly because the alternative meant taking a two-hour detour to the only slightly shorter Bay Bridge.

"I've already called him a dozen times," Reggie pointed out. As they passed the exit of the Topsail Hill Preserve State Park, she leaned forward, as eager as Erin was for her first glimpse of their house. "It just goes to voice mail, and I get a message that his inbox is full."

"Try. It. Again," Erin said through gritted teeth. She hadn't been able to reach Ron since their phone call had abruptly ended this morning. But not for lack of trying. Oh, how she'd tried. When she couldn't get an answer on his phone, she'd dialed the numbers of every single person she knew in Sugar Sand Beach. Most calls didn't go through. None of the people she had been able to reach could shed any light on why their conversation had been cut short.

Watching the news hadn't helped. The first images of the damage Hurricane Ursula had inflicted started rolling across the screen shortly after daybreak. The storm actually came ashore farther east than predicted, at Grayton State Park. It cut a path through the middle of the uninhabited 2000 wooded acres. And then, it simply calmed like a tired child at the end of a temper tantrum. Desperate for news, weathermen and reporters had excitedly shown pictures of a few downed trees, but when the same images scrolled across the screen time after time, Erin shut off the television.

"As soon as we know whether the house is still standing or not, I have to leave," she told her sister. "I need to find Ron."

"You really care for him, don't you?" Reggie asked.

"More than I want to," she admitted. She'd kept her feelings under wraps, but if there was one person she could be honest with, it was Reggie. "If he weren't leaving soon, I'd…"

She took a breath and let it out slowly. What would she do? Give him—give them—another chance? That wasn't going to happen. "It doesn't matter. He's leaving. This time, I'm the one who's staying behind."

"It doesn't have to be that way. You could go with him."

Reggie's response surprised her so much that

Erin swung a quick look at the woman in the passenger seat. "I thought you hated Ron."

"I never hated him, exactly. I hated that he broke your heart." Reggie pushed her hair behind her ears. "I hated that he was the reason you left. But I didn't hate him. If he makes you happy..." She shrugged.

"If I wasn't driving right now, I'd hug you," Erin said with a smile. "But no. It would never work with me and Ron. I have all the passport stamps I ever want. My goal now is to put down deep roots here in Sugar Sand Beach. If I gave that up to help Ron fulfill his dreams, it wouldn't be long before I'd resent him for making me leave. Eventually, that feeling would destroy our relationship, just like it did the last time." That was both the beauty and the curse of being older and a lot wiser than she'd been in her twenties— she had enough experience to recognize a bad choice when she saw one.

She gave her head an imperceptible shake. There really was nothing she could do...except brace for the inevitable heartache. In less than two months, Ron would embark on a round-the-world tour, and she would not. She'd made her choice. She was just as committed to her friends as Ron was to his new business venture. Her life, her future were tied up in the Sugar Sand Inn and

Cafe. As much as she might wish things could be different between them, she had to accept that they'd never have a happily-ever-after.

The headlights of an oncoming car blurred, and she swiped at her eyes.

"It's going to hurt when he leaves." A quiet sadness filled the truck cab when Reggie spoke.

"Tell me something I don't know." Erin followed Zeke's truck off the main road and onto the final leg of the journey home.

"The house is standing," Reggie observed.

"What?" She'd been checking the rearview mirror to make sure Michelle's SUV was still behind her and had missed out on her first glimpse of the house.

"Yep. All shingles and walls accounted for," Reggie quipped.

Amazed that her sister could still joke about the situation after all they'd been through in the last harrowing forty-eight hours, Erin looked ahead. The fading light from the setting sun bathed the two-story house in a rosy glow. Although palm fronds and branches littered the yard, the upstairs balcony was intact. Not a single one of the shutters had blown off. At least, none on the second floor. The window coverings for the first floor, though? That was a different story.

"Where are the storm shutters?" she asked. Driving right past the parking area, she stopped by the front steps.

Just then, the answer to her question rounded the corner of the house carrying a drill in one hand and a ladder in the other. Unshaven and still wearing the same clothes she'd last seen him in, her ex-husband had never looked so good.

"Ron!" she whispered as the realization of how deeply afraid she'd been for him slammed into her. She bolted from the truck. She had to touch him, to feel him, to make sure he was real. She ran to him.

"You're alive," she gasped, tears of relief streaming down her cheeks.

She was vaguely aware of the metallic clang of the ladder as it hit the ground. The drill landed with a thunk in the grass a second later. Then Ron's arms were around her, crushing her against his chest. She told herself she had to be mistaken when she felt him tremble.

"I thought for sure I'd lost you," he whispered into her hair.

"I thought the same thing," she admitted. They stood for a long moment before she tipped her face to his. "We were talking, and then there was an awful noise. And then nothing. I was afraid the roof had collapsed. Nobody could tell me what happened."

"It was a tree. It fell outside the community center," he said, solving at least one part of the mystery.

"But why didn't you call me back?"

"No service. No one could get a call out. After sunup we heard one of the cell towers had been knocked out. They're already working on restoring it."

The deep rumble of a big man clearing his throat kept Erin from asking any more questions. Aware that Zeke and Chris had joined them, she rose on tiptoes and lightly brushed a kiss on Ron's cheek. "I'm glad you made it," she whispered. "Glad we all made it."

Reluctantly, she backed out of Ron's arms to let the three men shake hands in that casual way men had of downplaying their emotions. Chris picked the drill up off the grass.

"Whatcha got here?" he asked. "Looks brand new."

More doors slammed as the rest of their little caravan spilled out of cars and trucks and Michelle's SUV.

"I bought the last power drill they had at the hardware store," Ron confessed.

"Ronnie and Frank are open?" Zeke's heavy eyebrows rose.

"Open and doing a booming business," Ron assured the contractor.

"Is there a lot of damage?" Michelle asked as she and the others in their group crowded around them.

"Not bad," Ron said, delivering the good news. "After the storm passed, I drove from one end of Sugar Sand Beach to the other, helping the mayor assess the storm damage. There are a couple of trees down, including that big oak outside Maggie's Diner. But we got off light. Most everybody even has power."

He let that sink in for a minute before he glanced at Chris. "Crews were already at work so there was nothing for me to do. I hope you don't mind that I got a head start on taking down the shutters."

Chris clapped Ron on the back. "Mind? Why would I mind? Give me an hour to get Mom and Hope home and settled, and I'll come straight back to help."

But Michelle shook her head. "There's no need to rush. We'll have all weekend to get things straightened around before our first guests arrive on Monday."

"But what about the open house?" Reggie

asked. "We aren't going to cancel that, are we?"

"Oh, I don't..." Michelle began.

Ron's features clouded. "It's not my place to argue, but I think that'd be a mistake. After a near miss like this one, everybody's going to want to celebrate. The whole town will probably turn out."

"You think?" Michelle's eyes narrowed and her lips pursed.

Erin studied the face of the man she thought she'd lost—forever, this time. That she hadn't, that Ron hadn't perished, filled her with a giddy joy. If the other citizens of Sugar Sand Beach felt one tenth as happy as she was at this moment, they'd be dancing in the streets.

"I have to side with Ron and Reggie on this one," she told Michelle. "We may have to scale down a few of the activities we'd planned—" The fishing tournament was out of the question. Regardless of how quickly the storm had died down, the ocean would remain turbulent for several days. "But we could go ahead with the rest of it."

"Except for the cookies." With Mr. Pibbs in her arms, Nina joined the group. "We'll save those for another time."

Michelle nodded. "Then it's decided. "We'll hold the open house as scheduled on Sunday afternoon."

"In that case…" Reggie clapped her hands. "Let's get to work."

"I'll help Ron with the shutters," Erin volunteered. There were a hundred other tasks she could tackle, but holding out her hand, she took the heavy drill from Chris. By sometime next week, or maybe next month, she'd grow used to the idea that Ron had survived the storm. For the time being, though, she wasn't going to let the man out of her sight.

Sixteen

Erin

"I don't know about everyone else, but this little one is beat." Reggie jostled a sleeping Hope on her lap. The sun still hovered well above the horizon, but a full day of playing with Dimella and Malcolm, Megan and Lily had exhausted the little girl. Reggie finger-combed the baby's damp, flaxen hair.

"She sure loved going down the slide at the end of the maze, didn't she?" Sitting beside Reggie on the rattan settee, Chris beamed down at his daughter.

Reggie nodded. "All the kids did." Time after time, their friends' and neighbors' children had raced through the maze to get to the end, where a plastic tarp spread over a sloped stack of hay bales created a fun exit. Reggie and Chris had taken turns going down the slide with Hope.

"The hayride was a hit, too." Erin nudged Ron with her shoulder. He'd made countless trips around the pond on the tractor, pulling a trailer filled with kids and adults.

"Megan—she's Zeke's oldest, right?" Ron waited for Erin's nod before he continued. "She started singing 'Row, row, row your boat,' and pretty soon, everyone joined in. When one song finished, she'd start another one. That girl's got perfect pitch."

"She does have a pretty voice. Sometimes, when we take the kayaks out, she'll sing while she paddles." Erin shook her head in wonder. "It's the neatest thing."

"I was surprised by how much food we ended up with," Michelle said. "I worried that no one would have time after the hurricane and all."

"Every cook in town truly outdid themselves." In the chair next to Michelle's, Dave patted his flat stomach. "It sure was nice of Maggie to bring all that chicken." The diner had contributed two huge trays of perfectly fried breasts, thighs and wings.

"Still, it's been a long week." Chris stretched.

"I, for one, will be glad if we never go

through another one like it." Erin sent Ron a meaningful glance. She hadn't completely gotten over the fear that had filled her when she thought he'd been injured—or worse. "We've been moving full speed ahead ever since we first heard about the hurricane." An agreeable rapport shone in the eyes of her friends and the men who, for one reason or another, had stuck around after they'd said goodbye to all the other people who'd shown up for the open house.

"It was good to kick back and relax a bit today," Ron prompted, looking at Erin. "You enjoyed yourself, didn't you? Every time I saw you, you were laughing at something someone said or did."

"Usually you." Erin poked him lightly in the ribs. Whenever he'd had a spare moment, Ron had spent it at her side.

"Speaking of things that struck me as funny—" Chris recrossed his ankles. "Yesterday, I had to get Jack Henson down from a ladder at Ruth Bees's house at seven in the morning. He was trying to pry off the boards over her windows with a crowbar. When I asked him what in tarnation he was doing there at that time of day, he said it was too dark in her house."

"Jack…and Ruth Bees?" Dave straightened slightly, his eyes widening.

"Oh, yeah." Michelle's smile spoke volumes. "The two of them have gotten quite chummy lately."

"What did you do?" Looking at Chris, Reggie whispered so she wouldn't wake the baby in her lap.

"Jack is eighty-six if he's a day. Maggie would have my head if I left him up on a ladder. I had to stop right there and then and pull those boards down myself." He turned to Reggie. "That's why I was late getting here." She'd already finished picking up the downed branches and other storm debris by the time he arrived. They'd spent the rest of the day putting the final touches on the hay maze.

"It's sweet that they found each other. It's nice to know love doesn't have an age limit." *And if you fail the first time, you can try again,* Erin added silently. She studiously avoided looking at the man beside her.

"We are lucky to live in a place where neighbors help each other. That's one thing I love about Sugar Sand Beach," Michelle said. Her attention focused on Ron. "You were right about moving forward with the open house. I'm glad you convinced us not to cancel."

Ron dipped his head. "This area has a strong sense of community. In a place like this, it's only natural that, after a scare like Ursula, people would want to gather together."

"I'm just glad this storm petered out like it did. Things could have been so much worse." Erin stared beyond the sand dunes to the choppy waters of the Gulf while the rest of the group sobered for a moment, each acknowledging in their own way the suffering and loss caused by hurricanes like Andrew and Michael.

The mood shifted when Nina's laughter trilled from inside the house. Less than a minute later, she stepped out onto the porch carrying an enormous tray of appetizers and snacks. Zeke was right behind her with two pitchers of sweet iced tea.

"Oh!" Reggie leaned as far forward as she could, considering the baby she held. "That looks yummy. I am so hungry."

"You're always hungry," Erin teased. A hint of spicy beef and seafood perfumed the air. She eyed the immense platter. "With all we had going on today, when did you have time to make meatballs? Or those crab things I like so much?"

"Ha ha." Nina faked a laugh. "I made these weeks ago. All I had to do just now was take them out of the freezer and pop them in the oven." The chef paused. "And before you ask, yes, I'm sure they didn't go bad during the storm. We only lost power for a couple of hours, not nearly long enough for the Subzero to defrost. Besides, Zeke taught me the neatest trick."

"Oh?" Michelle handed Dave a paper plate. "Do tell."

"You fill a cup with water and stick it in the freezer. When the ice is good and solid, you lay a quarter on top of it," Zeke began.

Ignoring the meats and cheeses, Dave filled his plate with crispy carrot and celery sticks. "They say if the power goes out for any length of time, you can tell by checking the quarter. If it's still on top of the ice, then nothing defrosted."

Bending forward, Chris loaded a plate with one of everything while he talked. "But if you find the quarter at the bottom of a cup of ice, everything in the freezer has defrosted and refrozen." He handed the plate to Reggie.

Dave selected another carrot. "There's a chance, too, that the water only partially melted and the quarter floated on top of a chunk of ice, and then refroze."

"No matter what, if the power was out for longer than forty-eight hours, you'd better toss it all," Nina finished. "Unless you happen to like food poisoning." Her mouth twisting into a wry grimace, she shook her head. "Personally, I don't recommend it."

Conversation flowed easily between the four couples while they sipped tea, and those who wanted a bite of this or that helped themselves. Eventually, the topic drifted to plans for the week ahead.

"The cafe is closed on Sundays and Mondays, so I have all day tomorrow to do laundry and watch TV," Nina reported. She held out one hand. "Maybe I'll do my nails."

Erin laughed at the obvious joke—unlike the first assistant Nina had hired, the chef did not wear nail polish. Nor did Erin think there was a chance in the world that Nina would lounge around all day. Dollars to donuts, she'd find her friend whipping up something marvelous in the kitchen before the day was out.

"I have that job to finish at Gus's," Zeke said. He and his construction crew had all but finished the expanded smokehouse behind the grocery store. Warmth shone in the look he gave Nina. "You could meet me for lunch," he suggested.

"Maybe." Nina shrugged, although everyone, including Zeke, knew lunch was definitely on her schedule. "The cafe officially opens for business on Tuesday. From then on, we'll have at least one table reserved for the inn's overnight guests. The first ones check in tomorrow. Right, Michelle?"

"The Winters—Sam and Diane." Michelle set her empty glass on the table. "I expect them around five." She rubbed her hands together. "By the end of the week, we'll have a full house." A note of wonder crept into her voice. "After that, we're booked solid through mid-December."

"Whoa! I did not know that," Reggie exclaimed softly. "Looks like we're going to be plenty busy for the next few months."

"Chris, I was thinking..." Erin broke a corner off one of the crab appetizers and nibbled on it. "If you have some spare time, I have a project I'd like you to take a look at in our apartment." She'd agreed to share a room with her sister while she weighed the pros and cons of accepting Ron's job offer. Now that she'd decided to stay in Sugar Sand Beach, she thought they both deserved their own, albeit smaller, bedrooms.

"I'll be glad to scope it out." Finished with his snack, Chris added his empty plate to a growing stack. "If it's more than I can handle, we'll get Zeke in on it."

Erin's gaze traveled around the circle of friends. Michelle and Dave shared an easy camaraderie. Reggie and Chris alternated between fussing over Hope and chatting about different tasks they each planned to tackle in the coming weeks. When they weren't trading heated looks,

Nina and Zeke's conversation ranged over a variety of topics, from his girls to a recipe she wanted to try. Of the eight of them, she and Ron were the only ones who didn't seem to have much to talk about. Other than a few remarks earlier in the evening, he'd actually said very little. Why was that, she wondered? Did he feel left out since his stay in Sugar Sand Beach was only temporary?

Pain lanced her at the thought of how soon he'd be leaving. She forced herself to move past it. There'd be time enough for sorrow later, after he was gone. For now, they needed to enjoy the time they did have.

Making an effort to include him, she asked, "Is the Preserve reopening tomorrow?" Like most businesses in the area, the state park had closed through the weekend so work crews could assess damage and remove debris.

As if he'd been lost in thought, Ron started. "Uh, yeah. I'm not planning to rent out any boats, though." His brows knitted. "I want to get out on Campbell Lake myself first. In case there's something I need to warn people about. A couple of years ago, one of my customers hit a submerged log after a big storm. Fortunately, no one got hurt, but it did damage my boat. I want to avoid that here, if I can."

"That's right." Zeke propped an ankle on one knee. "You run an outdoor sports business in Houston, don't you?"

"Well, I did." Ron ran a hand down one leg of his jeans. "I sold it this week."

"What?" Erin's head whipped toward Ron so fast, she thought she might have wrenched her neck. "When? Why?"

"I've been thinking about it for a while now."

"But, but wasn't that your home base for the global tours?" That was what he'd told her that first night when they'd spoken right here on this very porch. That he was expanding his outdoor adventure business to include trips all over the world. That he wanted her to join him. Selling the company didn't make sense unless...

Her heart skipped a beat.

"You're not leaving?" She studied Ron's face, hoping, praying for confirmation.

"Nope." A sly smile started at one corner of Ron's lips. It widened into a full-fledged grin. "Thought I might open a charter boat business right here in Sugar Sand Beach. You wouldn't have any objections to that, would you?"

He wasn't leaving.

"Um, no," she said, suddenly breathless. "So...this would be a permanent move?"

Ron's smile dimmed. His Adam's apple

bobbed. His expression turned serious. "How long I stick around is really up to you. I'll be here as long as you'll have me. Twenty? Maybe thirty years?"

His features shifted into an expression she'd never seen on his face before. Was it hope? Fear? She couldn't decipher it.

"What do you say?" he asked.

Erin stilled. He wasn't asking what she thought he was asking. Was he?

Her gaze bounced from Ron's questioning look to the faces of her friends and her sister. Which didn't help at all. Their expressions mirrored the same mix of confusion and surprise that swirled in her head. She licked her lips and faced him again. "Ron?"

Rather than answering, he stood. Before she had time to react, he bent on one knee and took her fingers in his hand.

"Oooohhhh!" Michelle's quiet gasp was the only sound that broke the stillness.

Erin stared into the face of the man she'd fallen in love with…the second time around. Her heart settled into a happy rhythm. This was happening. This was *really* happening.

"Erin. I came here hoping you'd agree to travel the world with me," Ron began. "That's what I wanted more than anything. To pick up where we left off. To follow the dream we had when we were young. I admit, I was surprised when you turned me down flat," he said with a half-smile. "I was afraid maybe you didn't feel the same way I did. But I convinced myself I could change your mind, so I didn't take no for an answer." His expression softened. "It took me a while, but I finally realized, I don't need to see the seven wonders of the world. I have all the wonders I need right here, right in front of me. See, I've never loved anyone like I love you." His eyes glistening, he took a beat, though his focus never wavered from her face. "And if you'll do me the honor of marrying me—again—I swear, I'll devote the rest of my life to making you the happiest woman in the world."

With that, he reached into his pocket. While Erin watched, he withdrew a small, black box. Inside lay a diamond ring so stunning it would have taken her breath away…if she'd remembered to breathe.

"It's beautiful," she choked. Inhaling at last, she said, "But you didn't need to buy a new one. I still have our old engagement ring."

"I love that you kept it," Ron said with the sweetest smile. "But a fresh start calls for a new ring." He blinked. "I take it that's a yes?" He lifted the ring from the box and slid it onto her finger.

"Yes," Erin said, not sure whether she wanted to laugh or cry, a problem that Ron solved by kissing her until her toes curled.

By the time the kiss ended, Reggie had shifted Hope into Chris's arms and stood at her side. "Let me see," she demanded. "Let me see."

Erin dutifully held out her hand.

Her sister barely glanced at the diamond that sparkled from Erin's third finger before enveloping her in a fierce hug. "I am so, so happy for you," Reggie gushed.

The next ten minutes passed in a happy blur of handshakes, slaps on the back and warm hugs as everyone tried to congratulate Ron and Erin at the same time. Once the initial excitement died down, Nina ducked inside the house, emerging a few minutes later with two bottles of chilled champagne.

"Ron stuck these in the fridge earlier. I guess he hoped we might have something to celebrate," she announced.

Corks popped. Zeke poured the sparkling beverage into flutes that, like the bottles themselves, had mysteriously appeared. Happy chatter and another round of congratulations followed.

The excitement was just beginning to settle down, and Erin was still trying to get used to the wonderful weight of the ring on her finger when twin beams of light appeared on the driveway. Nestled in the crook of Ron's arms, Erin eyed the headlights of an approaching car. "Do you have another surprise up your sleeve?" she asked the man she loved with all her heart.

"Not me. I'm fresh out." Ron kissed the top of her head.

She lifted her chin to Michelle. "Don't look now, but I think we have company."

"Really?" Michelle twisted in her seat so she could see the walkway and the parking area behind her.

As they all watched, a late-model sedan pulled onto the graveled pad and stopped. Thirty seconds passed before a man in pressed khakis and a polo shirt stepped from the car. He circled around to the passenger side, where he held the door for a woman wearing white slacks and a print top. She clutched the strap of her purse in both hands as they slowly made their way toward the front porch.

When they reached the steps, the man asked, "Is this where we check in?"

Michelle swung back to face Erin and the rest of their group while her eyebrows climbed so high they got lost beneath her bangs. "What?" Michelle mouthed. She pressed one hand over the lower half of her face before, hiding her shock, she stood and faced the new arrivals.

"Hi," she greeted the couple warmly. "Welcome to the Sugar Sand Inn and Cafe. I'm Michelle. How can I help you?"

"We're the Winters," the woman answered in a timid voice. "Our reservations aren't until tomorrow, but with the storm earlier this week, our plans got all discombobulated. Do you think we could check in tonight instead?"

With a graciousness Erin found amazing, Michelle didn't even hesitate. "Of course, of course," she said as if it were perfectly normal for their first ever guests to show up a full day before they were expected. "Let's get you checked in, and then I'll show you to your rooms."

A flurry of activity broke out on the porch the minute Michelle guided the Winters inside. After offering another round of congratulations to the lucky couple, Chris lifted his sleeping daughter to his shoulder and, with a quick goodbye to Reggie, headed for his truck. Nina and Zeke hurriedly gathered up the dishes and glassware while Erin straightened the pillows on the couches and chairs. Then, promising Ron she wouldn't be long, she dashed upstairs, where she double-checked that there were fresh towels and flowers in the Manatee suite. Satisfied, she trooped back to the porch, where Ron had two flutes of champagne waiting for them.

"Well, I guess it's official. The Sugar Sand Inn and Cafe are open for business!" she said, sitting close to him. "What a day, right? It's not every day you host an open house, guests drop in unexpectedly and the man you love proposes. I especially like that last part." She wiggled her fingers. The diamond on her third finger sparkled.

"Speaking of proposals." Ron lifted her hand to his lips. "Do you want a long engagement? A big wedding? Any ideas about a date?"

Erin snuggled into his arms. She and Ron were incredibly lucky. They'd been given a second chance at love and happiness, and she didn't want to waste a minute of it. "I think we should get married as soon as possible."

"Next week?" Ron suggested.

She laughed. Even a small wedding required a little bit of time and planning. "I was thinking more like Christmas. We could hold the ceremony here." She pictured herself walking down the staircase to marry the man of her dreams in front of her friends and family.

"Christmas," Ron repeated. His face softened. "A Christmas wedding at the Sugar Sand Inn.

It sounds perfect." He tipped his glass of champagne to hers, and they drank deeply. And then, for a while, they lost themselves in kisses filled with the promise of a long and lasting future.

Thank you for reading
The Reunion At Sugar Sand Inn!

If you loved this book and want to help the series
continue, take a moment to leave a review!

Want to know what happens next in
Sugar Sand Beach?

Sign up for Leigh's newsletter to get
the latest news about upcoming releases,
excerpts, and more!
https://leighduncan.com/newsletter/

Books by Leigh Duncan

EMERALD BAY SERIES

Treasure Coast Homecoming
Treasure Coast Promise
Treasure Coast Christmas
Treasure Coast Revival
Treasure Coast Discovery
Treasure Coast Legacy

SUGAR SAND BEACH SERIES

The Gift at Sugar Sand Inn
The Secret at Sugar Sand Inn
The Cafe at Sugar Sand Inn
The Reunion at Sugar Sand Inn
Christmas at Sugar Sand Inn

HEART'S LANDING SERIES

A Simple Wedding
A Cottage Wedding
A Waterfront Wedding

ORANGE BLOSSOM SERIES

Butterfly Kisses
Sweet Dreams

LEIGH DUNCAN

HOMETOWN HEROES SERIES

Luke

Brett

Dan

Travis

Colt

Garrett

The Hometown Heroes Collection

SINGLE TITLE BOOKS

A Country Wedding

Journey Back to Christmas

The Growing Season

Pattern of Deceit

Rodeo Daughter

His Favorite Cowgirl

NOVELLAS

The Billionaire's Convenient Secret

A Reason to Remember

Find all Leigh's books at:
leighduncan.com/books/

Want the inside scoop on Leigh's next book?
Join her mailing list for release news,
fun giveaways and more!
leighduncan.com/newsletter/

Acknowledgements

Every book takes a team effort.
I want to give special thanks to those who made
The Reunion at Sugar Sand Inn possible.

Cover design
Chris Kridler at
Sky Diary Productions

House photo used in cover illustration
Taken by Jerrye and Roy Klotz via Wikipedia,
licensed under Creative Commons
(link: https://creativecommons.org/licenses/by-
sa/4.0/deed.en)

Editing Services
Chris Kridler at
Sky Diary Productions

Interior formatting
Amy Atwell and Team
Author E.M.S.

About the Author

Leigh Duncan is the award-winning author of more than two dozen novels, novellas and short stories. Though she started writing fiction at the tender age of six, she didn't get serious about writing a novel until her 40th birthday, and she offers all would-be authors this piece of advice: Don't wait so long!

Leigh sold her first, full-length novel in 2010. In 2017, she was thrilled when Hallmark Publishing chose her as the lead author for their new line of romances and cozy mysteries. A National Readers' Choice Award winner, an Amazon best-selling author and recently named a National Best-Selling author by Publisher's Weekly, Leigh lives on Florida's East Coast where she writes women's fiction and sweet, contemporary romance with a dash of Southern sass.

Want to get in touch with Leigh? She loves to hear from readers and fans. Visit leighduncan.com to send her a note. Join Leigh on Facebook, and don't forget to sign up for her newsletter so you get the latest news about fun giveaways, special offers or her next book!

About the Cover

The minute I came up with the idea of writing about four best friends who open a beach-side inn, I knew exactly which house I wanted to put on the covers of these books. With its gingerbread trim and Queen Anne-style architecture, the Wood/Spann house is easily one of the most beautiful homes I've ever seen. Built in 1895 by F.S. Wood, the house is a part of Troy, Alabama's College Street Historical District and is listed in the National Registry of Historic Places. Best of all, it belongs to a member of my very own family!

Aunt Betty, thank you so much for letting me feature your incredible home on the covers of the books in the Sugar Sand Beach series!

Made in the USA
Coppell, TX
22 January 2024

28001057R00204